WOLF MOUNTAIN LEGACY

What Readers Are Saying about Linda Wood Rondeau's Books

- magical gift of words
- not your usual romance writer
- wise and gentle way of explaining how God moves in people's lives
- makes the reader part of the story
- using metaphor, description, and humor, this author is wonderful at setting a scene.
- characters that come to life
- creates quirky characters with finesse
- grabs and keeps your attention right from the beginning
- strong vibrant characters and great storylines
- doesn't fit neatly into any niche but one: Inspiring Christian Fiction!
- great mix of love, relationships, suspense & mystery.
- perfect in writing style, story theme, and characters
- not your typical cookie-cutter romances
- themes of mystery, romance and restoration, sprinkled with humor
- one of my favorite writers of Christian fiction
- liked the Upstate NY setting, especially in the Adirondacks, one of my favorite places.
- surprising twists and turns in her storylines
- satisfying endings are worth every tear
- be prepared to have your attention riveted
- draws you into the story early on and keeps you there.

WOLF MOUNTAIN LEGACY

LINDA WOOD RONDEAU

PUBLISHING THE POSITIVE
Plymouth, Massachusetts

COPYRIGHT NOTICE

Wolf Mountain Legacy

Cover and Interior Design: Derinda Babcock

Editor(s): René Holt, Deb Haggerty

PUBLISHED BY: Elk Lake Publishing, Inc., 35 Dogwood Drive, Plymouth, MA 02360, 2021

Library Cataloging Data

Names: Rondeau, Linda Wood | (Linda Wood Rondeau_

Wolf Mountain Legacy / Linda Wood Rondeau

284 p. 23cm × 15cm (9in × 6 in.)

Identifiers: ISBN-13: 978-1-64949-253-1 (paperback) | 978-1-64949-254-8 (trade paperback) | 978-1-64949-255-5 (e-book)

Key Words: mystery/suspense, millionaires, robber barons, investigations, loss of spouse, hallucinations, romance

Library of Congress Control Number: 2021938897 Fiction

DEDICATION

To all my Northern New York friends.
Thank you.
You believed I could when I didn't believe I could.

ACKNOWLEDGMENTS

No literary work is possible without the hidden efforts of many.

A special thank you to my Publisher and Chief Editor of Elk Lake Publishing, Deb Haggerty, as well as my editor Rene Holt.

I am eternally grateful for the years I lived in Malone, New York, north of the Adirondack Mountains. Its proximity to historical places and nearness to Canada, has provided me with a wealth of inspiration for my novels, this book included.

Thank you to my many friends who encouraged me along the writing journey.

A special thank you to my husband and friend in life, Steve. You have been housekeeper, cook, and chauffer as well as errand boy and encourager throughout this journey.

CHAPTER 1

The month of June crept upon Collins Bend like a steamy vapor. While brides walked down church aisles to meet their grooms, Marci Henderson trekked Wolf Mountain, seeking wholeness.

Wolf Mountain, the tallest in this section of the Adirondacks, was her favorite spot among all the trails. When she reached the top, she plopped onto a stone bench to enjoy the view. From her vantage point, she marveled at the panorama of azure apexes like soft ocean waves stretching for miles in all directions.

She wondered why she'd waited two years to return to this spot. Before Matt died—before her life changed forever—a hike had been her panacea for all life's ills, especially here on Wolf Mountain. Few tourists took the rugged, south-side trail. *Only for experts*, the brochure warned. A climb against this challenge never failed to boost her confidence.

She wiped her brow, satisfied she'd won the war despite her lingering memory loss. She longed for water, and her feet burned. In her rush, she'd left Matt's canteen and the extra pair of socks she'd put on the counter, along with her backpack of rations and flashlight. Eagerness to prove her wellness had trumped her good sense, a rookie mistake.

Though she'd made the climb without adequate gear, Dr. Solomon would be pleased at this accomplishment—that is, if she'd planned to keep her next appointment. No need—her success today proved she was sane once again. Her spirits soared with eagerness to return to work in the fall.

She gazed at the charred remains of the once bustling Wordsworth Mansion, her attention fixed on the right wing, Felicity's chambers. The remnants of an intricate, cast-iron balustrade jutted over the north drop, an endless abyss to the crags below.

A legend, haunted by tales of deceit and murder, accompanied these ruins. Marci closed her eyes and pictured the petite, young wife of the graying millionaire quilting in her sitting room. Perhaps she mentally prepared for her next charity ball to benefit the Orphans Guild. Everything Marci read about Felicity contradicted the rumors. A woman with her magnitude of philanthropy would never be guilty of running off with her husband's accountant.

Not all unhappily married women cheated.

Shadows lengthened. Not much daylight left. Marci took four deep breaths in preparation for descent. Only the foolish traversed the rutted trails in the dark.

A small child appeared from nowhere, his curly blond hair and oval blue eyes oddly reminiscent, as if a photograph she'd seen long ago. The child thrust a reddish pebble into her hand. "Here, lady. You can keep this. Nana won't let me have it in my room. It's too pretty to throw away."

"Yes, I agree. It's very pretty. Thank you."

A disembodied voice carried across the clearing, "Mark, come here." The child ran and disappeared behind the west wing ruins where the servants' quarters once stood.

Something seemed oddly familiar about the child. She pocketed the stone and followed the boy. When she rounded the building, she saw no one—the entire area was devoid of climbers except for her. Perhaps the boy and his companions left by way of the handicapped trail or took the elevator to the parking lot.

Had she birthed another delusion, or was this a hallucination? No. She'd been cured. There had to be another explanation.

She fumbled with the pebble in her pocket. Would a delusion leave her a gift?

She should begin her trek home now before daylight disappeared. Opting for the steeper trail to save time, she rose, feeling slightly dizzy from dehydration. Half-blinded by the descending sun, she tripped, catapulting toward the perilous slope under the balcony.

I'm going to die!

Apparently not.

She landed parallel to the cliff's edge, a boulder the only barrier between her and certain death. She took three deep breaths then examined her extremities.

Nothing broken.

Using the boulder as a crutch, she managed a wobbly stand, then scanned the slippery slope back to the apex. Nearly straight up. Impossible without gear or support of some kind.

She should sit by the boulder, call for help, and wait for rescue—the rational, reasonable solution if darkness weren't settling in too quickly. She'd be forced to spend the night, unprotected and with no light. She shuddered. No one knew she was here, except for a child who probably only existed in her imagination.

She reached for her cell, then remembered she'd left it on the counter with her canteen and backpack. The only option left to her—risk the climb to where she'd fallen.

She scanned the area in search of a limb she might use as a walking stick. Her gaze rested on a piece of crumpled cloth stuck within a group of stubbly pines. She could snap off a branch to use as a pick—make the climb on all fours.

She eased down to a prone position and sighed with relief when she snapped off the lower branch of a dwarf pine. As she plunged the limb deep into the wet clay, her hand rested on something solid. She looked back and gasped at skeletal remains, arranged like sticks of a bird's nest. Bony talons stuck together as if in prayer. Marci struggled to breathe. *First, the boy—now bones?*

A rush of fear propelled her forward. She repositioned her makeshift pick with the speed of an Olympian until, at last, she hauled her shaken form to the crest, then scurried to the elevator path, grateful no one was near to witness her hysteria. Tears of fright wet her cheeks as the elevator descended.

Once in her car, she took a dozen staccato breaths, closed her eyes, and leaned back against the seat. The boy—the nest of bones—neither made sense. She'd go home, guzzle a gallon of water, then go to bed. Chalk up the whole scare as nothing more than skewered perception brought on by overexertion. In Scarlet O'Hara's words, "Tomorrow is another day."

CHAPTER 2

ONE MONTH LATER

Marci's knuckles turned white as she gripped the car door handle. Must she attend this charade?

Her sister Anna pulled her Lexus into the valet circle. "We're here. At the very least, pretend to enjoy yourself ... for my sake."

Marci exited the vehicle and gazed at La Grande's gothic gargoyles, their masonic talons uplifted in derision, taunting, "You're still insane, Marci Henderson."

She hesitated at the stairway positioned between her tormentors, the only way to enter. This night could prove to be as disastrous as her climb up Wolf Mountain last month. She'd be better off home. No hallucinations there.

"Are you going to stand there all night?" Anna propped her hands on her hips, her nonverbal *tsk*. "I didn't fork out two hundred dollars for you to stare at the architecture. Please try to have fun—if not for yourself, then for everyone else. No one wants to be around a sour face."

Anna probably paid more for her diamond-studded clutch purse than what she shelled out for the alumni dinner. Still, she had a point. Marci was Anna's guest. A good guest should not make her host uncomfortable. She should shake off the feeling of being slighted. Not surprisingly, she herself had received no invitation to the fundraiser though she was as much an alumna as Anna. Only the wealthy alumni and prospective hefty donors had received a Dean Foster invite. Not many from her circle of friends would be there, not that she had many friends when she attended.

Marci adjusted her shawl, sucked in courage, and ventured into the lobby. *Baby steps.* First get into the lobby, then find a seat among strangers. That way she only had to offer an occasional nod. If questioned about her college days, she could feign memory loss. Certainly, she should be able to manage two hours of meaninglessness for a sister who'd been her rock for the past two years.

The incident on Wolf Mountain didn't mean she'd relapsed, and nothing out of the ordinary had occurred since then. If she hoped to return to work in the fall, she'd have to fight this tendency toward reclusiveness.

Tonight, Marci Henderson would prove to the world she deserved to walk among the sane.

She glanced at Anna, who wore confidence like a mink as she scanned La Grande's gala room. "I knew it'd be a packed house. Blake Montgomery is a much better draw than boring Dean Foster."

"Blake is tonight's speaker?"

"I thought I told you."

"No, you didn't. If I'd known, I never would have agreed to come."

"Well, now you know."

"Take me home, Anna."

"No. You're going to stay. You can avoid Blake if you want to, but you and your fifty-dollar coiffure that I paid for are staying put until I say it's time to go home."

"Fine. You win this round."

Marci sighed as she followed Anna's lead. Though a year younger, Anna had been the stronger sister—

determined and brave—while Marci lost herself in books. Even during their Briarcliffe years, the Vincent girls were bookends on the same shelf with nothing between them.

She turned toward Anna. "I hope no one remembers me." Her sister's popularity filled the fun pages of the yearbook. Not so for Marci. She'd buried her memories, especially those concerning Blake Montgomery.

Few knew Anna's compassionate side, a compartment of her complex personality saved for Marci alone. Anna's eyes misted. "You'll do fine, Marci. You need this night."

Anna thrived on attention, energized even by funerals. Three months divorced from husband number four, she might very well be scouting for her next pot of gold. Like priceless art, each of her failed marriages had increased her net worth by several million dollars.

Anna had already sabotaged Marci's best excuses to stay home. Though she expected the night to be more painful than a medieval torture chamber, she'd wrapped her psyche in steel before she left the house. But there was no weapon in her social survival arsenal fashioned against a close encounter with Blake Montgomery.

Call a cab and go home.

Anna's squeeze commanded obedience. "If you dare leave, I'll never speak to you again."

Marci gulped resolve, then moved deeper into the gala room, a mental walk on Blackbeard's plank. She scanned the room for a secluded table in the back, close to the door. Her gaze landed on a lean, middle-aged man who spoke with a group of alumni at the rear bar. Though his hair had grayed around the temples, he looked no different than the handsome history professor who'd stolen her heart so many years before.

Her knees wobbled as she grabbed Anna's arm. "Please. Take me home. I can't do this."

Crystal blue eyes met Marci's fear. "You're staying."

"What if someone asks about my job? Or Matt?"

"Matt died two years ago. That's all you need to say. As for work? You're not lying if you say you're between jobs."

Marci positioned her feet for flight, but Anna's firm pull propelled them forward. "Don't let a roomful of snooty people drive you back into seclusion. You're well, Marci. Let the world see the beautiful woman I know you to be. Look how far you've come—except for the little set-back after you climbed Wolf Mountain last month. What happened up there?"

"Nothing worth mentioning. Besides, I'm better now."

"I hope so. Go hide in a corner if you must. I came for a good time, and I fully intend to complete my mission." She released her hold and sauntered toward her former classmates, a model on her social runway. Her floor-length, blue-sequined, strapless gown glimmered as she passed underneath the chandelier.

Marci marveled at Anna's changed gait. Gone was her energetic prowl, a cover up for a once agitated spirit. Indeed, over the past few months, Anna seemed different in many ways. A gentler Anna was a welcomed respite, yet the cause for her metamorphosis remained a mystery.

For now, Anna surrendered the night to her personal agenda and left Marci with two choices—either face the dragons alone or be her sister's slinky shadow the rest of the evening. In this dim light, dressed in a black chiffon sheath, she could blend into the décor and remain invisible, no different than during much of her college years.

She scanned the crowd, voyeurism one way to survive group situations—easier to simply observe than to be engaged. Her attention veered toward a middle-aged man, standing alone at the bar. Dressed in a disco-era blue tuxedo, his retro John Kennedy haircut added to his mismatched aura. If nothing else, she could amuse herself by studying this human anachronism. *Who is he? Why is he here?* Like her, he might have been mentally bludgeoned to attend—and like her, felt horribly out of place. In that regard, they would be kindred spirits.

She scanned the crowd again, suddenly aware of her lower status as she compared her department store gown to the elegant designer fashions flittering about in the ballroom atmosphere. She reminded herself that only the wealthiest of the wealthy were invited to a Dean Foster fundraiser. Marci earned her admission only by invitation from Collins Bend's richest divorcee. A simple high school teacher rarely rubbed shoulders with the cliff dwellers who lived in homes nearly as opulent as the Wordsworth Mansion in its day. Maybe Cinderella didn't run from the ball because the clock struck twelve. Maybe she simply felt out of place. No amount of finery would change the fact that underneath she was a rag doll—her only true companions, the mice she fed.

Maybe that's how the man in the blue tuxedo felt. Maybe she could overcome her own discomfort by befriending someone as terrified as herself. She returned her gaze to where he had stood.

Gone.

She pursed her lips. *Get a grip, woman.* The man could have simply left to use the restroom.

Not every strange occurrence is a waking dream.

She found an empty table, sat and drummed her fingers in boredom. She should mingle. Parties had always seemed the bane of foolishness, even the few she attended with Matt. Like Anna, he loved the night life and went to some occasion or another most every weekend. Maybe that's where he'd met *her,* his liaison in death.

"Marci Vincent?"

She whipped around to meet the male voice. Blake's hazel eyes twinkled. Her breath hitched. This night would be easier if he'd gained a hundred pounds. "It's Marci Henderson now."

"Yes, I'd heard you married after graduation."

"Matt died two years ago." She spoke the words in the same manner as she had practiced them, only now sensing the statement's frigidity. Blake must think her unfeeling.

She searched his eyes, widened with—what? Pity?

"Yes, I know. Anna told me. I'm terribly sorry for your loss."

"You've already spoken with Anna tonight? We only arrived a few minutes ago." And what else had Anna told Blake? Hopefully, she hadn't mentioned Marci's hospitalization.

"I talked to Anna last week. I've rented one of her units at Glass Lake, near Wolf Mountain."

"Are you retiring to the area, or are you planning a vacation?"

"Neither. I'm taking a sabbatical while I write a book on Wordsworth's contribution to railroad development. Alfred Donahue helped me secure a contract with his publisher. And perhaps I'll get a chance to enjoy a bit of nature as well."

In the photo album of her soul, visions of Sorrel Pond resurfaced—their leisurely walks to an abandoned cabin, their secret place. "If I recall, you never needed an excuse to enjoy nature."

His ruddy cheeks faded as he took a sip from his glass. Whatever he drank refreshed his color. "I still love to do those things. In fact, I have a golf date planned with Alfred in a few days."

"How is Professor Donahue?"

"He's here tonight too." Blake pointed toward the other end of the room where a still nimble, eighty-something Alfred Donahue regaled a group of former students, most likely with a story or two about youthful exploits in Dublin.

"Is he in Collins Bend for pleasure or to promote his books?"

"Both. He retired last year and has been traveling the North Country to campaign for Will Forrester's senatorial bid while doing book signings. He's busier than the president. Alfred promised if I spent a sabbatical here, he'd find time to play a few rounds."

"How hard did he have to twist your arm?"

"No twisting needed. I've wanted to come here for years. I ran into Alfred during his recent speaking engagement at the college. He remembered my interest in the Wordsworth estate and suggested I summer here and complete my research."

Marci glanced at the floor, awkward perhaps, but necessary to avoid Blake's magnetic eyes. "I'd heard Alfred was supporting Will's bid for Congress." *Blake just said that ... why repeat it?* Nervous sweat beaded on her forehead as memories flooded and drowned sensibility. *Stop talking. Listen and nod the head from time to time.*

Minutes passed with Blake staring at her as if examining a Monet. Nor could she think of anything to say. Awkwardness filled the air until he blew the silence aside with yet another question. "Are you with anyone tonight?"

Marci glanced toward Anna who owned the further end of the gala room and was circled by a perky flock of former cheerleaders. "I came with Anna but ..."

Blake smiled. "No need to explain. You're welcome to join my table. Alfred will be sitting with us, and he brought a couple of guests—tourists—Tad and Bianca

Manning, brother and sister, who are also renting a cabin from Anna. Not far from mine, I understand."

"Alumni?"

"They aren't. But apparently, their father was Verne Manning, a friend of Dean Foster's during his notorious student days at Briarcliffe. And, of course, they come with a fat wallet.

"Tad claims his father attended many of these banquets, although I had never met the man personally."

"I ..."

"I do hope you'll join us."

No graceful way out. At least with Professor Donahue at the table, she wouldn't need to talk since the man would probably dominate the evening—entertainingly so. "That would be nice, but aren't you the main event?"

"Come again?"

"The scheduled speaker?"

Blake nodded toward the podium. "Only during dessert. Between you and me, I'd rather have all my teeth pulled than officiate at one of these things. Dean Foster does a far better job. Since he's tired of doing them, he only agreed to my sabbatical if I substituted for him tonight."

Blake took Marci's arm and escorted her to the head table where they were joined by Professor Donahue and a svelte brunette, her red, spaghetti-strapped dress more pasted on than simply snug. Marci assumed this woman was Bianca Manning, the tourist Blake mentioned earlier.

He introduced the table guests while everyone took a seat. Bianca batted her long lashes in Blake's direction, and he returned her attention with appreciative smiles. Bianca's brother, Tad, ping ponged his glances from Blake to Bianca. His large, oval eyes added to his mystique. Anna would have called them bedroom eyes. Curiously, and perhaps inappropriately, Tad's glances veered seductively toward his sister. He rendered an occasional, inexplicable scowl.

As if suddenly reminded of his role as host, Blake passed the bread to Professor Donahue. "Alfred, you remember Marci Vincent? I believe she took English classes from you before changing her major to history."

"I do. I'll admit, I can't recall the names of every student. But you, I remember. I don't forget defectors." He offered a wink of forgiveness.

Bianca let go of Alfred's arm and nibbled her salad, a rabbit at the feast. "Alfred tells me you're our speaker tonight, Dr. Montgomery. Care to tease us with a trailer?"

Blake blushed. "Believe me, Miss Manning—"

"Bianca, please."

"Bianca, then. I'm a poor substitute for Dean Foster."

Not so, Blake. As Marci recalled, she was not the only coed to adore Dr. Montgomery's lectures, resulting in a flood of converts to the glories of history.

Bianca leaned in, her flowery perfume as pungent as a stroll through a lilac garden. "Well, I'm sure your talk will be fascinating, Dr. Montgomery."

"Please, call me Blake."

"Oh, but Dr. Montgomery is so much more ... you." Her nasal tones scraped like metal on a ceramic floor. "And what do you know regarding the Wordsworth legend? Is it as fascinating as Alfred's tales?"

"Every bit, so I'm told."

Images of last month's climb resurfaced. Marci tuned out Blake's side conversation with Professor Donahue to study Bianca. Something about her voice rang familiar, as if a distant memory before Matt's death—before one day ran into another and her life became one gigantic blur. Maybe Bianca and Tad used to come to Collins Bend with their father, though Marci never recalled meeting anyone named Verne Manning or his children.

The seemingly perpetual sulking Tad piped up. "Dr. Montgomery, what do you think ever became of Felicity Wordsworth?"

"The meat of my book focuses on Wordsworth's contribution to the railroad expansion in the Adirondacks and the resultant surge in lumber trade. However, I must admit, the mystery surrounding her disappearance has always intrigued me."

Bianca slipped her hand on top of Blake's. "Oh, I so look forward to hearing about your discoveries. Perhaps you'd do Tad and me the honor of coming to dinner next week?"

Marci's thoughts bounced from curiosity over Bianca's too-familiar voice to Blake's descriptions of Wordsworth's contributions to North Country development.

When Blake paused, Professor Donahue winked at Bianca and added his own dime of knowledge. "Been to Wolf Mountain twice *meself*," he said. "Odd Wordsworth's accountant disappeared at the same time as Felicity. Theory is they had an affair and ran off together after setting fire to the mansion. Not a stretch of the imagination. She was beautiful, and Wordsworth was twice her age."

Bianca oozed interest, and Blake gobbled her *oohs* and *ahs* like mint-chocolate ice cream. "Perhaps I'll see the mansion while we're in Collins Bend." She sneered at her brother. "Of course, Tad is more interested in the Collins Bend Golf Course."

Tad brightened. "Don't kid yourself, Dr. Montgomery. Bianca's quite the golfer. Could have gone pro." He glanced first at Blake then at Professor Donahue. "Do either of you golf?"

Professor Donahue mimicked a short swing as he laughed. "I'm a duffer, I'm afraid. Blake has to give me a ten-stroke handicap."

Tad gazed directly at Marci. His long, dark lashes and smooth, milky complexion bordered on effeminate. "And how about you, Marci? Do you golf?"

"I went a few times with my late husband when we first came to Collins Bend. Two years before he died, he gave up the sport—said he liked fishing more."

Blake cocked his head to one side. "Maybe we could get a group together sometime?"

Bianca's lipstick glistened over a perfect smile. Something about her was as off as her makeup.

The conversation drifted from Collins Bend Country Club's challenges—ten out of eighteen fairways graced by an enormous water hole—to compliments toward La Grande's ambiance. When dessert arrived, Blake stood. "I suppose I'd better do my thing. If you'll excuse me."

He took the stage with a hesitant swagger, a familiar half-proud, half self-conscious gait that once made him the heartthrob of every coed and still the most interesting man Marci had ever known.

"Friends of Briarcliffe, thank you for your attention." He flashed a few charts and rattled off statistics. The audience shifted in their seats and fondled programs. A few didn't bother to hide their yawns.

Blake closed the PowerPoint, then dropped his index cards to the floor. "Facts and figures do not tell a story. People do."

The audience applauded with agreement.

"Briarcliffe is more than a seat of knowledge. For over a hundred years, the school's graduates have gone on to illustrious careers. Look around you—doctors, lawyers, and politicians. However, an education can do far more than simply prepare the privileged to take their place in the world. Let me tell you about Landon, a delinquent boy who found purpose in knowledge. As he studied the past, he found hope for his future."

Though older, Blake had lost none of his allure. Marci hung on every word. He had shared little of his past with her. Yet, as he spoke, she knew beyond any doubt Landon's story was in truth Blake's.

Admiration wafted through the room, as aromatic as freshly brewed coffee. No one brought history to life as passionately as Blake Montgomery. Not even their disappointing romance changed Marci's opinion in that regard.

His speech ended, and she stood with the rest of the attendees to offer a standing ovation. Though she could not deny her desire for him, she knew those days were past. She'd resist this resurgent infatuation, go home in a few hours, and this would be the last she'd see of Blake Montgomery.

CHAPTER 3

Her tablemates were long gone, and the *La Grande* had emptied faster than Friday night bingo at St. Michael's Church. Marci gazed at the few remaining attendees and searched for the man in the blue tuxedo. Since the cursory glance at the bar, she hadn't seen him the rest of the evening. Was he another figment of her imagination?

She glanced at her watch. Most guests exited within minutes of signing their pledge cards, except Anna and her entourage. She pranced and purred, a hungry cat devouring attention.

A limp strand of hair brushed against Marci's neck. Anna's gifted coiffure sagged along with Marci's determination to make the most of this dreadful night. She grabbed her purse, pulled out a small pad, and scribbled a note for Anna: *Gone ahead to the car*.

She readjusted her shawl, then scanned the event room for a hotel staffer to deliver the message, but the sliver of paper slipped from her hand. She bent to pick up her note. As she stood, she met Blake's broad smile.

"Why the rush? Anna doesn't appear ready to leave anytime soon."

Marci threw random glimpses about the room, anywhere to avoid Blake's eyes—gorgeous, dangerous, lake-blue eyes that pulled her into a place she didn't dare go—a destructively familiar place.

"I should throw a rope around her and drag her out the door. Otherwise, we'll be here all night."

Blake stepped closer. "Gives me time to ask you a question."

Don't ask. Go away.

"Since I'm spending the next few months here, I wondered if we could get together some time."

Get together? As in dinner and what dinner implied? Or as in, I'm just being polite to a poor widow? "I'm very busy."

"Maybe you could block me in for an appointment?"

She turned away. "Well, I'm ..."

Blake laughed. "Your sister already gave me your number. I will call you."

Not a question, rather a statement uttered with conviction. Maybe he truly intended to call, but this time she wouldn't sit by the phone.

When she turned to face him again, he was gone. If only he'd been a hallucination like the man in the blue tuxedo.

When she reached Anna's fan club, Marci tapped her sister three times on the shoulder, a signal used since their teen years, requesting to leave an uncomfortable situation.

Anna turned. Her cocked brow registered agitation. She shrugged, then turned back toward her friends. "Sorry, girls. Early morning tomorrow. Busy, busy, busy." She lifted her purse from the table. "Let's do lunch, girls. Soon. Okay?"

She saved her snarls until after the valet left to retrieve her car. "Honestly, Marci. What's your hurry?"

"Hurry? Hardly anyone left in there. Even Dr. Montgomery is gone."

Anna found her smile again. "I saw you two talking. And he sat with you. Isn't he as gorgeous as ever?"

"I suppose. I hadn't noticed."

"I doubt that."

"Is it true he's renting one of your cabins?"

Anna nodded. "Next door to the Manning siblings."

"I'm sure Bianca's pleased."

"Jealous?"

"Hardly."

"I thought for sure he'd ask you out. He never married, you know."

Marci bit her lower lip. "Well, he wasn't interested."

Anna cocked her head. "You're lying."

"If you must know, he sort of asked me to dinner but nothing specific. I told him I was too busy."

"So that's that?"

"He said he'd call me."

"And?"

"Even if he does call, I'm not ready to start dating. You of all people should know why."

Anna's eyes misted. "Look, Marci. We've both had sour relationships with men. If I haven't given up on romance, you shouldn't either."

"Who said I've given up?"

"So, you'll see Blake?"

"No, I can't."

The attendant pulled up with Anna's Lexus, and Marci slipped into the passenger seat, securing her seatbelt while Anna threw hers to the side. "Don't wall yourself up, Marci. Love is out there. For both of us. If I didn't believe in love, I'd curl up and die."

Two positives from Anna in a five-minute interval? Odd. In fact, over the last two months, Anna had been increasingly optimistic about life, strangely deviant from the self-absorbed social butterfly Marci grew up with.

19

Anna eased onto the open road while the radio played "Sounds of Silence." The songwriter likened quiet to an old friend. Marci did too.

Anna sighed, deep and thoughtful. "You know tomorrow's Sunday."

"Yes. Sunday normally follows Saturday."

"Why don't you go to church with me?"

Marci turned, expecting Anna to burst out in laughter or say something like, "Reeled you in on that one, didn't I?" Instead, her gaze was dead serious.

"You? Church? Since when?"

"I've been going since Robert and I divorced."

"Robert's gay. How did that push you toward religion?" Marci struggled to remember the last time she'd stepped inside a church. Not since Matt's funeral. He'd been the spiritual one. He'd preached to her about having what he called a relationship with the Lord ... enough so Marci knew all the language. She'd even considered letting God in as Matt had described. But his faith had not kept him from being unfaithful. What was the point of going all Christian if it didn't keep you from sin?

"Church would be good for you."

"I don't know—I haven't been since Matt—"

"God's not to blame for Matt's mistakes."

"The accident or the affair?"

"Both."

Anna never took no for an answer. Might as well agree so they could talk about something else. "Okay, if my going to church with you will make you happy, I'll go." She owed Anna. More like a best friend than a sister, she'd been Marci's lifeline back to reality after her hospitalization. A church service didn't come close to the level of challenge Marci had met at tonight's events—and she'd survived. "As long as the church has sturdy rafters, I'm in."

Anna smiled. "Don't worry. If the roof didn't fall on me, it won't fall on you."

Blake loosened his tie and swiped his hotel room keycard. One more night in these digs, then tomorrow he'd move into his furnished cabin. Not much to unpack. A computer, golf clubs, clothes, and personal items. Ten minutes, tops.

He yawned. How did Dean Foster do these dinners night after night? No wonder he took advantage of an opportunity to skip the Adirondack Alumni Association gala, according to Dean Foster, the most pretentious of all but also the most lucrative.

Blake's cell played "Rock of Ages." Dean Foster. He accepted the call.

"Blake, how'd it go?"

"We raised nearly ten million in endowments. You were right. The Adirondacks swarm with wealthy alumni and potential donors."

"Good job, son. Sure you don't want the gig permanently?"

"Absolutely not. Good night." Blake disconnected.

His stomach burned from a sea of acid. A ginger beer might help. Where would he find one this late at night? He grabbed his wallet and rode the elevator to the lobby and wandered into the lounge.

A bartender approached. "What'll ya have?"

"Ginger beer?"

"Sorry. Best I can do is ginger ale."

"Better than nothing."

As Blake tossed his payment on the counter, a distant voice beckoned. "Blake, *me boyo*. Come keep an old man company."

He turned and spotted Alfred as he waved from a distant table near the fireplace. Blake picked up his drink and joined his mentor. The monotone crackles of the fire and a misty smoke lulled Blake's senses. Hopefully, he'd sleep well tonight.

"Thanks for coming, Alfred. You have the gift of persuasion. I don't believe for one minute those folks' generosity was a direct result of my speech. I saw how you worked the crowd. No wonder Will Forrester hired you to spearhead his campaign funding."

"Glad to oblige on both accounts." Though the man regaled audiences large enough to fill Madison Square Garden, his modesty remained his most recognizable trait.

"How long will you be in Collins Bend this time?" Blake asked.

"At least the summer. Maybe longer. Writing a new book."

"What does this make? Twenty?"

"Twenty-four, but who's counting?"

"Another commentary on Irish folklore?"

Alfred laughed. "Thought I'd write a collection of immigration stories. A large Irish population in these hills, especially Collins Bend."

Alfred always seemed to find an Irish community wherever he set down his hat. "So, Alfred, when are you going to write your autobiography—finally spill the beans on your mysterious past?"

Alfred leaned back in his chair, his face etched in seriousness. "Not so mysterious, Blake. An angry, hungry lad makes a good rebel. The day I left Ireland, I vowed to the Almighty I'd fight a different war—a war against ignorance. I'd write books instead of building bombs."

Blake knew the pain of war all too well. "I suspect there's much more you're not telling."

"Blake, lad, we all have something in our lives we wish we could change. I believe those dark moments can ultimately lead to good. Cain murdered his brother but went on to build a city. Moses killed an Egyptian but led a nation to freedom."

"I suppose our pasts have a way of shaping our future."

Alfred raised his glass of O'Doul's. "I liked your speech tonight. I never knew you were such a rascal. Pegged you as the quiet type—prep school and a bourgeoisie heritage."

"How did you know Landon was me?"

"I think Landon is both of us. So, what's your story, *boyo*?"

From anyone else, the question would have prompted a quick exit. But Alfred Donahue, more than a mentor, deserved honest answers. "Always been a bit of a coward, Alfred."

"Is that so? Not the Blake I've come to know."

"And the Blake you knew before you led me to a better way?"

"Maybe ... the young Blake wasn't as much a coward as he was self-absorbed. Don't be so hard on yourself. Isn't a man or woman alive hasn't experienced a time when courage vanished."

Blake sighed. Coward should be branded on his shirt like a scarlet letter. "War changes a man, Alfred."

"That it does, *boyo*."

"After the Army, I tried to change, to earn self-respect. I wanted to think of myself as a good person." Blake tapped his chest. "Got a scar stretching from arm pit to arm pit. Not a day goes by but what I'm reminded of my true character—like Landon, the boy who robbed a fruit market and rolled on his friends. They went to juvy, while I only got a slap on the hand. I was just as guilty."

Alfred leaned in. "Sounded like a sane move to me. God embedded a survival instinct in the human spirit for a good reason."

"I hoped I'd find danger when I enlisted. Thought maybe if I faced a challenge head on and won, I'd finally be free of self-hatred."

Alfred snickered. "Didn't work out as you planned?"

"I volunteered for a mission to drop propaganda on Iraqi villages. As the leaflets fell like hail, the enemy appeared out of nowhere."

Blake could still hear the *tat-a-tat-tat* of repetitive fire as he cringed with fear, his screams as loud as the gunfire against the helicopter. "While my comrades fought back, I hid behind the parachutes."

"Chances are you weren't that old. What? Nineteen?"

"Eighteen, actually. I heard the crunch of metal, smelled burning flesh. Seven of my buddies died in that crash. Every day since, I ask God why he spared a coward, and better men perished."

"God's mercy is independent of our goodness. A truth you should never forget. Forgive yourself as God forgives you. He erases our past and turns our regrets into legacies."

Blake raised his glass. "Well, then—to our dark pasts. May they be remembered no more."

They clinked glasses and agreed in unison. "Here. Here."

Alfred set his glass back down and hunched over the table. "So, Blake. Given any thought where you'll go to church while you're in Collins Bend?"

"Not really, though I should make church shopping a priority."

"There's this wee community church across from the police barracks that a history buff like yourself might enjoy. One of the first churches built around here, I understand. Complete with a belfry. Services cater to tourists but are still inspirational."

"Why not? What time?"

"Pick me up at nine. We can go out for a bite afterward. My treat."

"Deal. I'm moving into my cabin in the morning."

"Need help?"

"No, doesn't take long to unpack two suitcases, a computer, and a golf bag." He downed the rest of his beverage. "If I'm getting an early start tomorrow, I should try to get some shuteye."

They rose and walked toward the elevator. Alfred sighed. "Might stop at the cemetery tomorrow morning. Want to pay respect to my boy who's buried there."

"I'm sorry, Alfred. I didn't know you'd lost a son."

"Five years ago. Settled in Collins Bend after he retired from the military. My daughter-in-law moved back near her folks. Shame my boy's grave doesn't get looked after much."

"Is that why you keep coming back here?"

"Why I accepted Forrester's offer to help with his campaign. He and Ryan, if he'd lived, would be the same age."

"What about the other children? Eleven all together, if I remember?"

Alfred grinned. "Most of them do me proud, and none of them are in jail. The youngest graduated law school this year. Just started working for the DA's office in Chicago."

"I remember your older son, Paul, from college days."

"He still owns more businesses than I can count. Don't know if all his wealth has done him any good, though. His wife left him two years ago."

The elevator stopped at Alfred's floor. "Rest well, Blake. I'll see you in the morning." He exited, turned right, and vanished down the hall.

So much about Alfred to admire, a man who lived a life most could only dream. His progeny could populate a hamlet. What legacy would Blake Montgomery boast? Having no children and disillusioned by his short military career, he'd hoped to be remembered for his academic achievements. Lately, though, not even his promotion to department chair eased the gnawing restlessness.

Dean Foster apparently noticed the bags under Blake's eyes caused by too many sleepless nights. Perhaps this was why the dean honored Blake's request for a sabbatical. "Take the breather, son. Go to Collins Bend. Solve the mystery on Wolf Mountain you're always talking about. Look for your pot of gold. While you're there, maybe you'll find yourself."

Until then, Blake hadn't realized he was lost.

CHAPTER 4

Marci stared at the cupboard until her eyes blurred. What to eat? She'd promised Dr. Solomon she'd down a good breakfast every day. Frosted bran? The sugary coating might compensate for cardboard. She reached into the refrigerator for milk. Only two tablespoons left in the container. She'd have to eat the cereal dry or go out to get more milk. No eggs in the fridge either. How she hated to shop, but errands at sunrise provided less opportunity to run into people she knew.

She glanced at her watch. She still had an hour before Anna picked her up for church. Gray's Convenience Store would be the least trafficked this time of day—and only a five-minute walk. Better if she drove—less likely to run into Sunday morning strollers. As she backed out of her driveway, a white Osprey, parked two houses up, sped off—dangerously fast for this neighborhood, too fast to see who was driving.

She turned onto Main and searched for a parking space. Not a one near Gray's. She drove around the block once more and found an empty spot in front of Bert's Tackle across the street from the market. As she stepped onto the sidewalk, she caught sight of an older gentleman dressed in kakis and a fishing vest. He sat on the cast-iron bench in front of the store. Not so unusual, yet she stared at him. No one she immediately recognized, yet he seemed oddly familiar. One of Matt's fishing buddies?

The man glanced up and waved as if he knew her. No time for idle chatter, so she crossed to Gray's just as another white Osprey accelerated down the road. She gulped, then chided herself for her paranoia. Of course, there would be more than one Osprey in Collins Bend, especially with a dealership on the corner of Main and Third. In fact, she'd been thinking of trading her Honda for an Osprey next year, perhaps a white one. This might be an explanation of her sudden awareness.

She dashed into Gray's, picked up her milk and looked for the fisherman, feeling remorseful for her previous snobbery.

Gone.

Another hallucination? If so, what about the two Ospreys? Was anything real? Was she truly on Main Street right now or asleep in her recliner? She pinched her arm.

"Ouch!"

The pain seemed real enough.

Anna honked the horn. Marci hesitated. If she were seeing things today, should she try to go to church? Maybe her next hallucination would be a spiritual visitation. She might be more believable if she saw angels rather than fishermen on benches and white Ospreys racing down village streets, not to mention bones, curly-headed toddlers, or men in blue tuxedos.

All her visions could be real. The curly-headed little boy might have simply escaped her peripheral vision.

The bones could have been nothing more than animal skeletons, and Marci's imagination took over from there. The man in the blue tuxedo probably got bored and went home. The friendly fisherman most likely went to get something to eat.

Foolish to feel afraid. She'd promised Anna she'd go to the worship service. Besides, churches were safe places.

"So, what's the name of this church?" Marci asked as Anna pulled out from the driveway.

"Collins Bend Community, now. Originally, it was an Anglican church, the first built in the area. Now it's an historic landmark."

Marci fell into silent mode while Anna gibbered about last night's banquet, how much money she donated, and about every former cheerleader's gown.

After they parked, Marci headed toward the historic marker while Anna walked ahead, her lack of interest in history no surprise. Tourist plaques made poor pathways to new husbands. Marci let her imagination escape into the past, a place she'd much prefer to be, especially after these strange imaginings. Her mind crashed against her crested thoughts. Wolf Mountain, once her place of assurance and solace, wooed her, begging her to solve its mystery—to exonerate the estate's maligned mistress.

For years, she'd studied every inch of Wolf Mountain's apex. There she felt at home, even more than her house. There she wrapped herself in nature's symphony as history danced in the annals of her psyche. Yet, she could not return. At least not for the foreseeable future—not until she could explain these hallucinations, or delusions, or however Dr. Solomon would decide to classify them.

Matt preferred music over nature. His gospel quartet became a favorite at North Country churches. At first, he begged her to attend his performances. Perhaps he tired of her constant refusals, for the invitations suddenly ceased. Maybe, if she'd gone as he'd asked ...

Stop conjecturing, Marci!

She recalled Dr. Solomon's counsel. "Don't dwell on what you perceive as past mistakes." All the regret in the world could not right the wrongs—hers as well as Matt's. She'd wanted to love Matt as much as he said he loved her. Did he really? If he did, why did he have an affair? Or was his perceived devotion part of the delusion that had driven her to insanity?

She squinted at the sign again, still unable to pull away from what she could not change. The year before Matt died, she'd determined to go to church with him as a good wife should. Didn't matter. He still cheated on her. Maybe Matt had a chance to whisper a prayer of penance before he died, and maybe God forgave him. Good for God. Why should she have to?

Did Anna expect going to church would force Marci into forgiving Matt? She could count on one hand the number of times she'd entered a sanctuary—her wedding and Matt's funeral included. Why join the hypocrites with phony hallelujahs? She was here, and she'd made a promise. No way out now. Since pinky swearing as children, neither sister had broken a pledge made to the other.

Marci caught up to Anna, waiting by the entrance. "Come on, the church is filling up fast. This is a popular tourist attraction."

They sped to an empty pew near the back of the church. Likely, Anna intended to fish *for* men rather than become a fisher *of* men. Maybe she thought her pool was here because she'd run the gamut of all other local marriageable men—at least, any who would fit her criteria: handsome, rich, well-educated, rich, socially connected, and rich. Now independently wealthy and nearing middle age, perhaps she'd settle for alive and heterosexual. Vigor and community standing were no guarantees of happiness, as she'd already discovered.

As she sat, Marci whispered, "What's the real reason you come to this time warp?"

Anna straightened. "I don't blame you for being suspicious. I know my former way of life doesn't mesh with the church-going crowd."

"Let's just say when the word gets out you claim to be a Christian, more than one jaw will drop."

"Maybe, at first, I came here hoping to meet a man with staying power. Pastor Rick introduced me to *the* Man and said He's got staying power for sure."

"I'm assuming you got—what Matt termed—*saved*?"

"If you mean, I prayed the prayer of repentance and made a personal commitment to the Lord, then, yes, I'm saved."

Heat surged. "You sound like Matt. He preached to me all the time. Didn't keep him on the straight and narrow."

Anna squeezed Marci's hand. "My dear, Marci. I'm only just beginning to understand being a Christian doesn't make a person perfect or even prevent them from making mistakes. Only God knows if a heart loves him or not."

"I'll never forgive Matt."

The pipe organ crooned "Bringing in the Sheaves," and all chatter quieted to a respectful hush. Pastor Rick came to the pulpit donned in intricately bordered white vestments.

"Greetings in the Name of the Lord."

Marci sat with rigid resistance, refusing to join in with the congregation as they echoed, "Greetings in the Name of the Lord."

Anna swatted Marci with the bulletin, punching the line, *Order of Service*. "The service is only an hour," she whispered. "Even you should be able to pay attention that long."

Pastor Rick projected his arms in a congregational entreaty. "Open your hymn books to number 543, 'A Mighty Fortress Is Our God.'"

Marci listened to Anna's sweet soprano, reminiscent of when she'd sung solos in the school choir. How could they be biologically connected? When Marci sang, she harvested a crop of incredulous glances. Mama could sing, but their father had a tin ear. Why couldn't she have inherited Mama's voice as Anna had?

Rather than join the congregational singing, Marci surveyed the bevy of worshippers. She craned her neck toward the opposite side, spotting a young man who looked like Tad Manning, hunched along the wall. Odd. Good he was alone. If Bianca had come, the proverbial roof would definitely have collapsed from the presence of these two unlikely souls in the Lord's house.

A duet of male voices boomed from behind, one an unmistakable Irish tenor. She managed a quick glance. Blake and Professor Donahue. No surprise to see the professor at church—his faith was a well-known fact at Briarcliffe. His theological debates put the most devout atheist at a loss for words. Blake? His anti-religion rhetoric resonated from the meeting rooms of Briarcliffe's political left-wing caucuses.

She pulled her attention to the hymnal. The words squirmed like tiny, black worms. She raised her head, and the walls heaved as she gasped for air.

No. Not a panic attack! Not now!

Before she could grab the pew to steady herself, she slumped into unconsciousness.

Blake scooped Marci from the pew and carried her outside. Placing her on the bench, he slid in next to her, braced her limp body with one arm, then rested her head against his shoulder.

Anna paced back and forth. "Need any help?"

An elderly woman came from the church and approached them. "I noticed the poor girl passed out. You're a nice lad to help her to fresh air." The woman handed Blake a vial. "This should help. My friends laugh because I carry smelling salts in my purse just in case of emergencies like this one."

"Thank you."

The woman left as oddly as she had appeared.

He thought smelling salts had gone the way of the dinosaur. Mustn't look at his angel with suspicion, even a ninety-year-old one. He broke the vial under Marci's nose. Within seconds, her eyes fluttered. "Anna, she's coming around."

Anna sighed in relief. "Glad you were here, Blake. I don't know if I could have handled the situation as discreetly as you. If I'd called an ambulance, my sister would never have spoken to me again."

Blake smiled. "Got that right."

Anna sat on the other side of Marci. "Are you okay?"

Marci nodded.

"I'll let the ushers know you're okay." She left.

Marci took three deep breaths then sat up. "Did I pass out?"

He nodded. "I carried you outside. I thought the fresh air might help." Her cheeks pinked slightly. "I'm so embarrassed. Sometimes, I can't breathe in tight places. I'm fine, now. Really."

"Since my tour in the Middle East, I'm a bit claustrophobic myself. Do you want to go back in, or would you like me to take you home?"

"I'll stay out here and wait for Anna. No need for you to babysit me any longer." Her brows arched. "Why are you here, anyway? A church is the last place I'd expect to see you. I thought you didn't believe in God—or, at the least, if he existed, he forgot about his creation and left mankind to his own devices."

How could he answer her without going into a long monologue of his sins, his treatment of her high on the list of regrets? "I came here with Alfred Donahue. He thought I might enjoy this place for its historical significance."

Marci inched toward the other end of the bench. She trembled as she rose. Blake stood and put his arm around her shoulder in case she toppled. She wriggled from his hold. "Please. Go in before you miss the whole service."

She plopped back down on the bench as she drew her lips into a half sneer. "Alfred might feel like you ditched him." Condemnation laced every accentuated word.

Sweat trickled down her cheek, and a stray brown strand of hair dangled over her eye. In her disheveled and miffed state, she grabbed his heart now as she had the first time he saw her.

Five minutes into his lecture, she'd run into his World History class, huffing for breath as she sat in the last row, then buried her face behind a textbook. He walked to her desk, took her book, and glared. "And why are you disrupting my class, Miss ...?"

"Vincent. Marci Vincent." Her luminous, narrow eyes, like a sparrow's, pecked at his heart.

She looked at him now as she did then, as if inviting the earth to swallow her whole. "This is ridiculous. I'm fine. Thank you for your concern."

"I'd feel better if I stayed here with you. Could I get you a glass of water?"

"Not necessary. Give me another few minutes before going back in. I should sit in the back pew on the other side. I think the pew was empty except for Tad Manning."

"Who?"

"The one who sat with us during dinner last night. Tad."

"Yes. I remember Tad, but I didn't notice him here."

When they entered, Blake glanced toward the back pew. No Tad. "The pew's empty."

Her face paled. "Tad was there ... I swear he was."

"Maybe he left, and we didn't notice."

"Yes. He could have gone out another door, I suppose."

"Very possible."

Blake held Marci's arm as he helped her into the pew, then slipped in next to her, his glance drawn to her pouty lips—lips he'd like to kiss again.

CHAPTER 5

Marci sank into her recliner and wrapped her hands around her cup of freshly steeped raspberry tea. *Home sweet home.* She warmed to remember how comfortable she'd felt in Blake's arms. Had he shown more toward her than gallantry? Maybe, or perhaps being near him renewed her delusions.

She shook her head, like a dog shakes after his bath. She was not crazy. No matter how improbable, whatever she saw, whatever she sensed, must have a rational explanation—even if exhaustion were the cause. That would be something she could accept.

The child, the bones, the man in the blue tuxedo, the fisherman, and Tad—all seemed real. If not, they were visions far different than the delusion that caused her hospitalization. Hallucinations were often based on physical causes. If they continued, she'd see her family physician. No need to bother Dr. Solomon yet. How would rehashing Matt's death help her now? She'd had enough therapy.

Marci folded her hands across her chest. "Look on the bright side, Marci. You are a Caesar. *You came, you saw, you conquered*—even if you fainted. You went back into that church, to the scene of your embarrassment. Growth! Huge growth!"

She stared into the living-room mirror, her favorite meeting place with herself. "A few setbacks don't mean you dove off the cliff again. You've had too much time on your hands. That's the problem. Tomorrow morning, you're going to call Dr. Solomon and ask him to give you clearance to go back to work in the fall." She missed teaching. Later today, she'd clean out Matt's closest.

She'd leave the house once a day, if only for a walk. And maybe, the next time Blake crossed her path, she'd not drown in the tsunami of bitter memories.

Alex's Diner, a cross between a retro fifties joint and a modern-day truck stop with all the conveniences, was bustling with hungry customers. The atmosphere, a mixture of memorabilia and modern décor, like Blake's life, converged somewhere between the past and present. How he wished he could go back to a time before he heaped mistake upon mistake.

Most times, he enjoyed breakfast with Prof. Donahue— his stories, his testimonies of faith, and his dogged constancy. Today, Alfred rattled on about Collins Bend and the influence of Alex's Diner on its history. He pointed to a photograph of Olympic legend Sonja Henie. "According to William Forrester, the current owner is the fourth Alex to run the place. In its day, this was a hot spot for Olympians of both 1932 and 1980."

Alfred's accumulated trivia on Collins Bend and nearby Lake Placid would prove useful to Blake's research but would pale next to what Marci knew. "Is Forrester from Collins Bend?"

"No. Until the railroads went out of business, the rich and famous vacationed in the Adirondacks, especially the area between Saranac Lake and Lake Placid. If tourism hadn't revived thanks to the Olympics, Collins Bend might have become a permanent ghost town. Now it's on the list of favorite American villages—low crime, clean air, and drenched in history."

Blake perused his menu. "Thanks for the church invite, Alfred. I enjoyed the service. Maybe I'll go again sometime."

Alfred leaned toward Blake. "I hope Marci will be okay. Panic attack, you say? Pity such a pretty lass is so trapped in fear. I'll keep her on me prayer list. You can be sure of that, lad. Let me know how she's doing."

"If I see her again."

"How's that? I thought I sensed a spark there."

"I don't think she likes me anymore." He sipped his coffee.

"Now, how could any lass resist a fine strapping lad like you?"

Blake coughed with the thought. "I'm hardly a lad anymore."

Alfred leaned over the table. "You say Marci doesn't like you 'anymore,' meaning, she did once? I'm sensing a story here."

Blake pushed back against his chair. "Not much to tell. We dated while she attended Briarcliffe."

"I heard rumors about you and a coed. So, the girl was Marci?"

"The dean found out about us during her senior year. When he threatened to fire me, I panicked and ended our relationship—badly."

"How so?"

"I suggested we see other people."

"And the truth?"

"I loved her. I should have defied the dean. At the very least, I should have explained my predicament, asked her to wait to resume our relationship after she graduated."

Alfred raised his right brow. "Why didn't you?"

"While I stayed in my quandary, Marci found someone else. A music student. They seemed happy. I convinced myself breaking up had been for the best."

Alfred rubbed his chin. "I get the feeling your purpose here is not limited to your research."

Like a prophet, the man read Blake's heart. "I might have hoped I'd see her, especially after Anna told me Marci was widowed. When I invited her to dinner, she looked like she'd sooner go out with the devil's brother. Where Marci's concerned, I don't think there'll be a rerun. I blew my chance twenty years ago, and I'll regret my decision the rest of my life."

Alfred winked. "Now hold on there, *boyo*. Don't run out on her again because she's built a wall for you to climb over."

Blake clicked. "You're a wise man, my friend. Okay, then, I'll call her. Better yet, I'll go see her. Anna gave me her address."

Alfred raised his milk glass. "There's a good lad." The waitress came with their order, and he dug into his big plate of pancakes. For a thin oldster, he packed away a lot of food.

Blake picked at his fare as he remembered Marci's determination. He'd have to find some way to circumnavigate her resistance. If he went to her house, she might very well shut the door in his face. Unless she'd mellowed over the years, he'd have better luck moving the Wall of China than getting a second chance with Marci Vincent Henderson.

CHAPTER 6

"Rainy days and Mondays," Marci sang, the first time she'd lilted a melody in more years than she could remember. Belting out sour notes of a sad song in the privacy of her own home somehow energized her. She should allow herself to exercise her voice more often.

She'd never sung when Matt was home; her off-key pitches provided no end of amusement to a talented vocalist like he was. After his funeral, singing seemed disrespectful somehow. Enough with letting those foolish feelings dictate what she did or didn't do.

She peered out the window. The early morning rain washed the ground. Droplets of renewal beaded on dandelions as the rising sun promised a glorious day and gave her courage to face the task ahead.

She stood in front of Matt's closet for a few minutes, then opened the door—not that she hadn't tried before.

This emotional ping-ponging must stop. For one minute, grief sucked her into a dark hole, then anger pushed her out. If only she were able to will those warring thoughts into the trunk along with Matt's suits, then maybe she could be done with regret. Cleaning out his closet would end the tug of war, wouldn't it? That is, if she could manage the task without another psychotic episode.

Her first attempt, too soon after Matt's death, had sent her spiraling into delirium like an out-of-control firecracker. She had very little personal recollection. But if what occurred were half as bad as Anna reported, she held her sister no ill will for calling the ambulance.

Marci's cheeks heated. How could she have sunk so low? She had convinced herself she was carrying Matt's child, even experienced morning sickness, and her periods stopped. She entertained the notion she'd name the child after his father—yes, a boy—Matt deserved a son.

How foolish she felt when the doctor told her the pregnancy was a delusion. Filled with rage, she rushed into Matt's closet with a pair of scissors. She'd wielded them like a warrior's sword, a litany of foul words her battle cry. That was the last she remembered. Nor could she recall the hours, days, and weeks that followed until she realized she'd been admitted to a psychiatric facility. As Marci had gained understanding through Dr. Solomon's tender treatment and Anna's faithful visits, the details of what happened pieced together as if reassembling a vase's remains after being hurled against a cement wall.

A sudden dizziness brought Marci to her knees. She hung her head with disappointment. Obviously, she still was not ready. She shut the closet door and cursed herself for yet another failed attempt. Her chest constricted, and her want of air prompted her to open a window and suck the air like a dying fish. Exhausted, she sat on the side chair next to the wall and stared at the closet door, her nemesis, another barrier to wellness.

Would her anger ever leave?

"Oh, Matt. I don't want to hate you anymore. If there is a God, help me!"

She brightened with the rational thought—a productive way to meet the need. She would hire someone to clean out Matt's closet for her. The result would be the same, the clothes gone along with the reminder of Matt's betrayal. "Now chalk one up for yourself, girl."

Enthusiasm over her solution quickly fizzled when she recalled Pastor Rick's sermon. "With God, forgiveness is not an option. He doesn't merely recommend we forgive those who have wronged us. He commands us to turn the other cheek, regardless of the harm inflicted upon us."

Easy enough for him to say.

She rose and forced herself to stand in front of Matt's closet one more time. "I forgive you." Empty words ... her heart knew better. Trying to remove her cloak of anger left her vulnerable to the gales of regret blowing in her subconscious.

To forgive Matt meant she must first forgive herself. She'd been faithful in word only. She'd ceased to love him, refused his embraces, and pushed him from their bed to his own room. He'd found love elsewhere. If he'd been more patient, perhaps they might have worked through her issues. Instead, he spurned their marriage and found an out.

So had Blake.

Maybe true forgiveness would come in time.

Not today.

Mentally exhausted, she wobbled to the kitchen. Her thoughts drifted toward an elderly, religious aunt who had visited on occasion, never without leaving tidbits of her wisdom. "Baby steps," her Aunt Betty used to say. "Sometimes God doesn't solve our problems with one giant leap of faith. Sometimes, he slides our feet a little to a time."

Marci yawned as she glanced at her watch. Only ten o'clock, and the day was dragging on like a soap opera. She'd give her entire savings, $200, to get one good night's sleep.

Dr. Solomon said sleep deprivation might have contributed to her initial breakdown.

She hadn't taken any sleeping pills since her last appointment with Dr. Solomon. He'd recommended she take them along with plenty of exercise. While she refused medication, she did enjoy the walks—until her scare on Wolf Mountain. She shook her head with resolve. "Starting today, you take your wimpy self out for at least a mile each morning. No time like now to start—a gorgeous day with temps promising to be in the mid-seventies."

Filled with pride at her newfound determination, she grabbed her keys from the counter, opened the door, and came face-to-face with Blake Montgomery, his hand raised to knock.

Marci's startled scream nearly split his eardrums. "Sorry, I didn't mean to frighten you." She didn't need to know he'd been at her front door for the last ten minutes rehearsing what he might say to her. "May I come in?"

She turned, left the door open, and went into the living room. An affirmative? Blake inched inside. "Did I come at a bad time?"

"No. I was only doing ... a bit of cleaning. I decided to take a break and get some fresh air."

"Oh." He rocked on his heels.

"Did you want something, Blake?"

"I ... uh ... that is ... well ..."

Marci giggled. "Since when did words escape the articulate Dr. Montgomery?"

A very good sign this might prove worth his while. He offered a smile in return. "I only seem to have trouble when I'm with you."

She pursed her lips as if chewing a retort.

He plunged ahead. "I was thinking about climbing Wolf Mountain this morning and wondered if you'd like to come along. I realize I'm being presumptuous to assume you wouldn't have other plans."

"I don't know, Blake. I'm not much of the outdoor type these days."

Still as slender as he remembered her, she looked healthy, with enough pink in her cheeks to highlight her remarkable hazel eyes, like chameleons, matching whatever she wore. Today, they were almost emerald, set off by an army green T-shirt and blue jeans. She looked ready for action of some kind. "I thought you loved the outdoors. Remember our walks around Sorrel Pond?"

She crossed her arms and gazed toward her carpet. "Barely."

Guilt revisited as he recalled their afternoon at the cabin where she first gave herself to him. He'd pledged his love. That night, he received the dean's warning. The following morning, just before English History class, he'd talked to her outside the classroom and blurted his cowardice. "I think we should see other people ..."

Before he could finish his rehearsed speech, she'd walked away ... out of his class and out of his life. He should have called her, told her about his dilemma. She dropped his course, a clear sign she was done with him.

In the days following his idiocy, he often saw her strolling along the college paths. Even then he lacked the courage to walk beside her, to confess his confusion. He knew full well if he spoke to her, they'd find their way back to the cabin, and Blake would be out of a job. He'd either quit, or he'd be fired. Either way, Marci's reputation would be ruined. No good would come of continuing their relationship ... for either of them.

By the time courage found him, she'd started dating a music student. Perhaps he hadn't broken her heart after all. His hesitancy cost him the only woman he truly loved. He comforted himself with the belief she'd be happier without him.

He now searched her eyes for a glimmer of retained affection. "I haven't walked around the pond since our last afternoon together."

"Why not?"

Because I never stopped loving you, Marci. Even though you married someone else. "It's a long story ... one I'd like to share with you. What a gorgeous day. Not too hot and no chance of rain." *A lame segue.* "Are you sure you won't come with me? You know this area quite well, and I could use a guide."

She returned his gaze, her face rigid with determined refusal. "I'd be better help around town than on Wolf Mountain, at least right now."

Not a complete rejection, Blake. Carpe diem! "Well, then ... show me around Collins Bend. I'll be living here for the next few months. We can stop some place for lunch. My treat. I insist."

"I don't know, Blake ..."

"Only for a few hours. Please say yes."

She hesitated, then nodded. "All right."

CHAPTER 7

Marci mused at Blake's enthusiasm. He explored the town like a wide-eyed, middle-school student, stopping at every corner, his child-like curiosity demanding answers to his bombardment of questions. When was this place built? How was it constructed? Who was mayor? City council members? Who was the economic backbone of Collins Bend? What caused Collins Bend to become a virtual ghost town, as Alfred had claimed?

When they stopped in front of Gigi's Chocolate Castle, they both marveled at the confectionary replica of Collins Bend. Blake coaxed her inside, then bought her a box of assorted creams. "A small token of my appreciation. I remember raspberry was your favorite."

Marci tucked the box into her tote. "You have a good memory, Dr. Montgomery."

Blake impulsively took her hand, the warmth of his grasp comfortable, yet the sensation confusing. "Come on. Let's get something to eat. This fresh air has stoked my appetite. I'm starving."

She released herself from his hold and adjusted her purse strap. "I'm a bit hungry myself."

Except for the impromptu hand holding, he'd been a gentleman. Several times he cleared his throat, then broached a change in conversation with, "Marci, I've been thinking ..."

Apparently not too hard. He'd stammer and then comment on the weather or the oak trees geometrically positioned next to cast iron benches. Like a toddler splashes in a puddle, he sat on each bench he spied. Was this walk truly about sightseeing, or something else? What did he want from her? Did he think he could waltz into her life as if nothing ugly had passed between them?

Dr. Solomon warned against piling up resentment. He'd said she needed to crack the hurt, as if garnering the meat of a Brazil nut. "Joy is encased within each traumatic memory. But before it can be released, you have to penetrate its protective seal." Could she?

Blake paused in front of Andrea's Coffee House. "Let's have lunch here."

Exercise normally dulled her appetite, but the blended aromas of freshly baked bread and cinnamon rolls called to her like a trumpet. "You're on. Andrea has the best selection of pastries in Collins Bend, not to mention coffee she should franchise."

"Works for me."

He pointed at an outside table. "Have a seat. What'll you have?"

"Mocha latte and a raspberry strudel. Cream cheese on the side."

"And what do you recommend for a stodgy professor?"

"And you want me to say, 'What stodgy professor?'"

He smiled.

Drip, drip, drip, the sounds of her melting heart. How easily she could fall in love with him again. A whisper told her to go ahead, explore a second round with Blake Montgomery. But a louder voice, more reasonable, warned her not to take the chance.

Blake nodded as if he'd made a crucial decision. "Guess I'll have a bear claw and a regular coffee."

"I remember your dislike for specialty blends."

He smiled as if she'd handed him a whirly lollipop. "You're right."

Marci scanned the horde of customers. "Looks a little crowded. I'll find us a table." She spotted one nestled against the white rail fence next to the sidewalk. As she sat, she glanced up to see Tad Manning sitting alone near the door. He turned in her direction and waved. Before she could return his greeting, a bird flew over her head. She instinctively ducked. When she sat upright, Tad was gone. Had she imagined him again? Or had he been following them. An insane thought reeking of paranoia.

Her vision blurred as nausea gripped her. She needed to go home. She searched for a scrap of paper to write a note. Too late. Blake emerged from the storefront and headed toward the table. What sane excuse could she make to orchestrate a quick escape?

"I'm sorry, Blake. I don't feel well. Stay and enjoy your bear claw. I think I should go home."

"I'll have these wrapped to go and walk you back."

"That's okay. It's only a couple of blocks. I'll be fine." She rushed off before Blake could stop her. Her rudest, yet most necessary action of the day.

The nausea left almost immediately when she entered her house. She stretched out on the sofa and propped her head with a throw pillow.

She'd been right to listen to the saner voice on her shoulder. Her leaving was for the best, though she regretted the abruptness of her departure. Much longer and she might have fallen into his snare. Perhaps Tad Manning's wave had been a cosmic siren, warning she should never see Blake Montgomery again.

Blake stared at his tray. Now what? Should he be concerned or angry? The day proved more encouraging than he'd hoped. She'd warmed to him, and for brief moments he'd managed to crack her resistance. When he held her hand, he'd sensed those unmistakable tingles reminiscent of their walks on Sorrel Pond.

Or had his hopes been so high, he misread the signs?

He sighed. If she wanted no more to do with him, then that was that. He'd made his interest clear. Why should he suffer any more humiliation? A wise man would go back to the cabin, grab his clubs, and take his frustration out on the golf course.

Blake never counted himself among the wise. Alfred's counsel echoed. If he wanted a relationship with Marci, he'd have to outlast her stubbornness and ride out her resistance like a winter blizzard.

How foolish to think he could reenter Marci's life after all this time and expect she'd welcome him with open arms, so easily surrender forgiveness to assuage his guilt. He'd obeyed God's nudge to come to Collins Bend, but to what end? Merely to offer a long overdue apology ... or did the Lord have another agenda?

"I'm sorry," was a simple statement. Then why so hard to say? When he rented the cabin from Anna, he intended to call Marci, invite her to dinner, and make his apologies. The rest of the summer, he would spend on research, golf, hiking, and canoeing.

That was his intention until he saw her again, an ember so easily ignited ... an old flame, true, but one that had never been extinguished. The afternoon afforded several opportunities to state his case and move on. Yet no matter how many ways he rehearsed his monologue, Blake Montgomery came out the bad guy.

Why not leave the past in the past? Why did the memories of Sorrel Pond haunt him, gnawing at his subconscious like an unreachable itch?

Whatever he decided, he'd left his truck on the street near Marci's house. No choice but to follow her tracks. He picked up his order and readied to cross the street. A white Osprey nearly clipped him as he stepped to the road.

He stopped at his truck, hesitated, then walked to Marci's door and rang her doorbell, muttering, "You're not getting away so easily, Marci Henderson."

No response to the chime.

He rang the doorbell one more time.

She'd said she didn't feel well and looked ghastly white. What if she'd fainted again? He checked the door. Locked. He took out his cell phone and dialed the landline number Anna had given him. "Come on, Marci," he said aloud to no one, "answer the phone, woman, before the coffee gets cold."

A click and then, "Anna?"

"No. It's Blake."

"Oh. I expected Anna to call. She usually does about this time."

"I was worried about you."

"I'm sorry to have left so abruptly. That was rude of me."

"Are you okay?"

"I'm better now."

"In that case, I'm outside your door with your strudel and my bear claw. Coffee's getting cold. Mind if I come in?"

She disconnected. A yes or a no?

Marci opened the door, and he entered. He'd have to gain her trust the same way he edged into her living room—one step at a time. He followed her into the kitchen. "Where should I put these?"

"The table's fine."

If her eyes hadn't contradicted her frosty tone, he'd have set them down and walked out the door, tell God he'd failed, and that was that.

She grabbed the napkin holder off the counter, put it on the table, then motioned for Blake to sit. "Again, I'm sorry I ran out on you like that. Don't know what came over me." She sat, crossed her arms, and pursed her lips.

Desire swept over him.

The last thing he should do is take advantage of her— what the old Blake might have done. He took a swig of coffee. "Anna tells me you're hoping to teach again in the fall."

She stiffened. "What else did Anna tell you about me?"

"That your husband died, and you've been on leave from your job."

"She didn't tell you why I'm still on leave after two years?"

Great. Should he confess he knew about her hospitalization? "I assumed you had health issues."

"A nervous breakdown is a pretty serious health issue. They don't call it that anymore, but that's what it was." She went to the window. "I'm a nutcase, Dr. Montgomery."

"You're not a nutcase, Marci. You've been through a tough time. Losing someone you love is a horrible thing."

Her eyes misted. "Thank you for saying that, Blake."

"Do you want to talk about what happened?"

"No." She turned to face him. "I appreciate your coming over, but I think you'd better leave now."

"Did I offend you?"

"No, I ... I'm tired."

If this wall were to crumble, he'd need a sledgehammer. "May I see you again tomorrow ... maybe go for a climb?"

"I can't."

"Can't or won't?"

"Both."

When he played baseball, his coach told him to step into the swing to obtain maximum power. Time to try for a base hit. "Please, Marci. Don't shove me away. At least, let me be your friend. I won't pressure you for more. I really could use your help with the book."

She turned toward the window. "You don't understand, Blake. Too much has happened since Sorrel Pond."

He fought the urge to go to her, take her into his embrace, but if he made a romantic overture right now, he'd permanently close the door. "I need a research assistant. I can't think of anyone more qualified for the job. I'll pay you, of course. If you want, we'll keep our relationship strictly on business terms."

She turned to face him again, her shoulders more relaxed. If he read her upward glance correctly, she'd moved from absolute refusal to thoughtful contemplation. "Would I have to go up Wolf Mountain?"

"What do you have against Wolf Mountain?"

"Don't ask, please. I can't go there."

"Then don't. I could use your help with the nitty-gritty research stuff … be my guide around town."

"You don't know what you're asking of me."

"Please?"

"What if I faint again?"

"I'll keep a supply of smelling salts in my pocket."

She smiled and turned to face him. "How much are you paying?"

"Two hundred a week, no more than ten to fifteen hours."

She offered a handshake and a smile—more like a thin parting of the lips—but a smile, nonetheless. "Deal."

He'd have preferred to seal this arrangement with a kiss and a date. "I'll see myself out. I'll pick you up at ten tomorrow. I'd like to go the library—maybe read whatever old newspaper articles I can find. If my suspicions are right, the philanthropist has skeletons in his past."

Marci's eyes widened.

"Something wrong?"

"No. I suspect, Dr. Montgomery, you may be on to something there."

"Tomorrow?"

"I won't disappoint you."

CHAPTER 8

Marci closed the door behind Blake and returned to the recliner. What had she done?

Her monthly disability check didn't stretch far enough to pay her expenses, and her savings were dwindling rapidly. Blake's offer was too good to refuse.

More than a survival instinct cemented her decision to work for Blake. Although the more prudent option would have been to run in the opposite direction, Blake's offer provided the opportunity to begin a fresh walk among the sane.

She turned toward her bedroom and reentered Matt's closet. "You can do this, Marci. You need to do this. Don't hire the work done." With newly found courage, she dragged up Matt's old trunk from the basement. "One shirt at a time even if that's all you can do."

She grabbed Matt's favorite shirt, an oxford with thin blue-and-white stripes. A faint scent of Stetson cologne assaulted her. She closed her eyes. *Let your mind go someplace else. Where?* She'd spent the last two years in the pit of resentment. She'd like to climb out, but the walls remained slick and high.

Dr. Solomon had taught her how to visualize happy memories when confronted with hurtful ones. Matt once loved her—of this she could be certain. They were happy in the beginning, until she realized she'd loved the thought of love but not the man.

She smiled at the remembrance of their first encounter, early spring of her senior year. Lilacs decorated the quad like fragrant balloons, and rose bushes graced the entrance to the academic buildings. As she walked the cement pathways about campus, she'd been refreshed by the signs of sunnier days ahead.

She hadn't spoken with Blake in weeks. When they'd made love by the fireplace, Blake declared he'd be hers forever. She believed him. But for Blake, forever meant until morning.

When she'd entered the classroom, he'd pulled her aside. "Miss Vincent, would you give me a moment, please." Then he motioned to talk with him in the hall. His face looked hard. "I think we need to see other people ..."

He might have said more, but she turned and walked away.

Though she had dropped his class, she hoped he'd call to say he'd made a mistake. His silence hurt more than their rash breakup. She'd been foolish to fall for his phony declarations.

She mourned their breakup for months, then spring brought renewal. Marci Vincent refused to play the victimized coed any longer. Anna would say, "Own up to your stupidity, Marci, and move on."

Then she met Matt. She had been sitting on the library steps reading *The Remains of the Day*. Tears trickled down her cheeks. She wiped them aside.

A deep male voice pulled her from her thoughts. "I thought I should warn you the fire alarm at the library will be going off in a second or two. You might want to move from the steps before you get trampled."

"Are you psychic?"

"No. I ..."

The siren blared, and the doors behind her opened. A mob rushed toward her.

Matt yanked her aside, narrowly avoiding the stampede, and ushered her toward the music building next door. His smile set off a reddish complexion—a Norman Rockwell innocence—and eyes, a composite of glistening quartz and topaz.

"Nothing to worry about. I'm sure the alarm was a prank," the stranger said. "I think somebody was bored and thought this disruption might be funny."

"You know this, how?"

His head bobbed—his laugh deep and resonant. "Okay, I confess. I had a friend set off the alarm. I wanted to meet you. I've been trying to figure out a way since I saw you on these steps last month."

"Well ... whoever you are—"

"Henderson. Matt Henderson."

"I'm Marci—"

"Marci Vincent. I know."

"What if you're found out? You could be in serious trouble."

"My friend works in the library ... a hopeless romantic. This was all his idea. I told him how I watched you on these steps every day. He said he'd set off the alarm and give me a five-minute head start. If I'm caught, well, any consequence was worth holding your hand, if only for a few minutes."

They both ditched their afternoon classes, spending the rest of the day discussing the absurdity of their meeting, walking, and sharing each other's hopes and dreams. She discovered his love of classical as well as gospel music. She couldn't carry a tune to the grocery market, and church was something she'd heard people do. "I haven't been to church since my mother's marriage to Ozzie, husband number three."

Matt didn't seem the least bothered over her fractured family history. "Marci, our heritage is only part of who we are," he said. "I believe God puts us within our families no matter how dysfunctional they might be."

"And why would God do that?"

"To shape us for his purposes. Sometimes, the very things we see as a weakness can be the thing that gives us strength."

"Must be God expects me to be Superwoman."

He kissed her hand. "Not likely."

At first, Matt's sermon tidbits intrigued her, making her believe God did care what happened to her and might someday use her heartache, maybe her failed romance with Blake, to some greater good. From then on, she and Matt became inseparable. He proposed on graduation day, and they eloped the next weekend. Though he'd won her affection from the first, he waited until they married to make love to her. Until Matt Henderson, no one had ever risked a fine and possibly jail to meet her.

Marci sank to the closet floor with the realization—Matt had been a good husband to her until his affair. More memories flooded in, like their vacation to Disney World. She'd been afraid to ride Space Mountain, but Matt coaxed her. Though the experience frightened her, she felt exhilarated and rode two more times. "Don't be afraid to try something new and different," he'd said. "Not everything will pan out to be memorable, and some things you attempt, you'll want to forget. Whatever the result, new horizons never fail to refresh."

During their marriage, Matt encouraged her to try many new things. At first, the challenge of the untried exhilarated her. And for a time, Blake Montgomery ceased to claim her waking moments.

If she'd been happy with Matt, why did her marriage fall apart? What made Matt betray their vows? Her heart knew—Matt's affection eventually failed to draw her, marriage became a duty—a burden she could no longer bear, no matter how much she pretended. She asked him to move out of their bedroom, a man who had loved her completely and without expectation, a love she hadn't deserved.

She finished folding the shirt and laid it in the bottom of the trunk. Tears streaked her cheeks. She could do no more today.

CHAPTER 9

Blake arrived a few minutes early. He remembered Marci's scare at the church. If he knocked and Marci wasn't expecting him yet, would the noise send her into a panic attack? He walked up and down the block and then circled behind her house.

The Federalist architecture suited her—white with black shudders—pragmatic but elegant. Marci understated everything, right down to her wardrobe: jeans, T-shirt, sneakers and only a hint of mascara on her long, brown lashes. Not like her sister Anna, a flash of fashion at every appearance.

Where Anna lived the dramatic, Marci dwelt in comfortable solitude, the world of literature her constant companion. Besides her beauty, Marci's spirited interest in history caught his attention. Looking back, he realized his offer to mentor her had been motivated more by attraction than a professor's wish to encourage an inquiring mind.

Yet, her insight never failed to amaze him. During her American History class, he'd re-read her term paper at least a dozen times. She'd interviewed World War II widows, showing freedom's sacrifices from the viewpoint of homeland hearts.

He imagined himself the shaper of her genius, a scared swan who had no concept of how beautiful she was—twice as attractive as her very available sister.

He'd hired her as his assistant, expecting their time together would be more than wonderful. He struggled against his need for her, knowing propriety demanded he keep his distance.

Some of the male faculty had no qualms against bedding coeds. Blake had thought himself above temptation until he met Marci. On Sorrel Pond, his want overpowered his deluded gallantry.

After Marci left Briarcliffe, he became the very professor he despised, luring young coeds to his apartment under the guise of scholastic assistance. He'd thought those lusts ended with his sinner's prayer and redemption. Until today. Where did faith flee when he held Marci's hand? Perhaps his old nature, as Alfred called his baser instincts, hadn't been purged—merely subdued, waiting for the right stimulus to reappear.

"God, help me be the man I should be, and not the man I want to be."

He rang the doorbell, and she let him in, her face taut, not even a pretend smile. "Professor."

"Mrs. Henderson."

A thousand and one things he wanted to say, but how does one defrost nearly twenty years of resentment in a single breath of regret? "Ready?"

"Ready, Dr. Montgomery."

"No need to be formal. You have called me Blake in our private moments since I've been here."

"Yes, however, now you're my employer."

"Then as your employer, I insist you continue to call me by my first name."

She grabbed a tote from the side table. "Remember, you promised to keep this a professional relationship."

Could he trust himself? "I'm a man of my word."

"Really? Since when?"

The memory of his deceit stung. "I am now."

She put her laptop into a tote then slipped one strap over her shoulder. "That remains to be seen. Let's go."

Marci scanned the main room of the Wordsworth Memorial Library, seemingly vacant except for Tina Langley, the librarian, and a few browsers in the reference area.

Blake raised his eyebrows, probably in disbelief, being accustomed to a comprehensive college library. "This is it?"

"Not very big, I know. Only two rooms downstairs, with the children's books in the alcove by the librarian's desk. The fiction section is upstairs and a separate room for first editions. I'm afraid this small-town library pales in comparison to what you're used to."

Blake smiled. "Yes, but Briarcliffe doesn't have old editions of the *Collins Bend Gazette*. Why don't you look through the reference books and catalog any articles or mention of Emerson Wordsworth."

Marci nodded, oozing a sigh. "Pity how much changed because of the railroads. Denuded forests and social upheaval, especially for Native Americans."

"Those who try to stand in the way of progress only get run over, Marci."

"Are you saying indigenous peoples should adapt or die?"

"Exactly."

Marci's back stiffened. "Permit me to disagree with his lordship. If that were true, why did Teddy Roosevelt establish the EPA to keep the Adirondacks forever wild? Too late to help the Mohawk tribes, but a wise presidential interference with progress, wouldn't you say?"

"Look at the reservations now, Marci. A lot of wealth. They adapted."

"Syndicated gambling and smuggling among the most profitable trades. Not much help to the majority of hardworking and honest Native Americans."

Blake shrugged his shoulders and offered a smile. "You've always seen history from the vantage point of those who actually lived through turmoil, how events shaped humanity rather than the economy. I wish I had your sensitivity."

"You do, Blake, but you shrug sentiment off like you do everything and everyone."

He ducked her emotional punch. "Ouch. Condemnation deserved." He chewed his lower lip, then, "I'll see what I can find in the *Gazette*."

Marci noted the influx of a few more patrons. A gray-haired, middle-aged man hovered over an issue of *Field and Stream*. Marci stared, intrigued by the man's attire— donned with a fishing hat covered with lures and a boat vest. On closer observation, she realized he resembled the fisherman in front of Bert's Tackle. Maybe he hadn't been a figment of her imagination. Or she was having the same hallucination.

She turned her attention away. Maybe the man would disappear as he had before. She thumbed the wall of spiral-bound local history books, the product of hefty grants over the years. Marci found one written in honor of Collin Bend's bicentennial, a two-volume history compiled in 2003.

She scanned through the first volume and noticed a segment on Emerson Wordsworth with a subparagraph headed: *Wordsworth's friendship with Rev. John Todd*. The name struck a familiar chord ... associated somewhere else besides the Adirondacks. She knew he'd been a missionary to Native Americans as well as influential in establishing a community for freed and runaway slaves. Where else?

She sat at the computer opposite the fisherman and googled *Rev. John Todd*. The fisherman sauntered behind her and glanced over her shoulder at her computer screen. He stroked his chin, then returned his magazine to the rack and left the room.

Curiosity made her follow.

Once she entered the adjoining room, the man was nowhere in sight. Fear gripped her, and the room began to spin.

Not again!

She caught the chair as she slumped and landed securely enough to avoid a scene. She cradled her head on the table, then after five deep breaths, sat back up. No fisherman.

If this sighting were an extension of a previous hallucination, she must admit, her visions were becoming very creative. Though she could think of no reason anyone should follow her, she'd rather be the object of someone else's interest than insane. Marci replayed the encounter. The complexity of the man's actions proved he was no hallucination. Something odd was going on.

Blake spun the handle on the microfiche. He wrung his hands with pleasure when he found three articles mentioning Emerson Wordsworth. The first announced the founding of the railroad extension connecting this portion of the Adirondacks to the Albany railroads and ultimately to New York City. The second article was Emerson Wordsworth's obituary. He died in 1865, a day after Lincoln's assassination, leaving everything to his son Erwin, Felicity's husband. Nothing unusual in the obit. The third article was a social announcement about Emerson Wordsworth's friendship with Rev. John Todd.

Blake recognized the name as the evangelist who led the prayer at the dedication of the Transcontinental Railroad. Beyond this tidbit, Blake knew very little about the man except the fact he was an abolitionist involved in the Underground Railroad throughout Northern New York and into Canada. His Native American friend gave away large tracts of land in North Elba to runaway slaves.

Blake had to admit to his scant knowledge of Adirondack history, even more so about the High Peaks. His lure to Collins Bend, besides Marci, was the intrigue of Wolf Mountain, an accidental discovery when he traced the railroads from New York City to Montreal for his doctoral dissertation.

Impure motives might have prompted him to ask Marci to be his assistant. However, her knowledge of the area would indeed be very helpful. He'd have to ask her what she knew about Reverend Todd. He sensed an important connection to the son, Erwin, though Todd's friendship was with Emerson. Nor would there necessarily be a connection to Felicity's disappearance. Still, a lead worth further investigation.

"Follow the money, Blake," he mumbled to himself.

Perhaps he should try to find any locals who might be descendants of the main players of the era. Felicity and Erwin had no children, and both Emerson and Erwin had been only children. After Felicity's disappearance and Erwin's death, the Wordsworth inheritance fell to Emerson's distant cousin and his descendants, who ultimately bequeathed the ruins to the county as a museum site. The House of History on the other end of town might hold more clues.

He'd never been one to follow instinct. He much preferred to study a matter from all angles before he acted on a hunch. He'd come to Collins Bend to research railroad history. Yet the unsolved case on Wolf Mountain seemed inexplicably connected to the Wordsworth's railroad empire.

Marci stood in the archway between the two sections. Her lips moved as if she were conversing with someone. Except, she was alone. She seemed visibly shaken. Blake hurried to her side. "Marci?"

She turned, her face ashen, eyes wild with fear.

"Are you all right?"

She walked, more like wobbled, to the other room where she picked up her tote. She heaved a sigh as she leaned against the table. "I'll be okay. The man in the fishing vest startled me a little. He stood behind me and read over my shoulder. Then, I remembered him from before, at Bert's Tackle. I'm sure he was the same man. I don't know why, but I'm certain people are following us."

"Who?"

"Please tell me you noticed the strange-looking man in the fishing vest. You had to see him. When he left the resource room, I followed him. By the time I got to the archway, you were the only one in the room."

Blake walked to the archway and cased the microfiche room, then returned to where Marci had propped herself against a table. "I don't see anyone in there now, unless he's hiding behind a stack of books. You may have thought he was going in there or else he skipped out when you weren't looking. I doubt he leapt out a window."

She scowled. "Don't make fun of me, Blake. I tell you I saw him. The fact you didn't doesn't mean I'm seeing things."

He wanted to believe her. Though his knowledge

of psychiatry might be limited, he feared Marci might be headed for another breakdown, as she called her illness. Paranoia often accompanied a psychotic episode, and there was no credence to her theory someone was following either of them. To what end? Collins Bend was a quiet town, not a haven for thugs or murderers. He'd have to give Marci a plausible explanation, or she might walk out on him like she did at the café.

"No, I didn't see anyone. Then again, I was preoccupied. I'm sorry, Marci. Your concerns are unfounded. Why on earth would anyone want to follow us?"

"I don't know. Call it a feeling."

She took out a bottle of water from her tote and took a sip. Her breathlessness belied her stoic stance. "You're right, of course. He probably was simply curious and ... and ... maybe I ... I ... only thought he came into this room."

Best to change the conversation. Get her mind off whatever did happen. "Did you find anything of interest in your research?"

She picked up an open book she'd left on the table and gently slapped it against his chest. "Read this. I'm convinced there is a connection between this Reverend John Todd and the Wordsworth estate. Felicity was known for her many charities. Perhaps she supported this preacher's missions."

Paranoid or not, Marci might very well be on to Felicity as the bridge between Erwin Wordsworth and the Reverend John Todd. "I agree. I found a reference or two about him in the *Gazette*. He frequented this area often and apparently had a friendship with Emerson. I suppose he may have influenced Felicity after her marriage to Erwin."

Marci nodded. "Might be worth digging a little deeper."

"Come into the other room with me."

Marci hesitated. "You go ahead, Blake. I can't breathe

in here. I need to get some fresh air. I'll wait for you outside."

She disappeared as quickly as her phantom fisherman.

The temperature outside was a balmy seventy degrees, and the air inside seemed quite comfortable to him. He shrugged his shoulders. Marci had been deeply troubled by whatever encounter she had, real or imaginary. Research could wait.

Blake stepped outside and joined Marci, who sat on the entrance stoop, peering up and down the street. "Okay, if we're going to work together, I need you to be more honest with me. What's going on with you? It's not just the quirky fisherman, is it?"

"I'm quite all right, Blake. See, I'm breathing better already." She stood, and the pink returned to her cheeks.

Her resiliency amazed him. Regardless of what she'd endured after Matt's death, she fought hard to come back, even now, when clouds challenged her sanity. He bent to kiss her, and for a moment he sensed her permission. Restraint conquered desire. He took two steps back. "The truth, Marci."

"If you must know, I'm still convinced we're being followed."

"Who?"

"Besides the fisherman, Tad Manning, and some woman driving a ..."

Marci's glance veered to the road as a white Osprey sped from the parking lot, too fast for Blake to see who was driving. Marci's face paled.

"No one's following us, Marci. It's your ..."

Too late to take back his cruel insinuation. Marci fell forward against his chest.

CHAPTER 10

Marci woke, cradled in Blake's strong arms. "Did I pass out again?"

"Only for a second."

Then she remembered. Another hallucination. What else could these strange sights be? As much as she willed the vision to be real, there was no other plausible explanation. Blake was right. Why would someone want to follow either of them?

"I'm sorry, Blake. I don't think I'm a very good assistant."

"Just because I didn't see Tad or the fisherman, doesn't mean they weren't present. And if you did see them, there may be a reasonable explanation we haven't thought of yet."

She pushed free of his hold. "Like what?"

"It's a very small town. Why wouldn't you run into the same people at various locations?"

"If I didn't see them, then I'm more than just paranoid. I've completely lost my mind. I think perhaps you'd better find a different assistant."

"I'm still convinced you're the right person. Please, give me at least a week. Then if you still feel you can't do the job, I won't hold you to your promise."

The warmth of his smile indicated genuine concern. Yet, he had almost kissed her. And she would have let him. Fortunately, he had more restraint than she at that moment. People do change. Perhaps time had taught Blake Montgomery to no longer take advantage of a woman's vulnerability.

Whatever almost transpired, this much was certain—a romance now was ill-timed. Blake might think himself noble, but what man would want to be saddled with a delusional lover?

Or maybe she hadn't gone bonkers. If only she could be certain. Nothing made sense. She barely remembered the episode causing her hospitalization. Yet, she could recall these recent events with minute detail, even the stubble on the fisherman's face as well as the gold watch on his right wrist.

She chilled with the realization. The man in the blue tuxedo wore an identical watch on his right wrist. Of course, the similarity between the blue tuxedo man and the fisherman ended there. The fisherman seemed more plump and a few years older. The man in the blue tuxedo was clean shaven. Still, she'd accept Blake's insincere but gracious out. There had to be some other explanation than a Marci Henderson psychosis.

Blake helped her to her feet. "Do you want to go home?"

That would be the smart thing. "No. I said I'd work for you. You can dock my pay every time I pass out. Okay?"

"We'll see. Do you feel up to going to the Collins Bend Historical Museum?"

"I think so. Why?"

"A hunch."

Marci marveled at Blake's boyish excitement—as tickled as a preacher with a full church—while they delved into Collins Bend history. Apparently remembering he was, after all, a dignified college professor, he stifled his exuberance and held the door open for Marci, allowing her first entrance into his wonderland.

So much about Blake to love. If only she could release the past and embrace the present. At the least, she could be friendlier. He deserved that much from her.

She forced her attention to the task at hand. "What do you hope to find here?"

Blake glanced at the display dedicated to the Adirondack railroad expansion. "If we're lucky, maybe we'll find correspondence or anything pertaining to a possible descendant who lived in the village during the Wordsworth era, or a descendant of a servant."

Finally, she could be of help. "Francine Bilow runs the place. Her ancestors' names are on the town charter. This house is one of the original homes built when the town was founded. If there's anything to know about Collins Bend, she'd be the one to ask."

"Then I guess we're in the right place."

Like psychic radar, Francine approached from the anteroom. "Hello, Marci. I'm surprised to see you here."

Before Marci could introduce Blake, Francine examined him like a priceless painting and met his gaze as she extended her hand. "I'm Francine Bilow, the curator. And you are?" She threw off heat like an overstuffed furnace.

Blake blushed. "Blake Montgomery."

Marci didn't fault Blake for his red face. There wasn't a man in Collins Bend who didn't salivate in Francine's presence.

Francine hooked her arm around Blake's. "And how can I be of service?"

Marci's inner heat emanated from revulsion rather than admiration. Francine Bilow was not available, or at the least shouldn't be available. Marci stepped closer—unable to distinguish the emotion—jealousy or protectiveness? "If I remember correctly, you and Darin have a second anniversary next week?"

Catty, she knew. Blake should be informed of Francine's marital status.

"That's right." Francine's response dripped like an icy rain on Saranac Lake.

Poor Blake. A monkey-in-the-middle of two snarling women. Marci wondered why she had thought Francine would help simply to help. Good ideas have a way of snapping back like an overstretched rubber band.

Shouldn't put all the blame on Francine. Blake didn't do much to extricate himself from Francine's familiarity. He fed on her attention like a starved kitten lapping milk.

Francine's perfume overpowered the air, but Blake didn't seem the least bit bothered. "Yes, well ... um ... Francine, I'm doing research for a book I'm writing. Marci thought you could be of assistance."

Francine arched her right brow as she glanced toward Marci. "Of course. What's it about?"

"The railroad expansion's impact on tourism in the Adirondack area."

"I love history." With one arm still wrapped around Blake's elbow, she rubbed his shoulder with the other. "I look forward to reading your treatise."

"I wonder if you, that is, the museum, has any letters or information about a possible living descendant to the Wordsworth estate. Someone I could interview."

Francine quirked a smile. "If you'll follow me, I might have something of interest. Of course, my family tree goes back to the days of our founding fathers, a group of farmers who migrated from Vermont after King George's land grant to Beaufort Collins. The town became chartered in 1803, then grew rapidly."

She continued with her obvious attempt at impressing a professor with her memorized encyclopedic knowledge of a small town whose legends held little interest outside of Collins Bend, except for history buffs. "The Wordsworths, as you know, were extremely important in the town's later history, a huge economic factor. They migrated from Vermont soon after the town was incorporated. They quickly established themselves both politically and financially. Emerson's father was a prominent businessman and well connected to the abolitionist movement. He represented the area at the first Republican National Convention."

"That would have been in Philadelphia in 1856."

"Absolutely!"

"I wasn't aware the Wordsworths were abolitionists. I'm surprised this bit of information got past me, though I'm not surprised about their abolitionist tendencies since John Todd was a friend of the family. I've long been interested in the Underground Railroad."

Francine released a hot breath. "Collins Bend played an integral part in the Underground Railroad. In fact, the Methodist church in the village still has cement vaults where they hid runaway slaves." She inched impossibly closer. "I'd be happy to show them to you."

Blake's cheeks reddened. "Perhaps some other time. I hoped to focus on the regular railroad for now."

"Emerson Wordsworth saw the railroad's potential to expand tourism, especially for the wealthy patrons in New York City. He invested heavily in transportation bonds and left his son a fortune. Tragically, or fortunately, however you look at history—since Erwin died leaving no heirs—a distant cousin inherited the estate. He saw no use for the property so gave the property to the town for a museum."

"What about servants or friends?"

"I do have a letter found in the ruins written by Felicity's maid, dated the day before the fire. Though charred around the edges, most of the letter is readable. There were two bodies found in the ashes after the fire. One was identified as Erwin by the ring he always wore. The second body was found in the maid's quarters—also burned beyond recognition. Of course, identification would have been difficult given forensic limitations of the period. Investigators determined the body to be the maid due to where she was found and her shoes, of course."

"Shoes?" Marci asked.

"Common boots worn by servants. Scraps of the leather were found near what remained of the body."

Marci listened intently, pained for the maid, if she indeed had been the second victim of the fire. Forensic limitations or not, likely little time was spent on confirming her identity.

With Francine glued to Blake's personal space, Marci trailed behind like the paid help she'd become. Francine stopped at an exhibit displaying memorabilia from the ruins. Pictures of Emerson and his son Erwin spotted the walls together with photographs of John Brown taken at North Elba and Reverend Todd who stood with Emerson Wordsworth. Francine pointed to a charred letter preserved under glass. "I can get this out for you if you want. You'll have to put gloves on, though."

Blake nodded.

Francine handed Blake a set of protective gloves, and eyed Marci with a slight bend of her head. "Will you be reading the letter too?"

Marci squared her shoulders. "But of course, I *am* Dr. Montgomery's assistant."

Francine scowled as she handed a glove set to Marci, then unlocked the protective case and gave Blake the letter. Francine pointed to an adjacent reading room. "You can take this artifact in there, Dr. Montgomery. Let me know when you're done so I can return the letter to the protective case." She glowered at Marci, turned on her heels, and left.

"Interesting woman," Blake said, as they entered the reading room. "Now let's see what we have here." He spread the letter between them on the table, took out a pair of glasses from his shirt pocket, and scanned the letter.

Blake squinted. "I can't quite make out the writing, even with these glasses."

"Do you want me to read it to you?"

Blake's cheeks reddened. "Go ahead."

Addressed to a nondescript person referred to as Madam, the letter started as most—inquiries into the recipient's well-being. The only unusual aspect was the writer's above-average command of syntax and language, atypical of a housemaid in that era, more like a governess. The content progressed to the writer's concerns she might have to leave her position.

> I fear, Madam, the situation here has become intolerable.
> My employers engage in such fierce arguments the volume of their disputes rock the foundations of the house.

Blake flashed Marci a wide grin. "Are you thinking what I'm thinking?"

"I don't know what you're thinking, but I'm thinking something might have been rotten in the state of Wordsworth Manor."

"Exactly. Maybe Felicity ran off with Wordsworth's accountant to escape her husband's abuse."

Marci empathized with the misjudged Felicity. How typical in bygone days to assign misdeeds to the wife rather than look elsewhere for blame. She didn't believe Felicity murdered her husband, in spite of this possible accusation against Erwin. Nor did she believe Erwin was the brute this letter seemed to indicate. "Erwin Wordsworth was a devout Quaker. I doubt he was given to alcohol. As for abuse, there is no indication anywhere he was cantankerous. Everything I've read about him indicates he was a good man. Biographies describe him as 'most congenial.' Besides, I'll have you know, an unhappy wife can remain faithful to her husband."

Blake's gaze remained glued to the letter. "I suppose so, especially back then. Women had few alternatives when they found themselves in a distasteful marriage. However, the man was considerably older. And she was very beautiful. I imagine she had a host of suitors. I doubt she married Erwin Wordsworth for his physical attributes. Is there anything else in the letter?"

Marci read through the remaining portions. "Nothing that I see. Normal closing:

> I trust this letter finds you recovered from your recent illness.
> Faithfully yours, Abigail Todd Fisher.

Marci met Blake's gaze, his eyes gleaming as if she'd handed him a bowl of ice-cream. They spoke in unison, "Todd!"

CHAPTER 11

They left the House of History in silence, Blake deep in private thoughts. He assumed Marci had a stew of her own going on. He'd behaved abysmally around Francine. He should have pushed her away instead of enjoying her flirtation, though he had no intention of taking her up on her offer.

He hadn't elicited attention, and what man doesn't like being fawned over? Interested in even a passing relationship with someone like Francine, especially a married woman? No. The old Blake wouldn't have thought twice about accepting her overtures. Thankfully, God had made him more introspective. At least he thought so.

No matter how much he minimized his reaction to Francine, on no level had his behavior pleased God. He'd used her attention to salve his wounded ego from Marci's resistance toward him. Whatever his motives, they were inconsistent with a surrendered heart.

Marci's displeasure, though, confused him. If she were so adamant she could not date him, then why did she care how he acted around other women? Foolish to hope she'd been jealous—how adolescent. Yet, jealousy meant she still cared for him. If she cared for him—even a little—there was hope.

He studied her taut brow as she slid into the passenger side of his truck. She was still pensive. He hoped somewhere in her contemplations she'd forgive his impetuousness and his attempt to steal a kiss from her. If she stayed on as his assistant, he would try to think twice before giving in to manly pride.

Her sightings teetered on the edge of insane, yet he shouldn't discount the possibility they were real. Certainly, the descriptions seemed odd. And, according to Anna, Marci's hospitalization had been the result of a complicated delusion ... not hallucinations.

He should call Anna and let her know Marci might be seeing things. Maybe all she needed was a medication adjustment. Except for her weird visions, she seemed fine.

And Blake needed her. With or without hallucinations, Marci scored high points for organization, a skill he lacked. With her at his side, he'd be able to complete his research in half the time.

You're selfish, Blake!

Or maybe he was the one with a mental problem, deluding himself into thinking he was the key to Marci's salvation. God didn't need a man so easily distracted by over-perfumed women to bring her to faith. Nor were Blake's motives so noble. He simply wanted to be with her, to be as they once were.

Was he pushing too hard?

He sensed her struggle. If he persisted while she was this vulnerable, what kind of man was he? She needed his protection, not his pursuit.

When he came to Collins Bend and learned of Marci's troubles, some part of him wondered if he'd been to blame. How egotistical. Perhaps her illness was an explosion emanating from a pressure cooker of disappointments, their romance one of many. If he was not the sole cause of her unhappiness, wisdom dictated his efforts alone would not bring her peace. He was bound to disappoint her again, as he had at the Collins Bend House of History.

If only he could behave himself and be patient. How long should he wait?

As long as it takes.

That was God's answer.

Blake sighed with the truth of his weakness. Obviously, the man he once was, what Alfred called the Old Man, had not died. He'd been dormant, waiting for the right stimuli to rebirth, a beast Blake could hear snorting in his subconscious as it raised its hoofs and whinnied, "You're still a coward, Blake."

Marci broke the silence first as he neared her street. "I think we should try to do a family trace on Abigail, but Todd is a popular name in the Northern peaks. We might not get far."

"And do you think as I do—the maid is the link between the Reverend John Todd and Felicity?"

"The idea is worth pursuing."

"I agree."

Marci yawned.

"You look tired. We can pick up the trail tomorrow afternoon if you'd rather."

"Okay. I'll see what I can find on my computer."

"Be sure to keep track of your time. I'll pay you on Fridays."

"Works for me."

He lowered his shield for one more try. "If you're not too exhausted, do you mind if we drive around town a little before I drop you off?"

"Why?"

"Besides *The La Grande*, Collins Bend Country Club, Alexi's Diner, and Andrea's Café, I'm wondering if there are any other hotspots around town where a single man can go eat. I'm hungry."

"Alexi and Andrea are brother and sister, so be careful you don't mention either name to the other if you decide to frequent both places."

He'd grown up in Brooklyn. Shops and stores in his neighborhood had their own brand of drama. The more he studied, the more he understood the role of family friction in local history—Cain and Abel revisited every decade in man's journey upon the earth.

"Do tell."

Marci snickered. "They had a falling out when their father died and left the restaurant to Alex. Andrea was so mad she took her small inheritance and bought a café of her own. If one runs a special, you can be sure the other one will too. The town benefits—keeps the prices low."

"American capitalism at its best. Any other eateries in town?"

"This town has as many restaurants as bars and churches, like most North Country towns."

Blake laughed. How he'd loved her acidic, to-the-point observations. "Same old Marci."

She gazed out the window, then turned to face him with an inquisitive, almost accusatory glance. "No. I'm not the same old Marci. Are you the same old Blake?"

There ... the window he had hoped would open. Still, how could he boast on how much he'd changed after his adolescent behavior at the museum? How could he profess a new being with the Old Man still parked in his soul? "In some ways, I'm not. If you'll have dinner with me, I'll explain how I feel I've changed."

She hesitated. "Not tonight, Blake. Thank you for asking."

He pulled into her driveway and parked. "Another time, perhaps?"

"I don't think so."

Her words said one thing, but her eyes, something else. "Marci, don't shut me out. I still love you. I never stopped loving you." He pulled her to him. She went momentarily limp in his embrace, then pulled away.

"You don't understand, Blake. Yes, I have feelings, but I can't let this happen."

"Fine. I'm sorry I hurt you so long ago. Sorry I didn't try to explain why I ended our relationship, something I'll regret to my dying day. I'd hoped you'd give me a chance. I see you're determined to close the door on anything between us. I don't know if—"

"Please, don't Blake ... I can't ..."

Forget his noble self-talk. This was too much rejection for any man to take. Blake clenched his fists as he walked Marci to the door. "I still need an assistant."

"I'm not sure I should be the one to help."

"If I promise to not try anything again?"

"We've already had this conversation ... to keep this a professional relationship. Doesn't seem to be working very well."

"I'll try harder. I need *you*, Marci."

He walked her to her door, and she stayed on the stoop with him. "I want to continue our work for personal reasons."

"Then you do still have feelings for me?"

"Those are not the personal reasons. Something about Wolf Mountain pulls me."

She hadn't denied feelings for him, yet she made her decision about them. He'd lost.

"I only hope I don't regret this. Call me tomorrow. Let's take inventory of where we are and decide our next steps."

Anger worked against reason, eroding any patience he had left. He sensed her want for him equaled his for her. He despised his weakness, the inability to simply be present for her. Common sense told him to give up and go back to Briarcliffe. If he didn't have a contractual obligation with a publisher, he would end the misery for them both.

With or without Marci Henderson, he must finish his book. He returned to his truck and slammed the door on his hopes.

Marci winced as she watched Blake spin out of her driveway. As she approached the door, a white Osprey, parked on the opposite side of the road, sped away.

How foolish to think every white car she saw had designs against her!

From Blake's reaction, she sensed she'd closed the door on anything between them. He got her message. Subliminally, however, it was not the message she'd wanted to send. Why couldn't he be more patient? Let her breathe. Not push against what they once had.

They were different people from when they walked the halls of Briarcliffe College. Why not explore who they were now, not try to resurrect something lost.

Blake claimed he had changed. In some ways she saw a difference, and perhaps she was more drawn to the new Blake than the old. With all this craziness going on, strange men in odd places and white Ospreys wherever she went, she couldn't trust herself, let alone Blake.

She needed more time—time Blake seemed unwilling to give her.

CHAPTER 12

Blake stormed into his cabin. He saw the evidence of his anger yet was unable to will the rage away, emotionally whipped. Why should he continue to hold onto hope where there was none?

He shouted to the ceiling, "Forget her. You've done everything the Lord required of you. This mountain refuses to budge. Find another assistant, and let Marci keep her warped, petrified image of you."

He grabbed his golf bag, let his cabin door slam on the way out, and threw his clubs into the back of the truck. As it was nearing dusk, he'd only have time for nine holes. At least the round would give him a couple of hours to calm down. No remedy like smacking a little white ball to bring his mind into focus.

Unless God intervened, he'd have to call Marci in the morning and agree with her assessment—hiring her was a bad idea. Francine would be willing to work for him. No. Another bad idea.

He jumped into the truck, started the engine, and peeled out of his driveway. In his haste, he nearly clipped the white Osprey speeding by his cabin. He could only determine the driver was a woman. He recognized the vanity plate—not unlike the one he'd seen earlier. Odd, he'd spotted two white Osprey's with similar plates in one day.

"Listen to yourself, Blake. Paranoia can be contagious." White Ospreys were everywhere, even in Collins Bend, and vanity plates were common these days. If he hung out with Marci any longer, he'd probably become suspicious of moonlight.

He gripped the wheel in confusion. Yes, he needed to move on. However, the why of Marci's persistent rejection niggled like a caffeine-deprived morning. Something other than bad memories had poisoned her toward him. Hurts he could only imagine had hardboiled her heart.

Perhaps God knew what Blake tried hard to deny. If she caved to his whims, his imperfect self would only hurt again—human nature—the stuff stunting every mountaintop experience of the believer. Though scripturally avoidable, the bane of living had brought as many failures as victories. Maybe that's the reason Alfred told him a Christian needed more time on his knees than anywhere else. Well, he could pray while he golfed, couldn't he?

As he pulled into the club parking lot, he checked the time on the dash. No opportunity to warm up or go to the driving range if he were to get nine in before dark. Supper could wait.

When he entered the clubhouse, Bianca Manning stood at the pro shop counter. Even the most committed saint would appreciate her long legs, accentuated by her short white sport skirt and filled-out green top. This woman was knock-out gorgeous. And unlike Francine, datable. He should ask Bianca out before she and her brother returned to Boston.

Blake gulped with admiration as she swayed toward him. "Good afternoon, Dr. Montgomery."

"Blake."

"Yes, you did say you prefer to be called Blake."

Especially by women as attractive as you. Her sensuality filled the room.

Marci's face loomed in his mind. She'd said she liked to golf. Maybe he should have asked her. Too late now. She'd made her opinion of him crystal clear, and she wouldn't even go for a walk with him. Why should he feel guilty about enjoying Bianca's obvious interest?

Bianca smiled as her cheeks pinked. "I'm embarrassed to ask, but are you here alone?"

"Apparently."

"My brother stood me up, probably for some blonde he met who knows where. I was so looking forward to a round today. And I hate playing by myself. May I join you? If my brother shows up, perhaps he could catch up to us at whatever fairway we're on?"

Another player would slow him down, yet who could refuse scenery like hers? Even if she were the worst golfer on the planet. Her swing would have to be poetry in motion if she never hit the ball.

"Sure. Hopefully, we'll get nine in."

She purred like a cat. "I suspect we will. Plenty of daylight left."

He paid their green fees, then hoisted Bianca's bag on his other shoulder, grateful when an attendant offered to load them onto their cart. Lugging one set of clubs was chore enough. He hoped Bianca hadn't noticed the slight bend in his posture before help arrived.

Blake normally tipped the staff with a couple of George Washingtons, but with Bianca watching, he pulled out a Lincoln.

The bag boy stuffed the cash in his pocket. "Thanks, mister."

A mild flower scent trailed Bianca, not like Francine's heavy jasmine, yet equally provocative.

Guilt blared. He silenced the sirens with his best rationalizations. He'd given Marci every chance. Bianca was no stone wall. Besides, he hadn't enjoyed a woman's closeness since his conversion. Did God expect him to live like a monk the rest of his life?

Bianca smiled as she slid slightly closer to him on the cart, a maneuver he recognized from bygone days, moves indicating her mind was on the same track as his. When the round was over, he'd go to her cabin, along with what was implied.

The Old Man snorted, strengthened and bold, digging his hoofs into the dirt, ready to charge. Blake dodged the horns, kicking at the beast. He needed to clear his thoughts. The new Blake should be revulsed. He believed he'd changed and had told Marci as much. But if the truth were told, he lacked the courage to fight for her, the only woman he'd wanted to marry. The others were escapes from loneliness. Even now, Bianca was a mere substitute, a pretty confection instead of the permanent fare he truly desired.

The starter signaled them to approach the tee.

Might as well play the round, then he'd go directly to his own cabin. Be a good scout like he knew he should.

He gunned the cart and drove to the men's first tee. He gazed at the ladies' 100-yard advantage. He took out his Calloway driver and teed up. The nonsensical idea that he'd somehow betrayed Marci weighed on his backswing, and his ball plopped into the pond on the right.

Bianca laughed. "Is that your best, Professor?"

Blake smirked. "Haven't been out in a while."

"Care to make the round interesting? Whoever loses has to buy dinner?"

There it was—the prelude to the invitation he imagined.

God, you can't really expect me to ignore her?

Yes, I do. This woman will bring you back to the place where I brought you from. Do not return to Egypt.

Blake pushed his driver into the bag. "I'll drop from the flight line."

"You can have a mulligan, you know. My brother and I allow one per nine holes."

"I don't believe in mulligans."

"Suit yourself."

He drove to the ladies' tee. "Let's see what you can do."

Blake's cheeks puffed with desire as he watched Bianca's swing. She'd played before—every nuance in her delivery spoke professional golfer or someone who'd had years of coaching. Her drive sailed nearly three hundred yards, landing in the middle of the fairway past the pond and a hundred yards from the green.

The words slipped out before his brain had time to counteract. "Tell you what, Miss Pro. We'll match play for breakfast."

Blake heated with anticipation. Bianca lifted her shoulders and took a deep breath, her eyes fixed on him.

"All square and one more to play, Professor. You're a good golfer. Are you sure you weren't a pro at one time?"

"Thought about being a professional golfer. Joined the Army after high school and had to work my way through college. How about you? You're too good to be an amateur."

She turned her gaze away as if steeping in a long-ago memory. "My brother and I grew up on the greens. I entertained the idea of going pro once upon a time."

"What happened?"

"Like you ... life got in the way. You're stalling, Blake. No more delays. Shoot."

Blake had checked the fairway legend as they drove up to the men's ninth tee, a par five, 510 yards. A stream crossed the fairway a hundred yards short of the green. He needed every inch he could muster on his drive if he had any chance for an eagle to win this match.

The women's tee would be an easy play for Bianca— only 425 yards. With her massive drives and a good second shot, she could easily be on the green in two. Blake took a deep breath. In the middle of his backswing, Bianca crossed her legs. Distracted by the movement, he topped the ball, and his drive landed deep into the woods.

Bianca laughed. "Can't take the pressure? We could leave right now." She turned toward him. "I'm hungry."

So am I, Bianca.

"Not on your life. You haven't hit yet. I'll take a provisional." His next shot sailed 325 yards into the middle of the fairway. He could easily reach the green with a short iron. If he sank his putt, he could save par. Wasn't over yet. He settled back into the cart and smiled. "Let's see what you've got."

Bianca teed her ball, took a practice swing, then hit her drive 275 yards into the right rough, behind a row of trees. She had no shot to the green and would have to chip the ball back into play. Her duffed shot landed in a fairway bunker.

Blake took out his seven iron.

"You an old man? Looks pretty heavy on the club, Montgomery."

"Yeah? Watch and learn, girlie." He eased his shot, and the ball landed in the middle of the green.

Bianca was only two in the sand. She topped her sand shot and landed on the left fringe. She'd have to sink a twenty-foot putt to make birdie.

Blake chortled. "Told ya. It ain't over till the fat lady sings, and she is nowhere to be seen."

Bianca came up short for her birdie attempt but made par. Blake would have to make a nine-footer for his par. *Definitely not a gimme.*

His male ego hoped he'd win. Either way, they'd laugh and joke about the round into the morning. Blake lined up, but his cell rang before he could execute his putt. He looked at the ID number.

"Sorry, Bianca. I need to take this call. It's Alfred."

She pursed her lips, propped her putter up like a cane, and leaned against it. "By all means, coward."

He cringed. The name, though well-deserved, brought back vivid memories. He shook them off. He turned and answered his call. "Alfred? Everything okay?"

"Not exactly, *boyo*. I'm in the hospital."

"That's not good. What's wrong?"

"They think I might have had a slight heart attack. Irregular EKG. Personally, I think it's a bad case of indigestion. The doctor insists I stay at least overnight to run a few tests. If everything's okay, I can go home tomorrow."

"Need anything?"

"That's why I called. I need to talk to you."

"About?"

"I overheard a very disturbing conversation at a campaign meeting last night. Might be a clue to solving your little mystery atop Wolf Mountain."

Blake glanced at Bianca ... so willing. A mix of curiosity and loyalty brought him to his senses. "I'll be there ASAP. Leaving the course now."

Blake pocketed his cell and smiled. Had God rescued him from himself?

Bianca slung her putter over her shoulder. "Why do I get the feeling I'm about to spend the night alone?"

"Bianca, I'm sorry. Looks like neither one of us will pack a bag tonight. Alfred called. He's in the hospital. Possible heart attack. I have to go. You understand?"

She sauntered back to the cart and plopped her putter into her bag. "I'm disappointed—but of course, I understand." She hitched her weight to one side, raising her slender hip. "Perhaps, we'll do this another time?"

"Maybe."

"Oh, we will."

"I'd have made that putt, you know."

"You think too highly of yourself, Blake Montgomery. You've missed shorter on this nine."

He met her determined gaze. How could he close her out completely? "All right, then. I'll declare you the winner by default. Meet me at my cabin at eight tomorrow morning. I make a mean omelet."

"Okay, but don't weasel out again. I'm not the forgiving sort."

CHAPTER 13

Marci paced. Why must she be so cold toward Blake? She drove him away just as she had driven Matt into the arms of another woman. Granted, their decisions should have been independent of her actions. Human nature was what it was. Only a greater power could salvage a relationship soured in her youth.

She should talk to Anna. Find out more about this faith of hers—one giving her a more positive outlook on men and life in general. Marci picked up the receiver, ready to speed dial Anna, when the phone rang.

Anna's giggle was unmistakable. "Were you standing by the phone? You never pick up without checking the ID."

"I was about to call you for a change."

"Miracles never cease. About what?"

For the past two years, Anna had called every day. Her faithfulness deserved gratitude. Time Marci did something for her sister in return. Right now, she'd start by initiating a phone call now and again.

"I started cleaning out Matt's closet today."

"Good for you."

"Didn't get very far though."

"One step at a time. Is that what you wanted to talk about?"

Time to celebrate minor victories. "I did more than start cleaning out Matt's closet."

"Is that so?"

"I spent the late morning and early afternoon with Blake."

She expected Anna's squeal of delight. "And?"

"And, that trampy librarian tried to seduce him."

"Are you jealous?"

"I don't know. Maybe."

"Why don't you admit you find him as irresistible as every other woman."

"All right. Yes. He's still very attractive."

Anna laughed. "There's nothing wrong with attraction."

"I suppose—but the timing couldn't be worse."

"There is no right or wrong time. Love is wonderful, however or whenever it comes."

Her optimism didn't make sense. If anyone had a right to be soured on men, Anna did. Then again, she'd always been the strong one, simplistic in her views, yet resilient when the world stomped on her heart.

"I'll admit I like being with Blake. He hired me as his research assistant. We're not dating."

"You want more than a business relationship?"

She could no more lie to Anna than God. "Maybe, but I can't date anyone right now. Especially not Blake Montgomery."

"Date him or don't date him. Why torture yourself with indecision?"

The world might view Anna as selfish and worldly—but Marci trusted her deepest secrets to her sister, her confidante since their toddler years.

"It's complicated."

Anna snickered. "Are you talking about your affair back in Briarcliffe? Good grief, girl. That was almost twenty years ago. And far from secret."

"You knew?"

"Everyone knew. I didn't say anything. I figured you'd tell me eventually. I didn't think you'd wait this long, though. What happened between the two of you? One day you're on cloud nine; the next, you're Queen Mopey. Then you met Matt and started smiling again."

"Blake dumped me."

"And I suppose you never asked him why? I'd have demanded an explanation. Not you. You soak up pain as if you're swimming in a bubble bath. Sounds to me like you never gave him a chance to work out your problems. Instead, you moved on. Did you ever think your marriage to Matt hurt Blake?"

Curt and self-centered, perhaps. Yet, Anna struck the proverbial nail, the same truth Dr. Solomon tried to help Marci understand. Some twisted need to suffer made her welcome pain, or at the least, usher in her self-prophesied disaster where men were concerned.

What was wrong with her? Why couldn't she welcome good?

She and Anna shared the same childhood experiences. Yet miraculously, Anna clung to an optimistic view of life. Not Marci. She was certain every gift contained a ticking bomb meant only for her.

"Look, Marci. Disappointments are not final. They are merely bumps in the road. When you fall, get back up. You'll be a little smarter—tougher."

"Life is not so simple."

"With you, Marci, nothing is. You overthink things."

"I wish I had your strength."

"You may not see a kaleidoscope world, but you have heart. Some say I bounce up from a fall like a cat jumps from barrier to barrier. Truth is, I learned to manipulate my falls to better my lot in life. Pure selfishness. Then I came to know Christ. He's changed me. I'm not who I was, nor am I who I will be."

"Funny. You sound like Blake. He keeps saying he's not the same man he once was. If that's true, then I'm not in love with who he is now, only the memory of him."

"If you ask me, you're afraid. Not because your husband cheated on you or even because Blake, like all of us, has a propensity toward stupidity. You're afraid to let go of your pain, Marci. You say you don't want to be hurt again. Only partly true. You're afraid you might be happy."

"You're wrong. Why wouldn't I want to be happy."

"You'll have to ask Dr. Solomon. All I know is this— happiness is a state of mind, not something dropped from the sky."

Though simplistic, Anna's logic was spot on. For whatever reason, before Matt, before Blake, Marci Henderson was stuck somewhere in a past beyond her sight, unable to forgive in the present. "You gave me a lot to think about, Anna."

"Good. Listen, sweetie, I've got to go. I have a date tonight."

"No way! Details, girl."

"A guy I met at the restaurant. Name's Herb Waycross. Says he's a friend of Tad and Bianca's father."

"And you agreed to go out with him before checking his story?"

"Where's the fun in that?"

"Still, be careful."

Anna giggled. "Funniest thing. I was having lunch with the girls at Tony's Bistro, and he came right up to me. Said he's an attorney who used to work with the attorneys who handled my divorce from Robert. He's visiting Tad and Bianca. He used to vacation in the Adirondacks with his family. But after his wife died, he didn't have the heart to come back until now. He retired in the spring and is considering a permanent move to Collins Bend. He's the one, Marci. I feel it."

"I don't know, Anna. The whole thing sounds too coincidental."

Anna groaned. "You'd be suspicious of a bunny rabbit. Marci, he's a delightful man. Not distinguishably handsome like Colin Firth or Pierce Brosnan—more like a pocked Brad Pitt. He's funny, and ... well ... I'm ready to take a new relationship out for a spin and see what happens."

"Be careful, Anna. He could be a gold digger, or worse."

"Worse?"

"Some crazed stalker or predator."

"Why can't a nice man simply find me attractive and ask me out? I'm not over the hill yet, Marci."

"That's not my point. You don't have a good track record with men."

"And you do?"

Marci tapped her fingers on the counter. *"Touché."*

"So, what if I fall down again? I always come back swinging. The most talented fighter doesn't always win, Marci. The victory goes to the one who remains standing at the end of the round. Besides, if Herb worked for Ludlam and McGee's law firm, he made good money. So why would he want mine?"

"Remember the fiasco with Donald Roundtree? Said he was a comedian and turned out to be a Casanova? Fortunately for you, I did a background check before you got too serious."

"I dated Donald between husbands one and two. I'm smarter now. Besides, just because Donald turned out to be a creep, doesn't mean Herb will. We really connected.

Get this. He studies landmarks as a hobby. He wanted to find out more about the Wordsworth Estate. I gave him Blake's number."

Marci gulped. Way too coincidental. "Anna, I know you think I digest paranoia like a pill, but please be careful."

"Look who's giving dating advice—a girl who can't climb out of her dead husband's casket."

No use arguing with Anna when her mind was made up. "Do what you want since you will anyway. Don't say I didn't warn you."

CHAPTER 14

Blake hesitated at the door. Alfred seemed at peace in his slumber. He lay amid a myriad of machines, each bleep a coded response to his body functions. Medications dripped down an IV tube in rhythm to his snorts.Yet, within the repose, an old man snored. Scores of wrinkles pulled at his face like hundreds of invisible strings. Could this feeble man be the same tower of strength he was just a few days ago? When had he aged?

Alfred opened his eyes, seemingly aware of another presence in the room.

"Clearly, Alfred, my friend, this is not the most desirable way to meet women," Blake said, as a nurse brushed passed him, taking visual note of medical paraphernalia while she took her patient's pulse.

When she let go of his wrist, she assisted Alfred to a sitting position. "So, this means I'm going home?" he asked.

The nurse smiled. She was young, probably even younger than Alfred's great granddaughter. "No. This means you're going up to medical. Doctor Jones will be in to talk to you in a few minutes."

"Great timing, lassie. My good friend has stopped by, and you whisk me away before I can even say hello."

Blake laughed as the nurse left. "Gauging by your sauciness, I'd say you're going to live."

"So they tell me."

"I suppose you enjoy giving everyone a good scare?"

"Not my intention at all, *boyo*. How's the research going so far?"

"Marci and I are trying to track down a distant relative of the maid supposedly killed in the fire that claimed Erwin Wordsworth's life."

"A poor maid who probably was never married? Not many prospects for relatives, even distant ones. What for?"

"A hunch. We found a letter written by her indicating all was not well in the Wordsworth home."

Alfred laughed between staccato coughs. "Not a new insight, Blake."

"Yes, but something tells me there was more than marital discord afoot."

"Most marital discord involves a third party. If Felicity were involved with the accountant—an unfaithful wife would cause any man to roam a house like a tropical storm."

"Perhaps. Marci's convinced Felicity wasn't guilty of adultery."

"Why the interest in the maid?"

Blake shook his head, unashamedly proud of his sleuthing. "Her name."

"Never knew what her name was ... guess no one thought her important."

"Nor did I until I read the letter and saw her signature."

"And?"

"Abigail Todd Fisher."

Alfred pulled himself up a little straighter. "Todd, you say? Interesting, indeed. Let me guess. You think there's a connection to Reverend John Todd?"

"Possibly. Last I talked with Marci, she thought she might be able to search on the Internet."

Alfred narrowed his gaze. "What do you mean by 'last'?"

Blake sat in the bedside chair, biting his lower lip.

"Blake?"

"We sort of parted on not so friendly terms, and I'm not sure she's still working for me."

Alfred shook his head. "Only you would be so uncertain." He leaned back against his pillow. "Never met a man who loved to stay in the dark as much as you. Good grief, lad, call her."

Blake stood and paced the room. "Probably should. I'll let the staff get you moved, and then I'll be up to see you after I call Marci. Before I go, you said you had information on Wordsworth you wanted to share?"

Alfred elevated the bed. "Funny what things will come to memory in the middle of the night. You see, Blake, the topic of the Wordsworth estate came up at our last news conference at Will Forrester's campaign headquarters."

"You meet a lot of reporters, Alfred."

"True, and I'm used to these sponges trying to corner me for a juicy tidbit."

"But this fellow was different?"

"Wasn't a fellow. A young girl, actually. Couldn't have been out of journalism school more than a year or two."

"And pretty? Never knew you to avoid the pretty ones."

"That, *boyo*, is an accurate observation."

"And she interested you other than her pretty face?"

"Very much so. When she found out I was staying in Collins Bend, she pulled me aside and asked a lot of questions about Erwin Wordsworth. She said she'd received an anonymous tip. Forrester was somehow connected to the Wordsworths."

"Digging for a scandal, I'll bet."

"Perhaps."

"Interesting. Is he?"

"Except for his campaigning, I don't believe so."

Blake settled back into the chair and leaned in toward Alfred. The man loved to cast his bait, and Blake never ceased to nibble. "From your tone, looks like your conversation didn't end there."

"Always knew you for a smart lad, Blake. Normally, I'd have brushed the reporter off."

"But, she was pretty, and ...?"

"And she said she'd always been fascinated by the Wordsworths, and like you, wanted to know more about their contribution to Adirondack history. She had visited the Railroad Museum in Long Lake ..."

"Probably baiting you, not letting you ditch her so she could drain what information *you* had on Forrester's connection to Collins Bend."

"Might be. As far as I know, Forrester has never set foot in Collins Bend."

Blake smiled. "The museum's not far from here. Maybe I should visit while I'm in Collins Bend."

Alfred nodded. "Might very well add some insight. I told the reporter I had a friend who was writing a book on the Adirondack railroads. So, I turned tables and interviewed the reporter. She gave me a veritable feast of information—information I thought you'd be interested in."

"You're a good friend, Alfred. A feast, you say?"

"Might have something to do with the marital discord theory of yours."

"And how's that?"

"Has to do with Wordsworth's management."

Blake leaned back in the chair. "Okay, I'm listening."

"The reporter—Patty was her name—said most of the ledgers had been destroyed in a fire. However, the town donated pertinent documents to the Long Lake Museum."

Alfred could turn a simple page of history into a five-volume report. "Tell me something I don't already know."

"Patty heard rumors that Wordsworth might have been hauling questionable cargo."

"Questionable, how?"

Alfred coughed again, a deep worrisome hack. "Opium."

"Morally questionable, perhaps, but hardly illegal. He wouldn't have been the only railroad giant to get rich from the poppy fields of the North Country."

"Not just the drugs, lad. Patty said Wordsworth was carrying human cargo as well."

"Now *that* I didn't know."

"Patty suspected Wordsworth brought women and children from the Indian reservations with promises of employment. He told his fares they could repay the transportation from their wages. A scam. Wordsworth got his money from smugglers who ushered these unsuspecting people into sweat shops and brothels."

Hard to believe, given Wordsworth's religious roots. The man might have done questionable business deals; however, human cargo seemed beyond debauchery. The reporter must be mistaken or else all the reports Blake had read on the Wordsworths were inaccurate.

"Emerson Wordsworth was a devout Quaker. I doubt he'd have been mixed up in something so vile. The drugs, maybe, since they weren't illegal. However, what you're saying is another kind of slave trade, something incongruent with the abolitionist philosophy."

"Patty said the cargo wasn't Emerson's. Rather, his son's, Erwin."

"Still doesn't make sense. Everything I read about the Wordsworth empire indicates Erwin carried on his father's idealism. The Wordsworth fortune built more hospitals and schools than any of the millionaires in the day."

Alfred clicked his tongue. "Don't let philanthropy fool you, *boyo*. You know as well as I do, the titans of industry all had their dark sides. Rockefeller and Carnegie, too. Greed makes thieves of us all, Blake. These men were as ruthless as mob dons."

Blake's arguments lost ground. "Maybe the industrialists justified their corrupt business practices by their generosity. Yet, I wouldn't be quick to lump the Wordsworths into the same category."

Alfred coughed, then rested back on his pillow. "Then maybe you should investigate for yourself."

"I will. Even if what Patty says is true, Wordsworth wouldn't have been the first railroad mogul to make a fortune off the evils of society. Still doesn't explain Wordsworth's death or Felicity's disappearance."

"Patty thinks Felicity found out about her husband's shenanigans. If he indeed was supplying slave-like labor under the guise of charity, it might be the source of disharmony between them and why she ran off."

"Could be."

Alfred adjusted his pillows. "One more thing. The reporter said the shipping manifestos listed no passengers."

"I wouldn't think so. If he were smuggling women and children for the sweat shops, he'd have covered his tracks by listing them as cargo." Two orderlies arrived with a gurney. "Speaking of transportation, I see your bus is here."

"Make the call, Blake."

"Call?"

"Marci."

Blake took out his cell. "I'll be back."

Alfred laughed while the orderlies transferred him to the gurney. He waved as they wheeled him away.

Marci opened her laptop and searched the name Abigail Fisher. Ridiculous to expect a simple Google search would garner anything worth following up on, and any research efforts might be futile. Her conversation with Blake ended on a tenuous note. By now, he probably realized their arrangement was a huge mistake.

Curiosity trumped practicality. If she found any useful information, she'd give what she learned to Blake to do as he saw fit. She sifted through the fifty irrelevant hits until she came across one holding promise, an advertisement for a used book—Abigail Fisher Tierney, author, *The La Grande*. She clicked the link to read the book blurb. "The author, once a maid at the famous resort, puts forth a compelling memoir of Adirondack history during the heyday of tourism." Marci noted the copyright year— written decades ago, making the author now a very old woman. Was she even still alive?

The cover art sported an unmistakable facsimile of the Lake Placid *La Grande*.

Too many coincidences.

She clicked to peruse the back cover. The terse biography mentioned the author lived in Herkimer. Decades ago. If she were still alive, what were the chances she still resided anywhere in the Adirondack region?

Won't know unless you try, Marci.

She checked the white pages and found a listing for A. F. Tierney, residing in Cold Brook, a small town in Herkimer County.

Marci punched in the number on her cell.

"Hello?" The voice sounded shaky, resembling someone of advanced age.

Where should I start? "Is this Abigail Fisher?"

"Oh my, I haven't been called by my maiden name for seventy years. Who wants to know?"

Marci chose to hope since the woman's tone seemed amicable. "My name is Marci Henderson. I used to be a history teacher at Collins Bend High School."

"How very nice. I'm sorry to say, I don't recall ever meeting you."

"No, you wouldn't have ... and I'm not teaching at the moment."

"Of course, dear. It's summer."

"What I mean is ... I'm working for a college history professor who is doing research on the Wordsworths, their railroad business, and the impact Wordsworth had on Adirondack development."

"That sounds fascinating, dear. But you're barking up a wrong tree. I don't think I could be of any help. I never worked on the railroad."

"I'm not calling about the railroad."

Abigail giggled. "Well, now, this is a mystery. How do you think I can help you?"

"Your book."

"I only wrote one book, so I assume you're referring to *The La Grande.*"

"Yes."

"Do you know the place?"

Perhaps not as intimately as she'd have liked. Many were the times she wished she could morph back to its glory days. "I was there only last week."

"Oh, I'm so glad it's still standing. Is it as magnificent now?"

"Probably not, but the building is still impressive."

"Have you read my book, dear? Or are you leading up to a different question?"

Abigail might be a super senior, but she had lost none of her insightfulness. "Your suspicions are correct. I did call for another reason."

"You said you were helping out a college professor? I don't see how my work at the La Grande would have any bearing on the Wordsworths."

"I'm calling about the Wordsworth mansion. Do you know anything about the ruins?"

Abigail's voice wavered as if hesitant. "Anyone who lived in the area knew something about the Wordsworths, dear. I climbed Wolf Mountain more than once when I was a young girl." She laughed, dissipating the momentary hesitancy. "I don't think I could climb it now, though."

Marci smiled inwardly. "Mrs. Tierney, although my employer's research is primarily about the railroads, we both have a keen interest in the tragedy at the Wordsworth estate. We're curious about the maid who died in the fire, Abigail Todd Fisher. I've been doing research in the hopes of finding someone with a historical connection. Felicity and Emerson had no children."

"Yes, dear, that's all common knowledge."

"All our efforts came to a dead end, until we found the maid's letter and learned her name. Her middle name led me to wonder if she might be connected to Reverend John Todd, who was a frequent visitor to the Wordsworth estate. When I came across your name ... well, you must admit there are a lot of similarities."

"Yes, quite possibly more than a coincidence."

"Then you are a distant relative?"

Abigail sighed as if giving more information to a stranger produced a struggle of conscience. "That depends on what you consider ... distant."

"Any connection at all?"

"I don't mean to be mysterious, dear. You do sound like a trustworthy person, a teacher, and obviously a very good researcher. So, I'll be honest. Abigail Todd Fisher was my grandmother."

Marci gasped. She'd struck gold. "Thank you for trusting me with this information."

"There's more, but I'm not comfortable talking about my grandmother's personal matters over the phone."

"May my employer visit you?"

"Certainly, but I insist you come too. You seem like such a lovely girl. I'd love the company. At my age, I don't get many visitors."

"Would tomorrow be convenient?"

Abigail sighed, more a joyous sound than sad. "Tomorrow is fine. I look forward to seeing you in person, though I don't know what my grandmother's tragic life could add to your research."

"Your grandmother's death was listed as a side note in the historical accounts. All the news items barely mention her at all, stating only a servant also died in the fire. The world should know she was more than a simple servant who perished with Erwin Wordsworth. If not for the letter found at the scene, no one would have ever known her name. Speaking for myself, I'd like to know more about her."

Abigail answered with short breaths. "Thank you for your sensitivity, dear."

Was she crying? Perhaps calling had brought back memories Abigail would sooner forget. Marci understood the pain of remembrance. "I'm sorry if my call unsettled you. I'm sure the last thing you expected was a call from someone sticking their nose into your family's past."

"It's quite all right, dear. Come for tea about nine o'clock."

"We'll be there. And thank you again for your time."

Marci disconnected and clasped her hands together, barely able to keep from galloping through her house. How exciting. This charming lady might be the long-hidden key to unraveling Felicity Wordsworth's disappearance, perhaps proving her innocence once and for all.

What if Blake refused to make the trip? Or refused to let Marci accompany him? Technically, she'd quit as his assistant. He wouldn't be obligated.

If need be, she'd conduct her own research on Felicity and let Blake concentrate on the railroads.

With or without Blake Montgomery, Marci would make a trip to Cold Creek.

Feeling confident after her luck with Abigail Tierney, Marci called Driscoll's Cleaning Service and arranged for someone to finish cleaning out Matt's closet. She managed to accomplish two important things in one day.

Moving forward was not beyond the realm of possibility.

A friendship with Blake, at least while he remained in Collins Bend, might also be possible. Twenty years is a long time—time enough to stop letting resentments rule her life. She knew very little about this older version of Blake Montgomery, the man who gave the speech at the alumni dinner. In fact, she hadn't really known him during the romance. They only made love once. Before then, Blake worked hard at keeping a professor/student distance between them, though she felt his struggle, relegating conversations limited to her research projects, his mentoring, and her school experiences.

If they started fresh, who knows what might develop? She would never know if she kept pushing him away. He'd been so angry when he pulled out of her driveway earlier. Had she waited too long?

She jumped when the phone rang. She checked the ID. *Blake.*

"Hello?"

Marci's cheerfulness took Blake by surprise. Had he not recognized the sultriness in her voice—a soft, yet soulful resonance like a lullaby—he'd have thought he'd dialed the wrong number. Sad he would have to dampen her welcomed good spirit. She'd want to know about Alfred.

They spoke in sync, "I've got news."

Blake laughed. "Maybe I should go first. Are you sitting down?"

She hesitated. "Okay. I'm sitting now. What?"

"I'm afraid I have some bad news. Alfred's in the hospital."

"Oh, dear. I'm so sorry, Blake. I know you think highly of him."

"He's like a father to me. Thankfully, he's okay. A mild heart attack. Of course, he sloughed the symptoms off as indigestion."

"I'm glad he's okay. I like Professor Donahue. He seems to have had a positive effect on you."

Blake's cheeks warmed as he remembered Bianca, how close he'd come to letting her seduce him. He recognized the game and became too willing to play. Alfred would have been disappointed in his protégé. Blake prayed for strength to cancel the breakfast date he'd made in weakness, knowing full well her flirtation came with a price.

And he'd been vain. If only he'd taken time to realize she must have had some other motive than his male magnetism. What agenda caused a beautiful young woman to lure a middle-aged man to her bed? He had nothing to offer her—no wealth, only his vast knowledge of history.

Yes, he knew she'd set a trap—one he'd walked into willingly. *Please don't let me be a complete idiot, Lord.* Knowing the right choice did not make choosing any easier.

Like an amputee's ghost pain, Blake's head ached with the force of Alfred's phantom scorn. *Don't go back to Egypt. Don't fool yourself into thinking a fling would hurt no one. Marci is the one for you. You need to give her more time.*

"Blake, are you still there?"

"Sorry, Marci. My mind wandered a bit. You're right. Alfred means a great deal to me. Someday I'll tell you why."

"I look forward to that conversation. Now, your turn to sit."

Blake plopped in a waiting room chair. "Done."

"You could tell me all about you and Alfred tomorrow, if you'd like."

Blake swallowed. An invitation from Marci? *Whoa!* "How's that?"

"I made an appointment for you."

"When. For what?"

"Since you didn't actually fire me, I took the liberty of arranging your calendar. Of course, I told her I'd have to confirm."

"Confirm? With whom?"

Marci gushed with excitement. "We're meeting with Abigail Fisher Tierney."

"Who?"

"Her grandmother was Felicity Wordsworth's maid."

Blake caught Marci's enthusiasm. "You're amazing. How on earth did you manage to find this out?"

"I Googled the name ... Abigail Fisher—a longshot, I know. I foraged through the numerous hits until I found a book authored by an Abigail Fisher Tierney, a memoir about her younger days as a chambermaid at ... ready for this?"

"Shoot."

Marci paused for dramatic affect. "*The La Grande* ... she traced its history from its heyday as a ritzy hotel for New Yorkers on vacation during the days of the millionaires and into the roaring twenties and beyond. She worked there toward the end of the depression and in the early days of World War II for a few years, then she quit to go to business school."

"I thought Felicity's maid was unmarried?"

Marci clicked impatience. "All will be answered when we visit, assuming you'll let me come with you."

A long ride with Marci could be the opportunity he'd wanted—the perfect chance to share his testimony. Or, the trip could prove to add more layers of frustration. "Of course, I want you with me."

The warmth in Marci's banter tickled his senses. Had she cracked the door open for a relationship between them? Whatever she offered, he'd accept—even if only friendship.

He resumed their conversation. "There was no indication Wordsworth's maid was married or had a child. I suppose Reverend Todd might have interceded to help Abigail gain employment. During those days, most employers would not have hired an unmarried woman with a child. Or, she might have kept the child a secret from her employer."

"You're speculating, Blake—although, you may be right. There may be more letters that can shed light on this mystery."

He'd prayed for an out from Bianca's clutches, and God answered in ways he could not have anticipated. Bianca's svelte form eerily loomed like a mental hologram, so real in his mind he could sense her presence even though she were nowhere near. As tempted as he was by Bianca's willingness, Marci's uplifted tones, even her breathing, called to him, a more portent beckoning, like surf pounding the shore.

"She seems very eager to meet with us. I got the impression she has a lot of information she wants to share."

"Marci, I love you!"

"Easy, Doctor Montgomery. Don't declare your undying affection until you've met Mrs. Tierney. For all we know, this venture could be a complete waste of time."

Not if I'm with you, Marci. "Or this might be the *X* on the treasure map. What time?"

"She invited us for tea at 9:00."

"In the morning?"

"She lives in Herkimer County."

God had given him the escape he needed. Why did he hesitate? Bianca's warning—explicit—she'd not forgive him if he stood her up. Why did he continue to stew in her temptation?

Maybe repentance began with the head, the heart lagging behind at a snail's pace. Lot's wife was rescued in spite of her devotion to the city. Though given a miraculous intervention, she glanced back, and the city devoured her. If he did not stop this roller coaster, he'd end up with a petrified heart.

"It'll take over three hours. I'll pick you up at 5:00. We can take our time. Pretty scenery between here and there."

"I'm so looking forward to meeting Mrs. Tierney. She sounds delightful."

"It's a date, then?"

"A date," Marci said, her repetition melodic and definitive.

CHAPTER 15

Funny how much like a date this trip with Blake seemed. She'd been up two hours already. Sleep was a privilege, one she rarely received very much of these days. She checked in the mirror one more time, satisfied her white satin blouse and black slacks would be appropriate for tea with anyone, let alone a fine lady like Abigail Tierney. Marci rummaged for her blush, putting on a few strokes. She needed sun to tone her pale skin. She'd been outside precious little since the fiasco on Wolf Mountain.

Time to confront her fear.

Smiling inwardly at her new-found courage, she vowed to take a daily, two-mile walk, starting tomorrow—right after the cleaning crew came to box up Matt's closet.

She peeked out the window as Blake pulled into the driveway. Punctual, as usual. He swaggered to the door—his signature hesitant, boyish, yet confidently distinguished gait so delightful to watch—even now.

She opened the door. Though still dark outside, the porch light illuminated his wide grin.

He laughed. "Don't know what young folks do these days, but I still prefer to pick up my date at the door and walk her to the car. Call me old-fashioned."

"I like old-fashioned." She looped her arm around his extended elbow, her cheeks warming, like a schoolgirl on her way to a dance. Her handsome escort might be driving a Ford Ranger, but at least he dressed the part—a gray sport jacket, blue oxford shirt, and black trousers.

"I didn't know if you'd have time for breakfast, so I stopped and got us a couple of bear claws and a mocha latte for you."

"Do you spoil all your employees like this?" She could easily get used to pampering.

Blake had not been so thoughtful in the past. She liked the improvement, whatever the cause. Curiosity took root. How had Alfred played into Blake's metamorphosis, although other than a kinder demeanor and a slight, middle-aged paunch, he seemed much the same as the man she loved so long ago.

Blake opened the door for her, and she slid in. Guilt niggled. She hadn't asked Blake how his mentor fared. "Did you have a chance to check on Alfred?" she asked as he hopped into the driver side.

"He's doing well."

Marci fastened her seat belt as Blake backed out of the driveway. She looked for the white Osprey she frequently spotted. Part of her recent series of hallucinations? If so, why didn't she see the car today? No more worries about her mental health. No sense dreading what the day might bring either.

She studied Blake's face. Was he glad to be with her? His smile said, "Yes." She'd accept Blake's desire for her, start anew, and appreciate the fact he still found her attractive.

Blake eased into traffic. Before long, nature lay before them in all its beauty. The rising sun shattered the mists, revealing budding trees and cold lakes. The scenery on Route 30 never disappointed. In winter, the pines glistened with frozen snow. In autumn, the circus of colors almost made her believe God cared for his creation.

The Adirondacks fielded abundant waterways, and their trip would take them along Saranac Lake, Tupper Lake, and Long Lake. She imagined the early settlers, trappers mostly, canoeing their hides to trade outposts. She was grateful for an insightful President Roosevelt, who loved the terrain as much as the native population and deemed the area "forever wild."

"I've lived in these mountains a long time, Blake. Whenever I travel these roads, I understand why locals call this region God's Country."

Blake smiled as he gazed out the driver's window. "Just thinking the same thing. Uncanny how our minds are so often in sync. When I retire from Briarcliffe, I'd like to settle in these mountains. A beautiful place to live."

"Are you sure? I remember how bundled up you'd get in October and complain about the cold Northeast. The Adirondacks will feel like northern Alaska compared to Briarcliffe. Are you sure you wouldn't rather live in Florida where you can golf year-round?"

"I like winter sports." He leaned in her direction, speaking in a near whisper. "I especially love the sound of crackling logs in a fireplace."

Like the cabin at Sorrel Pond.

Marci cringed at the memory, the recollection so intense she trembled at the sight of a woodstove. How foolish. Why did she cocoon herself in regret?

"Do you think you'll retire any time soon?"

"I am fully vested, so I could retire early. The idea of living in Collins Bend and devoting all my time to writing is definitely appealing."

"You *are* different, Blake. Yet, not so different. Boggles my mind. You still love history, and you were like a kid in the House of History, Francine's obnoxious flirtations aside. There's something in your bearing—a gentleness, kindness, and, dare I say, confidence—traits likely buried under the surface of a life still searching. Have you finally found what you were looking for?"

"I believe I have."

"What?"

Blake eased the truck over to the side of the road, parked, and then faced her. "Wow. You sure know how to open a door, Marci. I've been praying God would give me a chance to talk to you today about the Blake you remember and the man I've become. Not perfect, by any means. In fact, recent circumstances have shown how weak I am at times. Nevertheless, I have found something new—a life in Christ. I don't want to go back to who I once was, the man who hurt you. I never meant to, but I did. I loved you, Marci. Please, believe me."

"I suppose you did love me once. I've wasted too many years blaming you. The reality is that we are both at fault for losing what we had."

"Then there's hope for us now?"

"I can't say for sure. Like you said, you're different because of this faith you've found. My husband was a Christian, but that didn't stop him from being unfaithful. Forgive me if I don't congratulate you on your newfound religion. I am glad your convictions work for you."

Blake frowned. "Marci, I'm not Matt. I'm sorry he hurt you, but try to understand. Being a Christian doesn't make you immune to stupidity. Simply put, this faith I've found gave me an inner radar that helps me make better choices, although sometimes I fail to listen and end up in trouble— like Matt did, I suspect."

"I'm different, too, Blake. Not because I found faith. I like the idea of Christianity. I do believe there is a God. Matt had told me much about being saved and what this means. Sometimes, I think I'd like to take that step. I'm just not ready yet. I have so many doubts."

"Then what holds you back?"

"If I become a Christian, I'd have to let go of too many things."

Like resentment. Some days they are all that keep me afloat. If only this Christian thing was as simple as Blake and Matt claimed. To be free of bitterness.

"Marci, I've never stopped loving you."

"Then why did you break up with me the day after Sorrel Pond."

"I didn't break up with you. You walked out before I could finish what I wanted to say. And what I did say, I said badly."

"Then what did you want to say?"

"It's moot, but I'll try to explain. I owe you that. The dean found out about us and threatened to fire me if I didn't stop seeing you."

A lame excuse. "You valued your job over me. I get it."

"That's not true. I wanted time to figure things out. I thought I could keep both."

Marci looked out the passenger window. "Your plan didn't work too well, did it?"

"When you walked out on me, I wanted to go after you. I should have. I thought if I waited until you graduated ..."

"Matt?"

"Yes, Matt. You seemed happy. I knew I'd lost you. I didn't want to interfere. I kept in touch with Anna—I had to know how you were doing. She never told me about your unhappiness. For all these years, I thought you were better off without me." Blake took her hands in his. "Can't we start over?"

His eyes begged for a kiss.

"I know what you want, Blake. I'm not ready for anything physical. We each need to become acquainted with the people we are now—be sure we're not stuck in the past, in love with the memory of us."

"I know all I need to know, Marci."

She pushed back against the seat. "I don't think so."

"If you're referring to your hospitalization, I know the details."

"Anna?"

"Yes. Like I said, I'd call her from time to time."

"Then you must realize I'm not stable."

"You're stronger than you think, Marci."

"I thought I was cured. Then ... well ... recently, I've been seeing strange things."

He leaned back against the seat. "Like what? You mean like at the library and the café?"

She couldn't divulge Wolf Mountain. Not until she was sure she could trust him.

"And other things that make no sense."

"Your panic attack at the church and the donut shop aside, you seem fine to me. Whatever is wrong, we'll work through the problems together. Besides, there could be a rational explanation for the things you think you saw."

Oh, how I hope so, Blake.

"Take however much time you need ... just don't shut me out. I want us to be together again, and I'm willing to be patient—to see what the new 'us' becomes."

She could resist his pleading eyes no longer. She accepted his kiss, different from the demanding passion of yesteryear—this kiss, tender ... full of hope.

Blake restarted his truck, and they continued with only a few comments on the breathtaking scenery. They arrived at Abigail's home at precisely 9:00 am.

Marci scanned the living room while Abigail filled the flowered china teacups. Marci subdued the urge to burst into a gazillion questions, realizing the elderly woman might be sizing her guests up, assessing if she could trust them with family secrets, if indeed there were any to share. Best to let the conversation remain cordial, keeping to topics about the weather.

If she cajoled Abigail to talk about her life at the *La Grande*, Marci might be able to swing the discussion to what Abigail knew of her grandmother's tenure at the Wordsworth mansion. "Your book sounds fascinating, Mrs. Tierney."

"Please, call me Abigail."

"I tried to order a copy after we talked, but it's out of print."

"I have old copies here. I'd be happy to give you one."

"A priceless gift and an honor."

Abigail leaned back against her side chair. From the design and irregular marks on the wood, the chair was circa 1900. The craftsmanship was far too unique to be a factory piece, as was true for the settee where Marci sat and the paisley wing chair where Blake slouched. The marble-topped end tables added to the aura of a bygone era.

"I'm fascinated by your furnishings, Abigail. These are from the late nineteenth century and early twentieth."

"When I came here to live after my mother died, I didn't have the heart to replace her furniture. I still have her old four-poster bed. I'm afraid the modern stuff is not made to last, dear." She chuckled. "However, my mother's furniture will still be around in a hundred years."

Abigail placed her teacup on the tray. "You didn't come all this way to talk about my furniture. You hoped I could give you information about my grandmother's employment in Collins Bend."

Blake straightened to attention. "Yes. Do you mind if we ask a few questions?"

"I'll tell you what I know."

"Was your grandmother related in some way to Reverend John Todd?"

"I suppose in this day and age, there would be no shame for what my grandmother endured. Yes, Reverend Todd was a distant cousin."

Blake sipped his tea while Abigail talked, probably to contain his excitement at stumbling into living history.

"My grandmother was a typist for a wealthy merchant. He forced himself on her, and she became pregnant. In those days, the woman always bore the shame of rape. Though she'd only met Reverend Todd once, my grandmother was aware of his tireless work at North Elba and his charities for the downtrodden. She wrote to him out of desperation.

Marci ached for Abigail's grandmother. "In those days, the victim paid twice."

Abigail took a sip as she nodded, then continued. "Reverend Todd proved to be a man worthy of good repute. He arranged for my grandmother to give birth to her child, my mother, at the home of a discreet couple who fostered my mother until she was of age. Reverend Todd also used his influence with the Wordsworths to secure Grandmother's employment as Felicity's maid."

Abigail rose and walked to a side table, then pulled out a drawer. "You seem like an honest and fair main, Professor Montgomery."

"If we call you Abigail, then by all means you must call me Blake."

"Fair enough."

She retrieved a small chest. "In here is my Grandmother Abigail's diary. She was only twenty-five when she died and saw her daughter only three times."

Blake sat at the edge of the chair. "I'm surprised this diary survived the fire."

"Family legend says my grandmother sensed things were not well at the Wordsworth mansion. She feared someone would discover she'd been keeping a journal of her experiences on Wolf Mountain and might destroy or steal her diary. Her activities remained unsuspected since, in those days, few servants could read or write. My grandmother hid her education by speaking the vernacular of the other servants."

Marci imagined what life must have been like for poor Abigail, worked to the bone for little money, not able to see her child, and forced to hide her upbringing, all because of society's conventions. The times in which people live define their character. In Marci's esteem, Abigail Todd Fischer proved courageous.

"A month before the fire, she gave the diary to my mother's foster parents. They in turn gave the journal to my mother when she became of age. She passed it on to me before she died."

Blake's face reddened with excitement. "May I see it?"

"Of course. I'll do one better. I want you to have it."

He raised a hand as if to object. "This diary is worth a fortune. Are you sure?"

"I have sufficient wealth, Blake, and I can't take my money with me when I die. I want this to be put in the Collins Bend museum so the world will know about Abigail Todd Fisher—how she was a brave woman who struggled against the conventions of her day to do the best she could for her child—a child conceived through the lust of a sinful man, but thanks to the intervention of a crusader, brought up in a devout Christian home."

Marci gulped with emotion. "Reverend Todd?"

"Yes. Because of his compassion, what might have been a legacy of shame became a heritage of faith. My mother went to college and taught until she met my father, a circuit preacher. She didn't have me until she was in her forties. I was raised in a loving home and shown the way of grace my whole life. My husband was a doctor. In his later life, we served as missionaries in China. He has been gone for thirty years, and we had no children. My estate will be inherited by my husband's nephew who has no interest in this home or its belongings. I am certain he will sell everything. I'm over a hundred years old, so my time on earth is growing short." She clutched the journal to her chest. "So, you see? I will consider this a favor. I trust you will find a proper and safe home for my grandmother's words."

Blake's eyes misted. "I will."

Abigail heaved a deep sigh, then handed Blake the chest. He took out the diary and thumbed through its pages. "This seems to be in good condition. I'll make sure the curator takes every precaution to preserve this valuable document."

Abigail sighed again as she sat and leaned back.

Marci rose. "We've wearied you, Abigail. We should let you rest."

"Oh, my dear, I'll have plenty of time to rest when the Lord calls me home. You've made an old woman very happy."

Blake rose. "Perhaps we can visit again?"

"I hope you do."

"When I've completed this current project, perhaps my publisher would be interested in publishing your grandmother's story."

"I'd be honored."

Blake held the chest with both hands. "We should be leaving. I can't tell you how grateful we are for your generosity."

Mrs. Tierney rose. "I'll show you out." She led the way through the long corridor to the main entrance. "In the diary, you'll find references Grandmother Abigail made to conversations she overheard as she went about her duties. Visitors paid little attention to what they said around servants. If one did their job well, they seemed nearly invisible. The last few entries report Erwin and Felicity fought continuously ... and Felicity accused Erwin of using the railroads to traffic drugs and worse."

"Worse?" Blake asked.

"Grandmother didn't specify."

"I'm sure we'll find out the truth."

"Please understand, Blake, Grandmother Abigail was extremely fond of Mrs. Wordsworth. As you know, drug trade in those days was not illegal, but many groups began to champion the need for government regulation. Felicity, one of the most outspoken activists, believed the widespread use of these substances would corrode society."

Blake scowled his agreement. "Seems her predictions were on the mark."

"Grandmother's entries indicate her mistress considered her more than a servant—rather a friend in whom Felicity confided, to the dissatisfaction of Mr. Wordsworth."

"What did Erwin say when Felicity confronted him about her suspicions?" Blake asked.

"He vehemently denied trafficking of any kind other than purposes of tourism and transporting manufactured goods to and from New York City."

"A colleague of mine shared rumors Wordsworth might have been involved with human trafficking, luring young boys and girls, former slaves and poor Native Americans, with promises of employment in New York. The girls often ended up as prostitutes, and the young boys were forced into sweatshops. I hope Wordsworth didn't consider these young people as 'commodities.'"

Abigail sighed. "I've lived a long time, Blake. I am aware of how the laws have changed from my grandmother's era. As you'll see in her diary, Mr. Wordsworth was highly esteemed in the community. I can't imagine a man of his moral fiber would become involved in something that vile. Yet, Felicity said she had seen proof of his unholy business stored in a safe place."

Marci smacked her lips. "Unholy business indeed. According to articles I've come across, Felicity worked tirelessly toward improved working conditions and child labor laws. Though the perils of opiates were as hotly debated as the temperance movement, railroads became the link from supplier to customer, innocent children being the fodder for corruption."

Abigail smiled. "Sounds like you could write your own book, Marci. You are a teacher. And I suspect a good one."

Marci glanced at Blake. "His words, not mine. He has already written articles saying those exact words."

Blake's eyes widened. "You read my articles?"

"Some of them—the ones touching on the human condition."

Abigail leaned in as if to whisper a secret, though no one else lived in the home. "Apparently, however, Felicity began to believe Mr. Wordsworth's innocence ... well, you'll read her thoughts in the diary where my grandmother mentions Erwin pouring over ledgers into the morning hours, burning several candles each night."

Marci clasped Abigail's hand. "Do you suspect Felicity met with harm rather than running off with Mr. Wordsworth's accountant as believed by some?"

"Yes, I do. Though no one's been able to prove either theory."

Abigail turned with a gasp. "Oh, I forgot the book I promised Marci. And there's something else I want you to have. Wait here a moment."

She returned with her book and an alabaster cross displayed on a silver chain, handing both to Marci. "I can't think of anyone else I'd rather give this necklace to. A gift to Grandmother Abigail from Felicity. She had two made. Felicity always wore hers, even to bed. My grandmother gave this one to my mother's foster parents with instructions the necklace would be handed down in her memory. I would hate for this precious memento to end up on the auction block along with all the other antiques in my house."

Abigail's words stung ... the expectation Marci could bequeath such a treasure to anyone. Loneliness covered her, a cloud of unobtainable longing. "Like you, I'm a childless widow. I'd have no one to bequeath this to."

Abigail clasped Marci's hand around the cross. "Perhaps you could put the necklace in the museum along with the diary. If not, I believe you will find someone worthy to inherit something valuable but only to someone who cares enough to know my grandmother's story. I trust you to do the right thing."

Marci wiped away the falling tears. No one had ever shown her this much kindness before. "The book was more than generous—the heirloom more than gracious. I'll take great care to make sure the story behind both these treasures is made public."

Blake looked at his watch. "Thank you for everything, Abigail. Can you recommend a good place to eat?"

"The American Grill is a nice restaurant, if you like pot roast or chicken and biscuits."

Blake smacked his lips. "Sounds delicious."

As they climbed back into Blake's truck, his cell chimed.

"Blake, *mi boyo*, it's Alfred."

Blake turned toward Marci. "It's Alfred."

"Give him my regards."

"Marci sends her regards. How are you doing?"

"Seems I messed up my medication."

"You? I didn't think you were on any prescriptions."

"Only Lasix for fluid retention and a potassium pill. Doc says my potassium levels are way too high. Shouldn't be. I only have one banana a day. He thinks there might be some connection with the baking soda I take for my indigestion. I have to stay another day for more tests. Hopefully, I'll be back on Forrester's campaign trail before the weekend."

"Well, hurry up and get better. A good round of golf wouldn't hurt."

"You sound extra chipper today, *boyo*."

Why shouldn't his spirits be lifted when he sat next to Marci, her eyes trusting him, a chance to start over, or, at least to begin fresh? Besides, Alfred's indescribable snorts would lift the heaviest of hearts.

"If I get a chance, I'll drop by the hospital tomorrow. Anything you need?"

"Doc wants me to bring in my bicarbonate of soda to examine. Thinks it might have gone bad, might account for the odd readings in my blood work. Could you bring in the box for me?"

"Sure thing."

"That's a good lad." He coughed, raucous and hard. "Not the only reason I called," he said, after his cough settled. "Been doing a wee bit of research, *meself*. I stumbled on something interesting ... a mite pertinent to what you've been looking into."

Blake wanted to press Alfred for more information, however, he coughed again. Better to let the man rest.

"I look doubly forward to seeing you then. How about I bring your chess set."

"You'd take advantage of a sick old man?"

"My only hope of beating you."

Blake hit end call. As he raised his head, he met Marci's gaze. "You caught that?"

"Couldn't help but overhear since you were on speaker."

"Want to go with me tomorrow?"

"I would love to watch Alfred beat you at chess, although you used to be quite good. I noticed the trophies at the college library showcase. From your conversation, looks like Alfred has done you one better a few times."

"I'd like to say I let him win, or I didn't want to embarrass an old man. But yes, he beat me royally at the last alumni championship."

Blake enjoyed the easy banter, a comfort he wanted to keep. He vowed he'd never let Marci go again.

CHAPTER 16

Twenty patrons sat at various tables in the restaurant. "Must be a popular place," Blake said, as he glanced toward the filled booths. "I see an empty spot toward the back. Is that okay?"

Marci nodded. "Fine by me. Less crowded there."

Blake led the way as he pointed to a table for two near the window. Marci sat facing the front, the view of the door blocked by an array of potted trees. Blake draped his sport coat over his chair. "I'll be only a moment. Need to use the facilities. Go ahead and order coffee."

She watched him as he meandered to the restrooms, fascinated at his gait matching the whole of the man, a blend of confidence and humility.

The bright noon sun burned her eyes. She noticed an empty booth closer to the front, away from the glare. When she moved Blake's coat, a slip of paper fell from his pocket. Words in bold print popped out at her:

Bianca
518/345-9906

Jealousy or confusion? If he wasn't dating Bianca, why was her number in his pocket? He claimed he wanted a new relationship. She assumed they would be exclusive.

Anger crashed against her short-lived joy. She intended to invite Blake over for dinner tomorrow after he had seen Alfred or hiked up Wolf Mountain.

Stop jumping to conclusions, Marci. This slip might not mean anything. Quite possible Bianca gave Blake her number. This little piece of paper did not necessarily imply he'd been dating her. Or if he had, that they were still involved.

Until today, Marci had given Blake no encouragement. Why shouldn't he have looked elsewhere? Bianca was a beautiful woman. Understandable.

What now? Marci could not deny the resurgence of attraction toward Blake. She'd fought those feelings yet had lost the battle. She'd declared her affection, not knowing he might be seeing someone else.

Blake spoke of love, but how could he be so sure he loved this current version of her? She should step back and let Blake figure out what he wants. Ironic, since he had accused her of uncertainty.

They were close to solving the mystery of Wolf Mountain. She'd continue to help Blake with his work, regardless of where their relationship might or might not be headed. Marci took out the maid's necklace and draped it around her neck. How wonderful if she could help restore Felicity's good name.

The waitress arrived, and Marci ordered their coffees. She wished Blake would hurry back so she could put the uncomfortable question to him and be done with the matter. Her anger gave way to cynicism. So much for his declared intentions. If he chose to continue dating Bianca, she'd offer to finish the work as a friend. She refused to deal with a rival. Let Bianca have him. If Blake were truly involved with her, then they probably deserved one another.

Enough with bitter emotions. She remembered their kiss. Could he have been so deceitful, to pledge his intention for Marci while he held someone else in his heart? Should she give him the benefit of the doubt? Perhaps there was a reasonable explanation as to why he carried Bianca's phone number—an explanation as simple as his intent to call her with recommended reading. Perhaps she had expressed an interest in his work.

Her head hurt from clashing emotions. She glanced around the restaurant for anything on which to focus her thoughts rather than on petty suspicion.

The seating area in the front seemed to have emptied except for a trio of customers in the booth three tables ahead. She couldn't be certain since a large post blocked some of her view. However, she tuned in to their voices. They sounded familiar—a recent memory. Their tones seemed heated as if in an argument. Curious, she positioned herself for a closer look, hoping a tall, artificial tree would obscure their view of her.

Marci stepped back in disbelief. Bianca sat next to her brother, and a middle-aged man sat across from them. She snarled at Tad. "You needn't be so jealous, Trevor. Nothing happened between Dr. Montgomery and me. Not yet, anyway."

Why did Bianca call her brother, Trevor? Or maybe she'd addressed the man sitting across from them? Marci adjusted her stance to gain a better sightline. She'd seen the older man before ... but where? Not with Tad and Bianca.

Marci shivered with sudden recognition ... the man at the banquet, the one in the blue tuxedo. And he resembled the fisherman and the man in the library. If he were the same man, why the disguises?

He spoke. "Okay, you two. Stop acting like infants. We've got a job to do. Let's plan our next moves and get out of here before Montgomery spots us. Who knew he'd pick this restaurant."

Bianca laughed. "And what about the crazy lady?"

Tad sneered. "She's not the one we have to worry about—as long as nobody else sees us."

The older man leaned over the table. "You two have been fighting far too much. You're apt to get careless."

"Tommy, Trevor and I were only having a little disagreement."

Marci shook her head in confusion. Bianca had called the man Tommy. Then who was Trevor?

Bianca leaned over and kissed Tad full on the lips. *Creepy.*

Even creepier ... Tad kissed Bianca on her neck and shoulder. "I know the flirtation with Montgomery is only part of the job, but I don't like the way you look at him, or the way he looks at you for that matter. The two of you were far too cozy on the golf course."

"Don't worry. I wouldn't have gone the distance." Bianca nestled her head against Tad's shoulder. "You're the only man for me, Trevor."

"Are you ready to order?" Marci snapped back a step at the voice. A waitress stood next to her, probably wondering why her customer decided to hide behind a tree.

"I know this sounds crazy, but do you see three people at the table near the door?"

Her eyes bugged. "You want me to see if there are people near the door?"

Marci nodded.

The waitress strained her neck and looked toward the front. "Lady, there's nobody left in here but you and your gentleman friend."

Marci gasped. "I'm not sure what my friend wants. Can you come back in a few minutes?"

The girl walked away muttering, "Takes all kinds."

The whole scene was surreal, like a cloak and dagger mystery, only where could they have disappeared to? She'd only turned her head for a few seconds. If they were not a figment of her imagination, then they had been following both her and Blake. Why hadn't he noticed them? Perhaps they managed to stay out of Blake's sight better than they had hers. But why?

Bianca had called her "the crazy lady." Was that why they were not as worried about her noticing them? Or was this delusion so advanced, she'd imagined a complicated scenario where both she and Blake were victims of a trio of spies? Bianca and Tad were real, though.

Marci shuddered as she recalled Bianca and Tad kissing. Why did Bianca call her brother Trevor? Were they engaged in incest? Bianca had said she wasn't interested in Blake. Then why the flirtations? To make this Tad, or Trevor—or whatever his real name might be—jealous?

She peered toward the empty tables. These new visons were right after she'd discovered Bianca's telephone number in Blake's pocket. Was all this an elaborate delusion connived from her jealousy? If so, then she was indeed a crazy lady.

If she'd imagined Bianca and her brother, why dream up a different name for Tad?

Her knees wobbled. If what she saw was real, was Blake in danger? She should sit before Blake returned. As she wheeled around, she caught her hair on a branch at the same moment Blake came to her side.

He smirked, probably to avoid a full-scale guffaw. "Here, let me help you. Don't know why you decided to pick a fight with this tree." He untangled her hair and pointed to the table. "What did I miss?"

She grabbed her purse, anything to hold onto ... to touch ... to prove she was not in another dimension. "Not really."

"I see you've moved us."

"The sun was in my eyes. I must have tangled my hair when I put your jacket over the chair."

Blake veered his gaze toward his coat and cocked his head in disbelief.

Blake glanced about the restaurant. Something wasn't right. His jacket lay neatly folded on the chair, several feet from the tree. What was Marci hiding? He studied her demeanor, as cold now as she'd been warm only a few minutes before. She clutched her bag like a timid child.

He picked up his jacket, laid it across the back of the chair, and sat. "What happened, Marci? Don't tell me it was nothing. You're white as a sheet. You promised you wouldn't shut me out again.

She bit her lip. The waitress returned with their coffees and tapped on her order pad. Marci put her purse to one side but grabbed her cup so tightly, her knuckles turned as white as her face.

Blake turned toward the waitress who shifted on her feet. "I'm sorry, Miss. We need more time."

She stuffed the order pad into her pocket and left, muttering incoherently. Then he returned his attention to Marci, her face now gray. "You saw something again, didn't you?"

"I don't feel well, Blake. Maybe we should leave."

"No. You're going to tell me what you saw or thought you saw."

"I'm tired from the long drive."

Blake held her hand tightly and spoke sternly. "Talk to me, Marci."

Her eyes misted, and she pointed toward the front. "I thought I saw Bianca and Tad Manning sitting at that table. They were arguing."

"About what?"

"You."

"You must know how impossible this sounds. Why would they even be here in Cold Creek? Nothing here but a church, a few houses, this restaurant, and a gas station."

She stiffened. "They've been following us. Tad says he makes sure you never see them. They don't care if I see them or not."

Blake sighed. Should he take Marci to the hospital? This time her vision bordered on psychotic. "Marci, no one's following us. That they were here is as improbable as a snowstorm in August."

"Careful, Blake. This is the North Country. Snow squalls in the summer are not so impossible."

Her agitation increased. He'd have to humor her, find out more about what she thought she saw. "I stand corrected. You say they were fighting about me."

She nodded. "Tad claimed he saw you with Bianca at the golf course. He didn't like how friendly the two of you looked."

Blake leaned back against his chair. Impossible Marci had seen Tad and Bianca here. Still, how would Marci have known Blake had been with Bianca at the golf course?

Blake's cheeks burned with guilt. Friendly was not the word he would use to describe his antics with Bianca. He'd come far too close to a grievous sin. Had Bianca told her brother, and he assumed Blake had been a leech and called Marci? Did this prompt her to imagine Bianca and Tad had followed them to Cold Creek? Or was she so angry, she made up this story rather than confront him about his actions?

Marci's gaze speared him with deserved condemnation. "*Are* you friendly with Bianca?"

How much should he confess? Marci's white pallor had turned to crimson. Was this because of his intention toward Bianca or because he didn't believe she'd actually seen them?

He remembered their kiss in the truck. Would he lose what had only begun? He sighed, determined never to lie to Marci again. She deserved honesty, even if the truth hurt. He'd never take the coward's way out again. He'd have to risk all. "I won't lie to you. When I went to play golf yesterday afternoon, Bianca was at the club house. She said her brother stood her up and asked if she could join me since I was alone. I didn't see any harm."

"Are you attracted to her?"

Marci hit the nail on the head ... flattened it with her insightful hammer. "Yes ... and ... no."

She scowled. "That's not an answer."

"Fine. Yes. We'd made a date for breakfast, but I canceled."

Marci's eyes flamed. Her reaction went beyond jealousy. Disappointment? Fear?

He'd risk an explanation. "I don't want to be with Bianca. I want to be with you."

She handed him a paper with Bianca's number. "This fell out of your jacket. I thought you might still need it."

Blindsided.

Why had he put Bianca's number in his coat? Then he remembered. He'd been running late and decided to call Bianca from his truck on the way over to get Marci. He hadn't put Bianca's number in his cell, so he'd stuffed the slip she'd given him into his pocket.

"I don't know what to say, Marci."

"Then say nothing. You owe me no explanation."

He threw the paper to the floor. "I don't need this anymore."

Marci sipped her coffee. Her silence dug worse than fingernails.

He should never be in this position. He should have refused Bianca's attention ... not milked her wiles to feed his ego. Then why had he kept her number to begin with?

As to what transpired at the restaurant during his trip to the men's room, only God knew for sure. Whether imagined or real, whatever Marci saw had terrified her. She believed Tad and Bianca were stalkers. The idea was like a bad movie script. Bianca might be aggressively sensuous—but she wasn't a criminal.

Marci needed help. Serious help. More help than Blake could give her. He'd pledged patience ... to wait as long as necessary. What if she had relapsed? His best support might be to get her to a doctor.

"Not to change the subject, but—"

"I won't bring Bianca up again."

"That's not what I mean. I'm concerned about you, Marci, I'm sure you saw someone or something. However, there is no rational reason for Bianca and Tad to be in this restaurant. I don't know how you knew I golfed with Bianca yesterday, unless someone called and told you. You keep insisting they are following us along with some third party. I'm sure what you think you see is based on reality—"

"But there's no logic to what I report."

Blake shook his head.

"You think I've gone off the deep end again?"

"I wouldn't use those terms. I feel responsible."

"For my insanity?"

"No. Troubled is the word I prefer to use."

"And how are you responsible for my being ... troubled?"

"These things you think you see. They're only when you're with me. Right?"

Marci sighed. "Mostly. Except at the grocery store where I saw the fisherman who was later in the library."

"And you think you've seen him again?"

"Yes. Here. With Tad and Bianca. Only Bianca called Tad Trevor and called the fisherman, who wore a suit, Tommy."

That was all he needed to hear. Maybe he should call Anna. "Marci—"

"You don't have to tell me what I just said sounded ridiculous. You don't think I told myself the same thing?"

"Maybe you should talk to someone—"

"You mean my psychiatrist, Dr. Solomon?"

"He might have an explanation, or he could suggest something to help you."

Marci slapped the table. "I know what I saw, Blake. Just because I can't make sense of what I saw doesn't mean what I saw wasn't real. Yes, what I've told you sounds bizarre. Why do you think I hesitated to say anything? You had to go and drag it out of me and then accuse me of having a psychotic episode."

"I didn't say you were insane."

"Think about it, Blake. If I were losing my mind, would I have the rationality to realize what I'm seeing is irrational?"

"I don't know. I'm not a psychiatrist."

"I'm telling you they were here. And their behavior was not normal."

The waitress returned. "Maybe if you get something to eat, you two won't fight so loudly."

Blake sighed. "Bring us two ham sandwiches to go."

The girl arched a brow. "Okay. How do you want your sandwiches?"

Marci glared at Blake while she answered the waitress. "White bread, mayo, and with a slice of provolone. Please be quick. I don't think I want to be here much longer."

When the waitress left, Blake turned his attention to Marci. "I believe you saw something, Marci. Tell me more, and maybe I can help you figure out what you saw. Tad, whom Bianca called Trevor, and a man named Tommy, who you think is the same man you saw at the grocery store and the library."

"And at the banquet. He was wearing a blue tuxedo."

Worse than he thought. "Okay. What else happened?"

Marci leaned back, her agitation slightly subdued. "Bianca and Tad were ... demonstrative."

What was that supposed to mean? "Let's say they were here as you insist, and they argued ... about me. Some siblings are very close, even jealous of each other's romantic interests. Unhealthy, perhaps, but not so unusual."

Marci shook her head. "Blake ... they kissed ... not in the familial way. Their kiss was ... disgustingly erotic."

"And you say she called him Trevor?"

Marci nodded.

"Maybe that's his given name, and he goes by Tad."

Marci's jaws clenched tighter.

"I want to believe you. I really do."

The waitress came back with their sandwiches. Marci set her coffee down and picked up her purse. "Take me home, Blake. Until I can figure out if I'm completely off the wall, I think you should find a different assistant."

CHAPTER 17

Three hours can seem like eternity when the woman you love won't talk to you. Blake exceeded all speed limits to hasten the trip back.

Glad for satellite radio, he switched to a Christian station, the contemporary worship songs soothed his heart, assuaged his guilt of pride, the forbearer of many a downfall. A truth he thought applied to others. Foolish to think himself immune.

If Marci decided not to pursue a relationship with him after today, he wouldn't blame her. He reviewed his pomposity, his grandiose speeches, how he promised to wait until Marci felt ready. When they kissed, he knew he never wanted to be apart from her again. Yet a few hours later, they were at odds again. His stupid remarks about her imaginations and a not-so-thought-out confession sealed his fate.

He could take no credit for nothing happening between him and Bianca—according to Alfred, the mental entertainment of sin was as offensive to the Lord as the deed.

No one likes to stand before God's mirror. He supposed, though, the best of Christians needed a reality check from time to time. What was wrong with him? Why was he strong one minute and weak the next? Alfred said faith was not the result of good deeds, rather good deeds evidenced faith. He had a long way to go. Only God's grace could change him completely to the man he wanted to be. As the singer belted out the words to "I Won't Go Back," he lifted a prayer, *God, don't let me go back to Egypt.*

He checked his GPS. Only ten more miles to Collins Bend. Marci faced forward, her brows arched. He'd try to lighten the mood. "If you go any deeper into that stew, you'll drown."

She smirked.

"Is this station okay?"

"It's not the music. I'm still trying to wrap my head around this new-found religion of yours. Back in Briarcliffe, you were an outspoken agnostic. What changed?"

How could he answer and not deny the contradiction in his own life, especially the last few days? Did she really want to know about the man he became after they broke up?

"Somehow, whenever I try to explain the change in me, I come out sounding like a nincompoop. All I know, Marci, is I'm not the Blake you once knew or the Blake I became afterward."

"English, please."

"As I told you, a few hours after our time in the cabin, the dean came to me, saying someone saw us walking together. He reminded me professors were forbidden to date students. He gave me an ultimatum. If I didn't end our relationship, he'd fire me."

She sighed. "Not surprising you made the decision you did."

"That's the problem, Marci. I hadn't made a decision. I wasn't sure what I should do. I was worried for both of us. A scandal would hurt you too."

She eyed him with disdain. "Another rationalization?"

Though well deserved, her resentful tone stung. "I'm sorry, Marci. I can't turn back the calendar."

Her eyes filled with compassion he hadn't earned. "I didn't mean to condemn you. Please continue."

"I should have been honest with you. I'd give anything to go back and handle my fear differently, to have given our love a chance. After you started dating Matt, something soured in me. I'm not proud of the sinister professor I became. Nothing satisfied me … not alcohol … not drugs … nor pretty coeds. Yes, I did date other coeds and got pretty good at keeping those relationships a secret. Five years ago, before he retired, Alfred confronted me."

"About?"

"How I traveled a destructive course. He didn't know about the coeds, but he had heard from other profs I was acting very unprofessional."

She turned to face him. "I don't believe you could ever be unprofessional. Not Blake Montgomery. You cared deeply for your students, believed education was the key to making the world a better place."

"That man ceased to exist after I lost you."

Marci's lip curled. "Don't put your failings on me. If I've learned anything in my forty plus years, I know other people are not to blame for the poor choices we make in life."

This woman amazed him. As distraught as she might be, her insight was far superior to some of the brightest minds he knew. How much more amazing her wisdom might be if it were God-breathed.

"Spoken like a true philosopher. I tried to blame everything and everyone for my decadence. Warnings from my colleagues fell on deaf ears. Alfred's intervention proved to be the most effective."

"What did he say?"

"No condemnation at all. Rather than criticize, he helped me realize true satisfaction can never be obtained through possessions, pleasure, knowledge, or power. None of those things compensated for the natural man's separation from God. Only through a relationship with the Lord would I find what I craved."

"Sounds a little like hocus-pocus to me. Praise Jesus and everything's hunky-dory."

He nodded. "To me too, at first. I did want to be the professor everyone admired. I was once. I could be him again. All I needed was the right motivation. I didn't need God."

"What I've always chosen to believe—until recently. Now, I don't know."

"That's where we're wrong, Marci. Once under God's microscope, we begin to see the ugliness we hide from ourselves. The bent toward self is the basis of all wrongdoing. This is the thing we need to give over to God ... confess if you will. There is no hope otherwise."

She cocked her head. "If God changed you, why did you want to be with Bianca?"

Ouch. "I know it's a flimsy excuse, but I am still a man."

"You're right. That's no excuse."

He stared back at her. "I know what you're thinking."

"You're a mind reader now?"

"You're afraid, Marci. You're afraid I'll hurt you again."

"Possibly."

"I'd never hurt you intentionally. But I can't arm myself against my own stupidity. I say and do things every day that prove God still has a lot of chiseling to do in my journey. I don't know why Bianca is interested in me. Fish have to swim, and Bianca has to flirt, I guess. I'm not irresistible."

At last, a smile. "You're still handsome in my book. And any woman can appreciate your genteel ways, even a model-perfect beauty like Bianca."

"Thank you."

"Feel better now?"

"Yes ... no. I wasn't fishing for a compliment. I'm trying to say I can't date Bianca when God wants me to be with you."

He was supposed to be a gifted orator. Yet he'd blurted out ill-thought presumptions.

She grunted. "Now who's crazy? God told you I'm the one he wants for you? And because of your duty to God, you'll wait however long you need to for me to see your side of things? Hogwash. Are you sure this God thing of yours isn't another disguised ego trip to placate your guilt?"

No getting out of this without stepping into the goop. "Okay. I'll confess. Yes, yesterday, I was tempted to be with Bianca. For a few moments, I sank into old, selfish habits, thinking only of my wounded pride. But now I'm telling you, I'm done with her."

"The question is, Dr. Montgomery, is Bianca done with you?"

He gripped the steering wheel with all the frustration of a quadruple bogey. "I want a meaningful relationship. One with a future. I want to move forward ... to something better ... with you."

"Premature thinking, Blake. You've only been here a few days."

"You can't deny something's sparked. We deserve to find out what. We'll never know if you keep pushing me away." He pulled his truck into her driveway and parked.

Marci flexed her fingers, then sighed. "For the record, Professor, if I'd known about your dilemma, known you truly did love me, I'd have waited until graduation. There would never have been a Matt in my life. And neither of us would be dragged down by our regrets."

Yes, regrets fell like rain—for them both. "Are you saying you didn't love him?"

"I loved the idea of someone loving me. At the time, I didn't want anything more." Her eyes grew misty. He'd unintentionally brought her to a place of painful memory. She leaned back and closed her eyes.

"I'm sorry Matt hurt you. I'm sorry I hurt you. Those things are in the past, Marci. Can't you let go of them?"

Her sigh was thick with sorrow. "I can't date you, Blake, or anyone else, at least, not right now. This time, I'm dead serious. As much as I wish otherwise, I can't be your assistant. As for Bianca, I'm suspicious, not jealous."

"Suspicious of what?"

"I'm convinced she's not who she claims to be. There's something familiar about her. Like a melody ... one you know you've heard before but can't remember the notes. She claims she's never been to Collins Bend before. I think she's lying."

"For what purpose?"

"I don't know. All I'm saying is ... be careful."

"I will. I think the Holy Spirit gave me a big fat hockey check against my spiritual wall."

"There you go with all that Christian talk. You sound like Anna."

"I've not been the man I've wanted to be for you, and I'm sorry. You have every right to be perturbed."

"I'm not perturbed. I'm confused."

"Confused I can deal with. I promise not to pressure you. At least let me call to see how you're doing?"

She opened the passenger door and slid out. "Maybe I will see Dr. Solomon. Although, I'm convinced what I saw is real. No one believes me—not even you. But, if you call me, I won't hang up." She opened the truck door and climbed out. "I'll walk myself to the house."

CHAPTER 18

Marci had stayed up well past midnight watching movies, but sleep still eluded her. She forced herself to stay in bed until the first crack of dawn, then she arose and paced the house until seven. Should she call Anna or not?

As she reached to call, her landline rang. Anna. "I was just about to call you. You normally don't call before nine. Anything wrong?"

Anna nearly shouted with excitement. "Nothing's wrong! I wanted to tell you something!"

"And the news couldn't wait until nine?"

"I'm too excited. Marci, I'm in love."

Anna's being in love was nothing new. Who was the man of the hour? "Tell me, give me the details."

"Remember the date I had? I told you he might be the one. We had a great time! Now I'm convinced he *is* the one!"

"The guy you said had worked with the firm who handled your divorce from Robert?"

"Yes. Herb Waycross."

"Anna, you never saw him there, right?"

"The firm has at least a dozen or more attorneys. It's not out of the realm of possibility to have not actually seen him at the firm. Oh, Marci, he's wonderful. He's so charming. I feel like time stands still when we're together."

Not unlike Anna to fall in love at first sight. "You're going too fast, Anna. Slow down. Get to know the man a little better before you declare your love."

"True, we've only had the one date. Strange how he knew so much about me. I feel as if we've been friends forever."

"People aren't always who they seem."

"You're too suspicious, Marci. He's nice. I think I'm a fair judge of character."

Marci stifled a laugh. "This from a woman four-times divorced."

Anna huffed. "I admit, I've been fooled in the past. There's something genuine about Herb."

"You said he's vacationed here a number of times. Seems strange you never crossed paths before this. You own ninety percent of the short-term rental properties in town."

"Stop being so negative. Can't you be happy I've found someone?"

Marci crossed her arms. Was she suspicious or jealous of Anna's ability to move forward so quickly, to be able to fall in love at the drop of a hat? "If you're happy, then I'm happy."

"I know that tone. Is something wrong? I was so excited about my news I never bothered to ask how your date with Blake went."

Marci sighed and sat on the couch. "Not well."

"Why not? He's crazy about you. Why do you keep giving him the brush off?"

"I'm not like you. I don't fall into the arms of every man who shows interest in me."

Anna growled. "That's not fair, Marci."

"Isn't it?"

"A true statement once. Since I found the Lord, I'm not interested in romance."

"No? Then why are you ga-ga over a man you met only a few days ago?"

"I can't explain why. Maybe because he seems to understand me. He makes me feel like I'm special."

Marci sighed. Anna could be naïve. This smacked of reckless. "Sounds like a come-on to me. Men know how to charm for what they want."

"Herb's charm is not provocative. He was a perfect gentleman. He didn't even kiss me goodnight."

Marci despised her inability to trust. She should be glad Anna found someone to love. "Then how do you know he's the one for you?"

"Maybe he's not. But who's to say? I do know how wonderful I feel when we're together. I don't expect you to understand. Not when you have a man who is obviously crazy about you, and you shut the door in his face every time he tries to tell you how he feels. He won't wait forever, Marci."

"I suppose not. I'm not ready, and I don't know when I will be."

"Are you still going to work for him?"

"Under the circumstances, I don't think I should. Blake is unable to keep this relationship on a professional level."

Anna laughed. "I don't think the problem's all Blake. I think you still love him and won't let go of the past. You're both available now. No stupid college rules to stand in your way."

"But, I'm not available. Emotionally, that is."

"That's an excuse because you don't believe you're allowed to be happy."

"It's because I'm ..." How could she tell Anna the truth—*because I'm insane.*

"Because, why?"

Marci hesitated. Anna was happy. Why saddle her with worry over her sister? If she explained the fight, explained the craziness at the restaurant, she'd have to tell Anna the whole story. The boy on Wolf Mountain, the bones, the man in the blue tuxedo, the fisherman, Tad and Bianca's strange behavior, and how Marci didn't think anyone was who they said they were. Anna would whisk Marci back to the hospital if she confessed the strange visions of the last week.

Instead, she'd give Anna hope. "On a good note ... I think I will go back to see Dr. Solomon."

Anna cooed her pleasure. "About time." The phone line clicked from Anna's end. "I have a call. It's Herb. I'll check with you later. Let me know when you schedule your appointment with Dr. Solomon. I'll go with you if you want."

"You are a dear sister—now answer your call."

A bright sunrise sometimes indicated a later storm. Not a cloud in the sky. How could such a warm morning be a forecast for rain? At least for this day, Blake had woken with new clarity where Marci was concerned. He should give up hoping to revive a dead relationship. Neither he nor Marci were the same people. She was right. He loved the memory of her ... Marci Vincent. Did he love Marci Henderson, teacher and mental health patient?

Yes.

Could he be sure after so short a time together?

Yes.

If he were to gain her trust ... trust he never had from her before ... he must first be her friend. He'd call as he promised—every day.

He dressed and rushed off to Tobias's Bakery, supposedly the home of the best donuts in the North Country. Settling into a seat near the framed picture window, he gazed across the cobblestone road at the various independently owned shops and eateries on Market Street. He imagined the visiting New York society who once strolled the streets of Collins Bend—men in top hats and ladies in bustled gowns, parasols swirling as they meandered through stores filled with sounds and sights of yesteryear.

He'd like to hike Wolf Mountain, with or without Marci. Not likely, given the foreboding forecasts of heavy rain due to arrive later today and for the next few days. Too wet to play golf. Was there nothing he could do or say to convince Marci to come back to work for him? Even if she were delusional, he needed her help.

She'd been insistent what she saw was real. Could be she saw three people who resembled Tad, Bianca, and the fisherman. In her current confusion, she jumbled recent events together. Made sense. Still, as irrational as her descriptions may have been, her tone gave impossible credence to her claims. He wasn't there, and there was no way he could determine the veracity of what she said she saw.

There was one project he could do on his own. He could examine the ledgers at the Adirondack Museum in Blue Mountain as Alfred suggested. The trip would take a whole day and would keep him focused and less bored. If Wordsworth's bookkeeping practices were as questionable as Alfred's informant indicated, the find would be a great spin on his book. Well worth the trip. He also had the maid's diary to peruse before he donated it to Collins Bend Historical Society.

"Dr. Montgomery?"

He hadn't heard anyone approach him. The voice boomed in his ear. Startled, Blake knocked over his coffee, jumping up as the hot brew spilled onto his upper thigh.

He glanced at the intruder. The man wore an immaculately tailored navy suit, a white tuft of handkerchief in his pocket. The Rolex watch added to the aura of wealth. An oval, child-like face set off his salt-and-pepper hair, cropped and styled like a politician. Given the oddity of the man, Blake wondered if Marci's delusional sightings might be contagious. The stranger handed Blake a wad of napkins and flashed a gregarious smile. "I'm sorry. I didn't mean to startle you." He offered a firm handshake. "Name's Herb Waycross."

"You have me at a disadvantage, Mr. Waycross. You know me, but I'm afraid I don't know you."

"Please, call me Herb."

"We'll see."

Waycross nodded as if understanding Blake's hesitancy. "I'm an acquaintance of Anna Vincent. I knew her as Dechantes. I see she went back to her maiden name again after her most recent divorce. I rented a one-room studio from her—in the village, not far from this café. We dated. A charming woman."

Paranoia must be in the air. Blake warmed with caution. "Yes. I know Anna Vincent. Is there something I can help you with, Mr. Waycross ... Herb?"

He winked. "Not what I *need* from you, Dr. Montgomery. What I can *do* for you."

If the man weren't so mysterious, Blake might find him amusing. "How so?"

"Anna's told me about the research you're conducting on Wordsworth's railroads."

"Yes, for a book series."

Waycross handed Blake a business card. "I currently am an independent defense attorney, though I'm an amateur historian. Anna called me this morning. She was unsettled because her sister, your assistant, quit her job. I explained I knew a lot about the Wordsworths, information I've gained in my frequent visits to Collins Bend. I've been fascinated with the legend of Wolf Mountain. She suggested I talk to you. I might be of help."

"And how did you know I'd be here?"

"I didn't. I happened in for one of Tobias's marvelous pastries and saw you sitting alone."

"You recognized me?"

"From the college website."

"Oh." Reasonable answers.

Waycross motioned toward the empty chair next to Blake. "May I?"

Blake nodded, and Herb sat. He seemed attentive to his surroundings. His attire and aura fit an attorney's persona as far as Blake was concerned. Then again, he'd never had a lot of personal dealings with lawyers.

Blake speared Herb with an inquisitive glance.

"Sorry to be evasive. Really, there's no mystery. You see, I plan on moving to Collins Bend permanently in the next month. I used to vacation here with my wife. This is my first time back since she died. I had frequently hiked Wolf Mountain as well as visited the museum at the base. I thought maybe I could team up with you. You don't have to pay me. I would consider this entertainment. I could be your guide and, at the same time, learn from your amassed knowledge on the Wordsworths."

Was Herb an albatross or a godsend? He needed help. If Herb knew the area half as well as Marci, his help would be very valuable.

"Quite possible. The weather won't be cooperative for a few days, and I thought I might make a trip to the Adirondack Museum. If you're still here when I get back, maybe we could make the climb then." Blake looked at the card. "Is this a number where I can reach you?"

"My cell."

They shook hands like old-time farmers. Waycross offered a near-militaristic salute, did a one-eighty, and left. Blake found the man laughable until he remembered he often made similar gestures. Once a soldier, certain mannerisms were inherent.

Blake watched Waycross as he paraded past the picture window. Hefty and with an ambling gait, his physical bearing belied that of an outdoorsman. Curiously, Waycross came to stop at the curb and conversed with someone in a white Osprey. Blake strained to see who was in the car, but it sped away before he could distinguish if the driver were a man or a woman. Waycross remained on the curb while he checked his cell, then walked across the street and disappeared in the municipal parking lot.

Blake scratched his head and scrunched his brow, considering the similarities. Waycross fit Marci's description of the man she'd supposedly seen at the restaurant with Tad and Bianca. Were they indeed being followed?

Blake shrugged his shoulders. Marci's fears were rubbing off, and now he began to doubt his own sanity. He should verify Herb's story. He called Anna and told her of his unusual encounter.

"Herb's wonderful, isn't he!" Anna went on and on about Herb's humor and charm. Those characteristics weren't important in an assistant. At least, she confirmed Herb was who he claimed to be. Good enough for Blake to put his worries aside.

He shoved down the last of his donut, then walked to his truck. He glanced up just as a woman who looked like Bianca strode into a drug store. He remembered her long legs topped by a very short golf skirt. He imagined her voice in his ear. "I dare you to try another round, Dr. Montgomery."

He fought the engaging idea. Dangerous. Best defense would be a strategic offense.

CHAPTER 19

"Have a seat, Marci." Dr. Solomon's voice possessed the same calming vibrato as when he treated her at the hospital.

She scanned the familiar décor in Dr. Solomon's office, always fascinated by his collection of gothic paintings. "Thank you for seeing me on such short notice. I didn't want to wait past the weekend."

She chose the deskside chair rather than Dr. Solomon's couch, afraid of what she might reveal if too relaxed. Yet, she needed to be honest about the hallucinations or delusions or whatever the images represented.

She clutched her purse and gritted her teeth. "They're back."

Dr. Solomon met her gaze. "What's back?"

"Hallucinations."

"Marci, what you experienced before was a delusion. If you are rationally telling me you've had a delusion, then you haven't truly had one. What's going on?"

"I'm seeing people who aren't there."

"And that's why you think you're delusional?"

Wasn't this all semantics—psychiatric political correctness? No matter what label she put on her experience, the results remained unsettling. Naming the problem did not make the images less terrifying. "The thing is, Dr. Solomon, I'm the only one who sees these people. Am I schizophrenic?"

"No, Marci, you're not schizophrenic. You had a severe mental reaction to a highly stressful event. That does not mean you have an ongoing problem. Why do you think what you see isn't real?"

"That's the question I keep asking myself."

His smile reassured her. "If these were true hallucinations, you'd be convinced what you saw was real beyond anyone's opinion otherwise. Yet, you yourself are questioning what you have seen?"

"Yes and no. I believe I saw what I saw. I can't reconcile what I saw with what's reasonable."

"That's not so uncommon."

"It's not?"

"For example, people with cataracts may see inexplicable things, but they know what they are seeing is inexplicable. Just as you believe what you saw has no basis in reality. My mother used to see giants in her living room. We laughed many a time. The giants disappeared when she had the cataracts removed."

Marci smiled. "If surgery makes my giants disappear, then I'd be all for it." She gazed at his somber face. "It's not that simple, though ... is it?"

She sighed with hope. A medical explanation for her visions was far more palatable than a resurgence of mental illness. One rational explanation for the irrational things she saw.

"I haven't been sleeping well."

"Lack of sleep could be part of what's going on."

Marci nodded. "No one else seems to notice what I say I've seen. Yet these events are so vivid, I remember every detail like a photograph. I don't remember many details of my hospitalization or what I experienced after Matt died—only what Anna tells me. But if I'm having another breakdown, I think this is different than before."

"I see." Dr. Solomon crossed his legs, a gesture Marci remembered as getting ready to delve into the nitty-gritty of the visit.

"You don't seem surprised I'm here. Did my sister call you?"

He set his notepad on his lap. "As a matter of fact, she did. She's been worried about you. You were doing so well until you took a hike up Wolf Mountain last month."

She set her purse beside her. "Do I need to go to the hospital again?"

Dr. Solomon offered a reassuring smile. "Perhaps not. Sometimes it's not what we saw. We need to determine the significance of how you interpreted what you saw. You're right. This current issue is much different than your original difficulties after your husband's death. As you said, you were not aware of those ideations, nor were you cognizant of the erratic behavior causing your hospitalization. At that time, you suffered a complete divorce from reality. At this point in time, you are lucid and in control of your thoughts."

"Then, what's happening to me?"

"Your interpretation of your surroundings may be skewered from lack of sleep. Or an unmet need or fear could cloud your interpretation of events as they unfold. Sometimes we struggle against the rebirth of an unpleasant memory. Deeper still, your interpretations could be impacted by repressed memory."

"Like a waking dream?"

"In a way."

Dr. Solomon leaned in. "Tell me what you think you saw."

She revealed all, withholding only the toddler and human remains on Wolf Mountain—too horrible to revisit.

She fidgeted with the clasp on her purse.

"What else, Marci."

She closed her eyes. She must tell all if she hoped to be well. "Something I saw on Wolf Mountain." She told him about the child, her fall, and the discovery of a pile of bones. "Why would I dream about those things?"

"What was on your mind before you saw the child?"

"I was thinking about Matt, how sad he died before he could have children. Then I thought about Felicity's untimely death."

Dr. Solomon leaned back and smiled. "Well, there you are. You probably did see a friendly child who managed to escape your view. When you tripped, you may have seen a partially decomposed animal as well as a discarded piece of clothing and filled in the blanks from there. You did say you were dehydrated. Dehydration can cause your vision to be distorted."

Marci sighed as her muscles relaxed. "Thank you. While what you say may explain Wolf Mountain, why then did I see people I've never met before? And why do I constantly see white Ospreys?"

Dr. Solomon didn't respond. Instead he leaned forward once more, his gaze like a sledgehammer to her resistance. "Tell me about Professor Montgomery."

Marci clutched her purse as tightly as she possibly could. "Did Anna tell you about Blake?"

He nodded. "A man with whom you were once romantically involved?"

"We broke up in my senior year. I met Matt shortly after we ended our relationship."

"I see."

"See what?"

"Dr. Montgomery's arrival in Collins Bend may have triggered unresolved feelings both for him and for your husband. This emotional strain may have clouded what you saw at those places, so your imagination is taking over your senses."

"Isn't that rather simplistic?"

Dr. Solomon offered a gentle laugh. "Life generally isn't complicated, Marci. We make life complicated by our refusal to simply live life. What are you not telling me about Dr. Montgomery?"

"Why do you ask?"

"You've been clutching your purse to your chest and fidgeting in the chair ... things you did during our counseling sessions at the hospital, nonverbal barriers. I can't help you if you're not completely honest with me."

Marci unfolded her arms, overwhelmed as she burst into sudden, violent sobs.

Dr. Solomon put his pad on a table, his face a portrait of patience and understanding. "Whenever you're ready, Marci."

The sobs subsided and the shaking eased. She blurted her history with Blake, past and current, including their afternoon at Sorrel Pond and how they parted ways the very next day. "I walked out of the lecture hall and dropped out of his class. I'm surprised he didn't give me a failing grade. He probably felt guilty. I would see him occasionally around campus. I know he saw me too—but he made no effort to talk to me."

"Did you try to talk to him?"

"No. Why torture myself?"

"Interesting."

Like a flicker of a candle, awareness dawned. "Could Dr. Blake's former treatment of me have anything to do with my breakdown after my husband's death?"

"From what you've told me, you started dating your husband a few weeks after your breakup with Dr.

Montgomery. Many people harmfully jump into a new relationship before they've healed from the hurt caused by the former one. Did you love your husband?"

Her whole body stiffened. Truth hurt. "Not the same as I loved Blake. I thought I loved Matt enough to marry him. I tried. At first, I didn't mind our lovemaking." Marci gulped, surprised at this release of her intimate thoughts. Yet not so surprising. She trusted Dr. Solomon with her pain. He'd helped her once. Perhaps he could help her again.

"I tolerated Matt's touches. Soon sex became unbearable, though I despised myself for my inability to make love to my own husband. Matt was a good man, good to me, and he tried hard to be a good husband. At first, I made excuses: 'I'm tired' or 'I have a headache.' I'd wait to go to bed until he'd fallen asleep. Matt must have known I avoided him. He never said anything or asked what was wrong. Finally, he moved into the guestroom. Shortly afterward, Matt started his weekend fishing trips. I suspected another woman. A part of me was angry, but mostly I felt relief. Now I had a good excuse to avoid intimacy."

Dr. Solomon wrote on his pad, then looked up. "Your feelings about your husband's affair are not uncommon, Marci, especially in situations where sexual difficulties permeate the marriage."

Matt hadn't deserved her treatment of him no matter how many people experienced the same feelings.

Dr. Solomon met Marci's gaze. "Let's talk about your frigidity." Though she'd rather not have to answer the doctor's direct questions, Marci respected him for his insightfulness.

"I dislike that word, though I suppose the description is accurate during my times with Matt ... cold ... distant. I felt duty required me to perform. My heart felt a million miles away."

"Trust me when I say, I think your feelings about intimacy may be connected to something you experienced long before your relationship with Dr. Montgomery. How many times were the two of you intimate?"

"Only once."

"How did you feel afterward?"

"I loved him, but I felt ashamed. I blamed my reaction on the fact we weren't married. But I've never been religious or heard anyone preach sex outside of marriage was wrong."

"Intimate relations before marriage is still a taboo in many subcultures today. Society as a whole has become extremely permissive. Neither here nor there. Your guilt may have been due to some cultural influence."

"When Blake suggested we see other people, I was glad I wouldn't be intimate with him again." Marci felt her eyes well with tears. "What's wrong with me, Dr. Solomon? If I loved Blake, why did I feel that way?"

"I think it's time we talk about your father—how you felt after he left your mother."

"What does his abandonment have to do with anything?"

Dr. Solomon handed her a box of tissues. "Maybe nothing ... maybe everything. You were twelve, an impressionable age."

"How did you know?"

"Your sister came to see me a few times while you were in the hospital. Your treatment required a better understanding of your family dynamics. You'd clam up every time I tried to discuss your childhood."

"Then you know we never heard from him again. My mother remarried—three times. Between marriages, she had several live-in boyfriends. I'm not surprised Anna takes after my mother. Even in high school, Anna jumped from one boyfriend to another. I always wanted something more permanent."

"You and Anna are close, though?"

Marci hesitated. How could she confess those memories without admission of her sin? Anna's sin? Mother made them promise never to tell.

Dr. Solomon's voice touched her spirit like the coo of a nightingale—soft, reassuring, compassionate, and uncondemning. "I know it's hard to talk about, Marci. If you ever want to be well, you need to remember."

She dabbed her eyes with a tissue. "I cried a lot after my father left. A month before I went to college, Anna and I learned he'd died a year after he deserted us. I don't know if Mother knew or not. She died during my sophomore year and Anna's freshman year. After her death, we were on our own."

"Have you always depended upon one another?"

"I'm the older sister by one year. One would think I'd have taken care of her. She was the strong one."

"I'm going to ask this straight out, Marci. Did any of your stepfathers or your mother's paramours make advances to you or your sister?"

Marci felt her body go limp. "What did Anna say?"

"I want to hear your version of what happened."

Marci sobbed, deep and uncontrollably. "Yes. Mother's first boyfriend after Daddy disappeared. His name was Ron. One night he came into my bedroom and lay down on my bed beside me. He didn't touch me, but he slept next to me all night. I was very frightened. The next day, I told Anna what Ron had done." Marci hitched her breath. She didn't want to speak of what followed ... to betray Anna ... to break the pledge they made to one another.

"Then what happened, Marci."

Through labored breaths, she forced herself to speak. "Ron ... never came into my room again. Instead ... he went into Anna's room."

"And how did their being together make you feel? Toward Anna? Toward Ron?"

Marci screamed as she balled her fists. "I hated him. I told Anna to tell our mother. When she finally tattled, Mother made Ron leave."

"And then what?"

"Mother yelled at Anna all the time ... called her awful names ... said if Anna weren't evil, Ron would still be around."

"And how did your mother's rants make you feel?"

Marci squeaked an answer from a dry throat. "If I'd have let Ron back into my room, Anna might have had a better life. I was the older sister. I should have protected her."

"Marci, you were both children who didn't have the wisdom to know how to handle an adult who behaved inappropriately. Neither you nor Anna is guilty of blame. Your mother couldn't handle her own grief and didn't know how to help her daughters. Anna says she's forgiven both Ron and your mother. Maybe we should start there to help you find peace with all you've endured since then."

"What does my experience with Ron have to do with Blake or Matt?"

Dr. Solomon glanced at his watch. "Our time is nearly done. I want you to realize something as we work toward your healing. Because of what happened with your father's abandonment and Ron's sexual abuse of Anna, you learned not to trust men. Intimacy, true intimacy, cannot be realized without mutual trust."

"Is that why I felt guilty when Blake and I made love? Why I couldn't be intimate with my husband?"

"I think so. You've made an important first step today, Marci. Confronting those memories took a great deal of courage. Since you've turned a corner, I think you are on the way to wholeness."

"Then why am I so filled with resentment? Will those feelings last forever?"

"Marci, some people find peace through faith."

"Anna's the one with religion now. Are you a religious person, Dr. Solomon?"

He smiled. "I am a Christian. I believe in the power of forgiveness found in faith. Though difficult for many people to accept, forgiveness is the first step toward absolute healing. Not only forgiving others, but forgiving ourselves."

"And do you pray for your patients?"

"Of course."

"Thank you. I've often thought I'd like to be one—a Christian—though I didn't think I was good enough. Then when Matt had the affair, I figured being a Christian didn't make him a better person."

"Or maybe you feared if you became a Christian, you'd have to forgive all those who hurt you, as well as yourself. Someday you will. From what I've observed, you have more faith than you realize."

The memories, like vampires, sucked all will to keep them at bay. "And what about my visions."

"Your episode two years ago may have been a result of a heightened sense of anxiety, unresolved feelings of abandonment, first caused by your father's leaving, the abuse, your mother's succession of partners, and Dr. Montgomery's rejection. Your husband's affair may have been the proverbial straw that broke your emotional back. I suspect Dr. Montgomery's reappearance has brought all these issues to the surface again."

Dr. Solomon's explanation seemed plausible—yet she reconnected with Blake after she climbed Wolf Mountain. The doctor's theory did not explain the things she saw there. "How do I get better?"

"You need to confront the initial pain and work your way forward. Grieve, if you will, in a healthy manner instead of denial."

"Do I have to take medication?"

Dr. Solomon stood, signifying her appointment time was over. "Do you feel you need medication?"

"Maybe not. If I can find some other way to deal with my imagination."

"Medicine might make you feel better. Sometimes drugs give you a false sense of well-being and prevent you from doing the hard work of true healing. Let's see how you do without medication, at least for now. If you continue to have trouble sleeping, let me know. I'll prescribe something for you."

Marci rose, confident to return home and face whatever the day brought. "Thank you, Dr. Solomon. At least now I know I'm not crazy. Maybe merely highly imaginative."

"Confused, hurting, perhaps. I wouldn't say you're psychotic. I'd like to see you on a weekly basis for a few months."

Marci walked toward the door and sighed. "I won't cancel any more appointments. I promise."

"Good. You've come a very long way in two years. Once we get past this current roadblock, I don't see any reason why you can't go back to work. Make sure you take a long walk every day. Consider it a prescription."

She gazed toward the window. "It's still raining."

Dr. Solomon smiled. "Marci, I promise you. Rain doesn't last forever."

CHAPTER 20

Marci had eaten a hearty lunch, surprised at how hungry she felt after her morning session with Dr. Solomon. One would think emotional duress would strip the appetite. She stacked her dishes in the dishwasher and looked at the clock. No reason she couldn't go for a walk, as Dr. Solomon had suggested. Not a long one today. Still, half an hour would be good for her soul. The deluge had passed, but the clouds remained darkened. Should she stay at home in her sanctuary or keep her promise to Dr. Solomon?

She picked up her umbrella, then put it back. If it rained, it rained. Enough shops and eateries she could duck into if needed. She stepped from the house onto the sidewalk and walked six blocks into the heart of the village where small cottages intermingled with independently owned shops. She hadn't been in this area of town in a number of years. The fresh air after a rain stoked her appetite. Deciding to go for one of Andrea's cinnamon buns, she headed toward Market Street.

Deep in contemplation, Marci didn't see the preschooler until he rammed into her with his tricycle. "I'm sorry, lady."

Marci rubbed her ankle. "It's okay." Her gaze caught the boy's impish smile, blue eyes and curly blonde hair. "Mark?"

The boy laughed. "How do you know my name?"

"I think we met before. On top of the mountain? You gave me a pebble, and I still have it."

"I climbed the mountain with Grandma and Grandpa."

A woman, probably in her mid-fifties, called him from two houses down. "Mark? You're not supposed to be riding on the sidewalk. Get back to the driveway, right this instant."

"I gotta go, lady."

"Mark, is that your grandmother?"

The boy nodded.

"May I meet her?"

"Sure. Come with me, lady."

"My name is Marci."

"Come with me, Marci."

She followed Mark to his house. A woman, most likely Mark's grandmother, stood on the front stoop and stared at Marci with uncertainty. "May I help you?"

"I'm sorry. I don't mean any harm. I know it's an intrusive question, but I have to know. Were you on Wolf Mountain last month?"

"Yes. We climb there often."

"Mark came to speak to me, then disappeared. I thought I had been seeing things, but here he is."

The woman eyed Marci as if suspicious. "Yes ... we saw him talking to you. I'm sorry if our hasty departure caused you uncertainty. We're trying to teach Mark not to talk to strangers."

Something shone in the woman's eyes—something like sympathy. But why? Had they met before? Did she know the woman she was speaking to had once been insane?

The woman glanced up and down the road while she spoke, seeming to avoid direct eye contact. Her voice squeaked, as if she spoke a half truth. Could she be hiding something?

Remembrance slowly surfaced. "I'm sorry to stare, but I believe we know each other from somewhere."

The woman pursed her lips. "I won't lie, although I hoped, for your sake, you didn't recall us. I didn't whisk Mark away because I feared him talking to a stranger. I know who you are. Marci Henderson."

"Forgive me for not remembering who you are."

"My name is Gabriella Lopez."

The name registered as if in a dream, a *déjà vu*. "I should remember you. I'm sorry."

Gabriella's dark eyes gleamed with compassion. "Elena was my daughter."

Elena, as in Matt's mistress, the young woman who died with him in the accident? "You were at Matt's funeral? Is that where I've seen you before?"

Reality hit harder than imagination. Marci's knees buckled, and she sank, preventing a fall by grasping the rail. She gazed back toward Mark, now playing on the steps with a Tonka truck. Matt's features rebirthed in his son, his sandy hair down to the dimples in his cheeks.

Gabriella opened the door to her home. "Please, come in. I know this must be a shock to you."

Marci accepted Gabriella's kindness and followed. The home was small, one story with most of the house, except the bedrooms and bathroom, visible from the living room. Though neat and orderly, the furnishings were simple and sparse. Pictures of Elena and Mark decorated one wall. "Elena was your only child?"

Gabriella nodded as she took Mark's hand. "I need you to play in your room for a little while so Marci and I can have a grownup conversation."

The boy puckered his lips. "Grownup conversation means little kids can't hear it. Okay. Bye, Marci. Will you come watch me ride my tricycle again?"

"If it's okay with your grandmother."

Gabriella nodded. With that, Mark disappeared as quickly as he had on Wolf Mountain.

Perhaps Marci's expression told Gabriella no explanation was needed. "Marci, are you all right? You look very pale."

"This may sound strange. I'm glad I've met you ... and Mark."

Silence went up like a brick wall, neither woman brave enough to say the necessary words. Marci stood to leave. "I've intruded long enough."

Gabriella took a step forward. "Wait, please."

Marci sat back down.

"I've wanted to meet with you many times. I'm so sorry for the pain Elena may have caused you."

"You are not to blame for what Elena did."

"Maybe this is God's timing. I wanted to let you know about Mark, but I feared the pain would be too much."

Marci marveled that she embraced relief more than betrayal. Strange not be broiled in resentment. "To say this encounter has been a shock is an understatement. Yet, I truly am relieved on several levels. Although the affair did hurt, there is some comfort to know part of Matt lives on. I always wished I could have born him a child. He loved children."

Perhaps Gabriella's oozing compassion held shock at bay. "I wanted to talk to you at the funeral. I was too ashamed and couldn't bring myself to approach you. I prayed for strength to find the right time and place. Then the weeks became months and soon years. I suppose God knew now was the right time."

Marci glanced at Mark's photographs. A beautiful child—the child she would have wanted to give Matt— compensation for her inability to love him as he deserved to be loved.

"May I get you tea or anything?"

Marci leaned back against the couch, barely able to breathe. She wanted to feel sorry for the woman who sat across from her. Marci had lost a husband, but Gabriella lost a daughter. "No thank you. I had tea before I took my walk. I'm sure you're as troubled to see me as I am to see Mark. Please know I'm trying hard to forgive both Matt and Elena."

Gabriella wrung her hands. "You're right. This is difficult. We are very ashamed of Elena's affair with Matt. My husband and I are Christians and brought our daughter up to know better than to become involved with a married man. Their affair lasted only a few months. Matt said he'd made a mistake and wanted to give his marriage another try."

Marci thought back on Matt's sudden frequent fishing trips, fabricated music gigs, and errands taking several hours. She'd been suspicious. Lack of proof, however, made pretense easier. Perhaps she should have confronted Matt ... offered to give him his freedom to marry Elena. After a few months, Matt stayed home more often, became very attentive with flowers and gifts. However, several months later, Matt resumed his long absences. The accident brought the affair into the open. No more denial.

"Unfortunately, Elena became pregnant. We did not believe Matt should divorce you and marry Elena simply because of the pregnancy. He insisted on supporting his son. And he did. Most of those weekends he told you he was away, he spent with Mark at our house, not with Elena."

Marci's head spun. She'd assumed Matt had resumed whatever tryst he'd started. Perhaps if she'd known he was trying to make a bad thing better, forgiveness could have come sooner. "With both parents dead, how are you able to support Mark?"

"We get by. Elena had a small life insurance policy through her employment, and Matt had taken out extra insurance for Mark's support in case something happened to him. The benefit did not amount to a lot of money, though the cash payouts help to supplement my husband's military retirement. He does yard work on the side. We are comfortable. As you see, Mark is a healthy and happy child."

A heaviness weighed Gabriella's words. Marci Henderson was not the only victim of Elena and Matt's affair and untimely deaths.

Gabriella revealed more, and Marci soaked in the words. She found odd comfort in the fact Matt had wanted their marriage to work, to at least try to overcome the barrier between them. "Matt and Elena talked to us and decided they needed to let you know about Mark. Your husband didn't want to hurt you and put off the truth. The day of the accident, Matt had taken Elena to buy Mark a birthday present. The police said he must have skidded on black ice into an oncoming truck. Matt died on impact. Elena never regained consciousness."

Tears streamed down her cheeks, and Marci tasted their saltiness. Not bitter tears—rather tears of release. Matt and Elena had made a horrible mistake, compounded by their secrecy. Marci wondered if knowing the truth when Matt died would have made the last few years more tolerable. Or perhaps her breakdown had been long overdue, as Dr. Solomon indicated.

If Matt had been given the chance to admit his sin, would she have found the grace to forgive him? Or would she have used the knowledge as an excuse for a divorce? Foolish to mull over choices she never had the opportunity to make. Dr. Solomon said some things need to break before they could heal.

"Thank you for sharing all this with me, Gabriella. I'm glad you were there for Mark. He's a precious boy."

"Sometimes God's greatest blessings emerge from our deepest wounds."

Wise words from an apparently wise woman.

Marci rose. Shouldn't she be weak from shock? How could she feel so composed in view of this discovery? Was some power at work in all this?

Gabriella showed her to the door.

"Tell Mark I'll be by tomorrow, if that's okay with you."

"You may see him whenever you'd like."

"I'll tell him I'm his daddy's friend."

"Mark would like to know someone who knew his daddy. I didn't know Matt very well, and I think Mark would benefit from stories about his father. I hated Matt for a while, especially after Elena died. I blamed him for her death, for Elena's unhappiness, and her pregnancy. Forgiveness came hard, but it did come."

"How did you find the courage?"

"I realized Elena had made poor choices too. Then I look at Mark, and I see goodness."

"Matt was a good man who made a very bad choice."

"God showed me none of us are without fault. How can I expect God to forgive my sins if I don't forgive the one I most wanted not to forgive?"

Gabriella's words were like a slap to the soul. She called for Mark to come into the living room. "Mark, Marci is a friend of your daddy's. Would you like her to come visit you sometimes?"

"My daddy and mommy are in heaven," he said in a matter-of-fact tone, then ran back to his room, presumably toward his toys.

Marci wondered. Was Matt in heaven? If a righteous God could forgive a husband's infidelity, perhaps she could find the power to forgive Matt too.

"Thank you, Gabriella. The truth helps more than you could know."

Marci stepped outside. The downpour had resumed, yet as she walked, the rain seemed more like a baptism. Fresh thoughts swirled in her heart and mind. Anna would say God had allowed her to fall apart so he could put her back together, better and stronger.

As she walked, the years of anger toward a God she resented seemed to dissipate. She thought of all those in her life who had tried to convince her God was Love—Aunt Betty, Matt, Anna, and now Blake. Somewhere within the torrents of confusion, regret, relief, and understanding, she felt prayers go up—prayers of repentance and gratitude.

Could God possibly turn all the wrong in her life to something good? Could he turn a legacy of regret into one of hope?

If this beautiful child was a hint of what God could do in the face of human failing, then perhaps He could salvage ... no better yet ... build Marci's future from this day forward. What had Dr. Solomon said? Intimacy required trust. First, she must learn to trust the Lord.

Another thought interrupted her newfound peace.

If Mark had not been a delusion, then perhaps the rest of her visions had not been her imagination either, rather totally accurate—the odd man whom she suspected of following her, seeing Tad in peculiar places, the white Osprey, and, in all likelihood, the remains on Wolf Mountain. Human or animal? She must know for sure.

CHAPTER 21

After three attempts to reach Blake with no response, Marci left one more message. Nothing to indicate urgency. Still, she wished he'd return her calls to put her mind at ease. Irrational fear of danger gnawed. *Please Lord, if I can't reach him, keep him safe.* She thought of Bianca. *Safe from temptation too.*

She tried once more to call Blake—still no answer. She went into Andrea's café, then pocketed her cell. The phone vibrated just as she sat. Maybe Blake finally decided to return her call.

"Marci?"

No. Not Blake. Anna.

"I almost forgot the number. I don't think I've called you on your cell in two years. I'm glad I couldn't reach you on your landline. You're out of the house!"

"I promised Dr. Solomon I'd take more walks."

"Where are you now?"

"At Andrea's, about to order a cinnamon bun and hot chocolate. I also promised Dr. Solomon I'd find one pleasurable thing to do each day. Decided to fulfill both promises with one walk. Oh, and a strange thing happened today that I'd like to talk about."

"Now there's a coincidence. I called to see if I could drag you out of the house for coffee. Coincidentally, I'm across the street. Had to stop into the drugstore to pick up my blood pressure medication. Be right over."

From her vantage point, she could see Anna nearly sprint across the road, waving. Marci entertained herself by guessing what her sister would order this time.

She sighed. No one could predict what Anna Vincent would do next. Marci struggled to vary one routine in her life. She always ordered a cinnamon bun at Andrea's, a bear claw at Alex's, and a glazed donut at Tobias's. She mentally tripped through every restaurant and café in Collins Bend and what she'd order at each place.

Time to mix things up.

A youngish blonde waitress came to her table. "I'll have a blueberry muffin. My sister will be here shortly. I don't know what she'll want. Might as well wait until she gets here to put our orders in."

"I'll be back as soon as I see your sister come in."

Everyone in town knew Anna Vincent. Marci had lived in Collins Bend for twenty years, taught at the same high school as Matt, yet could count on one hand the number of friends she had made since they moved here. "To make a friend, be a friend," she'd heard said.

The college-aged Marci Vincent had hated conformity, deliberately defying the latest fashion. When did she change? If Blake fell in love with a woman of mystery, how could he be so in love with Mrs. Henderson, a middle-aged portrait of predictability? Yet, she believed his declaration of affection. He desired her in full knowledge of her confused, rattled state.

She'd like to see where this new romance would take them since she now knew her sightings had not been delusional. Perhaps they could try again—if she hadn't pushed him away for good.

Anna joined her, toting a chocolate éclair, French vanilla coffee, a cinnamon bun, and hot chocolate.

"Thought I might as well get our order at the counter, then find you. I brought you your usual." She oozed a loud sigh as she plopped into a chair. "For once I'm chasing you down instead of trying to get you to go somewhere with me."

"Everything okay?"

She giggled like a high school ditz. "More than okay."

"Herb?"

"Every time I'm with him, I'm more convinced God has brought him into my life."

Marci shook her head. "That's what you said on the phone the other day. Anna, your romances are like Alex's coffee flavor of the day. I can't keep track."

"Herb's different. Not exactly handsome, yet attractive in his own way. A slight paunch, white hair at the temples. An absolute combination of adorable. We talk and go for walks. He's a fascinating man. Very knowledgeable. Went on *Jeopardy* a few years back."

"Anna, slow down. How do you know he's not after your money?"

Anna's smile vanished, and she squeezed her lips into a fake pout. "Why can't you be happy for me? You don't think it's possible for me to find a man who will truly love me?"

"I thought Jesus was the only one in your life now."

"There's no harm in an earthly romance, is there?"

"Not as long as you're happy. Where is Mr. Wonderful now?"

"He took your place as Blake's assistant, and the two of them have gone to the Adirondack Museum."

She'd been easily replaced. So much for his declared need for her expertise. "Why there?"

"To examine old railroad ledgers. Herb said Blake called him early this morning to see if he'd like to come along for the ride. Pity you gave up on Blake. Otherwise you'd be with him, and I'd be with Herb."

"I didn't give up on Blake."

"Then why is Bianca with them?"

Marci's throat closed. She squeaked the name out with alarm. "Bianca?"

"Herb said Blake invited her since she loved history."

"I don't trust her."

Anna snickered, obviously amused. "Jealous? Good grief, Marci. She's twenty-five and Blake is closing in on fifty. I hardly think she's after him."

"Perhaps instinct is giving me a warning. Hard to explain."

"Then don't. Besides, Herb's driving her Osprey. Not enough room in Blake's truck."

"Osprey?"

"What are you deaf? Yes."

"White?"

Anna took a bite of her éclair and sipped her coffee, then leaned back against her chair.

Marci kicked Anna's shin. "Anna? Is Bianca's Osprey white?"

Another coincidence?

"I don't know ... maybe. What difference does the color make?"

"You don't think her wanting to come along is odd?"

"She's young and curious."

"Not to mention gorgeous."

"So what? Doesn't prove anything. Besides, Herb said she's engaged. She seems very interested in Collins Bend. I've seen her out driving around town quite a bit."

Marci bit her lower lip. "Did you see her anywhere else?"

"Yes, since you asked. I hired a repairman to do some work on the empty cabins. As I was showing him around,

I saw Blake carry his clubs to his truck. He threw them into the back and tore out of the drive onto the main road, a Mario Andretti wannabe, I guess. Seconds later, Bianca rushed out of her cabin. Since she was dressed in a golf skirt, I figured she was heading up to the country club too."

"Strange coincidence, don't you think."

"That's exactly what it was. Why read something more into it?"

Had Bianca feigned being stood up by Tad to trick Blake into playing with her? Had she gone deliberately to seduce? Why?

"For your information, Blake told me he'd considered dating Bianca after they shared a round of golf together. He's changed his mind since then."

"There. Nothing to worry about."

"I think she's chasing Blake for some reason other than attraction."

"And why should you be concerned? You had your shot with Blake and blew him off. You should have gone to the club with him instead of sending him off rejected. I've never played golf. However, if a man like Blake Montgomery asked me on a golf date, I'd take a private lesson before I admitted my ignorance. You, on the other hand, do know how to play."

"He didn't ask."

"Whatever her reasons, if Bianca's really interested in Blake, you'd better let him know how you really feel about him."

"And you have no concerns she's with Herb?"

"Herb said he was friends with her father. Probably an uncle figure to her."

"Ron was a father figure too."

Anna threw her napkin on the table and stood with a huff. "Don't go there. Herb is nothing like Ron. I trust Herb. You on the other hand can't trust anyone."

"Here's an interesting factoid. For the last week, I've seen a white Osprey wherever I went. Not today."

"Doesn't mean anything"

"I think Bianca has been following both me and Blake. And Tad shows up frequently too."

"Do you have any idea how ridiculous this sounds? Have you talked to Dr. Solomon about all this?"

"I have."

"And?"

"And he thinks what I see is real. According to him, my interpretation is at fault. But something happened earlier today. I know what I have seen is not a matter of misinterpretation at all."

Anna sat back down. "I don't doubt you've seen Bianca and Tad around town. Collins Bend is hardly a metropolis. When do you go back to see Dr. Solomon?"

"I'll have weekly appointments to start."

"Promise me you'll keep them."

"I promise."

"That's good."

Marci shook her head. "I'm not delusional, Anna. Something isn't right."

She'd not admit the full truth to Anna—jealousy mingled with fear for Blake. She'd rejected him too many times and drove him into Bianca's arms just like she drove Matt into Elena's. Only Bianca was like the mythical Sirens, ready to woo a weakened heart onto a reef.

Anna pulled out her iPhone and fiddled with her apps. "Look, I'll show you. Herb has a face you can trust." She shoved the phone two inches in front of Marci's face. "See? I took this selfie of us in front of the Town Square fountain. He tried to wrestle the phone from me, but I dropped it into my bra. How can you distrust a face like his?"

Marci gasped.

Anna put her phone back into her purse. "What? I said he wasn't exactly handsome, and this picture doesn't do him justice ..."

"Anna ... that's him!"

"Him, who?"

"The man at the banquet, in the library, and he was with Tad and Bianca at the restaurant in Cold Creek."

"What restaurant ... when? Marci, you've got three seconds to start talking, or I'll never speak to you again."

CHAPTER 22

Marci handed Anna a tissue. "I'm sorry to burst your bubble about Herb."

"You're absolutely sure the man at the banquet, in Cold Creek, and the fisherman were Herb? You said they were similar yet looked different."

"Only the hair and clothing, and the fisherman had a beard."

"Herb is clean shaven."

"They are all the same person. Believe me."

"How can you be sure?"

"Let me see Herb's picture again."

Anna handed over her iPhone "There. How can you doubt such a sincere smile?"

Marci studied Herb's facial features. "The eyes. The eyes were the same. Herb's eyes. I'm telling you, he is the same man I saw in each place."

Anna dabbed her eyes. "Let's say your suspicions are right, that he's following you, along with Bianca and Tad. And, apparently, he's a master of disguise. Why?"

"I don't know."

"He said he knew I lived in Collins Bend, and he'd worked on my case when I divorced Robert. Not to sound like an egomaniac, but suppose he followed you to find me?"

"Then why disguise himself? Why not simply ask me if I was your sister and how could he contact you?" Marci held Anna's hand. "I don't know why Herb, if that's his name, is following me or Blake. Nor do I know why he's decided to date you. Whatever he's up to, you can be sure Bianca and Tad, if those are their names, are part of the masquerade."

"The fact you heard the Manning siblings call him Tommy doesn't necessarily mean Herb is involved in an elaborate plot to rob me."

For Anna's sake, Marci hoped Herb—aka who knows— had been truthful about his affection for her sister. Protective rage surfaced. She prayed for a clear head. Anger at this point would not solve anything or bring answers to a growing puzzle. Fear for Blake intensified. Perhaps he was in danger as well.

"Anna, do you remember Herb from your lawyer's firm? He might be lying about his employment."

"I vaguely remember the name. It's a large firm, so the fact I don't remember isn't anything to make me suspicious. But there's one way to find out."

"How?"

She took back her cell and hit a number, then hit speaker. "Calling my lawyer's office now." After a series of beeps and a few rings, a young female voice answered. "Dawson & Dawson."

"I'd like to speak to Herb Waycross, please."

Hesitation, then, "I'm sorry, Mr. Waycross is no longer with us."

Anna covered the mouthpiece. "See, I told you he'd retired." She returned to her call. "When did he leave?"

"Two years ago."

"This is a crazy request, I know, but important. Can you give me a description of Mr. Waycross?"

"One moment please."

Anna raised a brow and drummed impatient fingers.

A different, more sultry voice came online. "The receptionist said you'd like a description of Mr. Waycross. May I ask why?"

"There's a gentleman here in Collins Bend who claims to be Mr. Waycross. I need to confirm his identity."

"Not possible. Mr. Waycross didn't leave us by choice. He died."

Anna's face paled. "Thank you." She disconnected and put the phone in her purse, then met Marci's gaze. "You're right. The man I kissed last night was not Herb Waycross from Dawson & Dawson." She touched her lips. "That man was definitely not dead. Satisfied?"

"Of course not. I'd rather have been proven insane than to see you hurt again."

Anna shrugged her shoulders. "So, another one bites the dust. Plenty more fish in the sea, my dear."

Marci expected more platitudes to follow. Instead, Anna's resiliency shone brighter than ever before. "I told you, God's my main man now. Am I hurt? Yes. Do I feel foolish? Yes. This, too, shall pass."

"You've always been the strong one, Anna."

"No. I've always been the foolish one. I ran from one relationship to another, and this time was no exception. I didn't pray about Herb. I should have. Something I'll do from now on where men are concerned." She shivered. "I'm grateful I found out before ... well, nothing more than a kiss."

"What should we do now?"

Anna crossed her arms and leaned back in her chair. "What we will do, my dear Marci, is nothing. We'll play this man's game and try to figure out what he's up to. And his marionettes as well. What did you say they called one another at the restaurant?"

"Tad called Bianca *Sis*. Bianca called Tad *Trevor*. And they both called Herb *Tommy*."

"Sounds like a convoluted plot for a B-movie. Pity is, I really thought he liked me."

"I'm sure he does. Even scumbags can fall in love."

"If Herb or Tommy, or whatever his real name, has attached himself to Blake ... is he in danger?"

Marci pushed her uneaten bun to the center of her table. "We might all be at risk. I've tried to reach Blake to tell him about my ... my experience ... this afternoon. Oh, Anna, you don't even know what I discovered today!"

"Call Blake first. By the smile on your face, your news is good. I could use a happy thought about now. It *is* good news?"

Marci nodded. *Mostly.* To know Matt had ended the affair with the intention to save their marriage brought relief. And she was strangely comforted to know Matt did have a child to carry on his name.

She took out her cell and hit Blake's number. "What do I say? Herb's a fraud?"

"We don't know what Herb is up to. Warn Blake to be cautious because Herb isn't who he says he is." Anna grabbed the phone away from Marci. "I'd better talk to Blake. He won't believe you."

Anna pushed speaker and waited until she heard the voicemail prompt, then disconnected. "Should we leave a voice mail?"

"I've left three. I asked Blake to call me. That's all. He probably has been busy and didn't check his messages." *Busy with Bianca?*

Anna punched alpha keys. "We could send a text."

"What if Herb sees it?"

Anna stopped her text, then pulled Marci to a stand. "We need to get out of here. Figure out what to do."

Marci tried Blake's cell one more time as she headed toward the exit and motioned Anna to wait outside. Directly to voicemail again. As they headed toward the parking lot, Tad Manning, aka Trevor somebody, scooted across the street.

Blake scanned the ledger one more time. This information may have been worth the long ride, including Bianca's unwelcomed flirtation. His head told him he wanted nothing to do with this beauty next to him. He glanced at her long, black hair, traced her curves with his eyes. Her jeans and knit top fit snuggly to a model-perfect form. What man wouldn't be tempted?

Of course, Herb was the one who asked Bianca along for the ride. Yet, Blake had made no objection. Had he unconsciously desired to see Bianca again? Blake had prayed for a Holy Ghost intervention to stay clear of her hooks. Then why was he snared? Maybe he needed to bask his prayer in more sincerity.

Bianca could have any man she wanted. He'd like to think of himself as attractive, even with a few extra pounds and distinguished tufts of gray on his temples. Nice to have his ego stroked, though common sense dictated a lack of innocence in Bianca's interest.

He turned the ledgers toward Herb. "You're an attorney. What do you think? These entries are vague at best. Looks as if someone other than the usual cargo manager logged these in. The other manifests are meticulous."

Herb shrugged his shoulders. "Doesn't mean anything."

"The cargo entries state simply, 'large crates.' And look at the other columns for specified geographic origin and destination, quantities, and signed verifications of receipt along with arrival times. These entries specify nothing, are merely checked off rather than delineated. Definitely not standard protocol, even in more lax times."

Herb scratched his head. "Could be the cargo officer had a substitute who was careless."

"Or perhaps the cargo manager was hiding something. I read the maid's diary last night—"

"I'm not aware of any surviving diaries." Herb's eyebrows arched above his reading glasses.

"This was one Mrs. Henderson and I received from the maid's granddaughter. Before her death, the maid gave her journal to her daughter's foster parents."

Herb took off his reading glasses. "I also wasn't aware the maid had descendants. I thought she was unmarried."

"My research with Marci proved productive. We found a granddaughter who lives in Cold Creek."

"So that's why you went there the other day?"

Blake had told no one except Alfred about his trip. "How did you know?"

"Anna told me you'd taken a drive to Herkimer County. She wasn't aware of the nature of your business."

Possible explanation.

"So, there's a diary. Interesting. Do you have it with you?"

"No."

"I'd love to read it when we get back."

"I promised the granddaughter I'd donate the journal to the Collins Bend Museum."

"Thoughtful of you. I'm sorry, I interrupted your ... forgive the pun ... train of thought. As you were about to say?"

"The maid paints Wordsworth as a very honorable man. She made reference to an argument she overheard with Wordsworth and his accountant. She wrote that she could only make out a few words ... 'unconscionable' ... 'how could you do such a despicable thing' ... 'stop the shenanigans or you're fired.'"

Herb rubbed his chin, one eyebrow cocked. "Anything specific as to what the aforementioned shenanigans might be?"

"No." Blake turned his attention back to the ledgers. "Sometimes orphan trains, supposedly going out west to adoptive parents, were actually a cover for human trafficking. Drugs may have been legal, but human trafficking was not."

"Are you insinuating Wordsworth's railroad was used for these evil designs?"

"Possible."

"Proof?"

Spoken like a true attorney. "Not yet. Maybe I should climb Wolf Mountain soon. Poke around the ruins."

Herb closed the ledgers. "The ruins have been thoroughly combed. What wasn't destroyed in the fire is in the site museum or the House of History. What do you think you could possibly see that hasn't already been uncovered?"

"A hunch. Anna said her sister used to hike up the mountain several times a month before she took ill. After her recovery, she wanted to restart the tradition and made the sojourn last month. Strangely, Marci hasn't returned since and refuses to say why. Thought I might have a look around, perhaps off the beaten paths."

Herb laughed—more like a disturbing, goose-bump producing screech—creepy and unexpected—out of character for a laid-back, newly retired divorce attorney. "Marci Henderson's a nut case from what Anna tells me. Who knows what she might have imagined up there."

Blake stepped back. "Nutcase is a very unkind description, Herb. True, Marci's had her troubles of late.

I'll tell you, I'm not so sure everything she saw was caused by psychosis. The Marci I knew years ago had more spot-on gut feelings than Sherlock Holmes."

This time Herb's laugh seemed like feigned pleasantry, betrayed by an accusing glare. "Forgive the cynicism, Blake. Sherlock Holmes is a fictional character."

"Yes, I know, but it doesn't change the fact Marci is very intuitive. I'm telling you, Herb, she saw something—something too frightening to share. She's always believed in Felicity's innocence. After Abigail's entries—"

"Abigail?"

"The maid."

"Never knew her name. Interesting."

Blake scoured Herb's countenance for sincerity. His surprise seemed genuine enough, although his inquisitions were more like an interrogation. Then again, perhaps his direct approach came from years of legal work.

"Anyway, after reading Abigail's entries, I'm inclined to agree with Marci. I don't think the mistress of Wordsworth Mansion ran off with her husband's accountant."

Herb chuckled. "Are you writing a mystery book, Professor, or a documentary on the railroad? Doesn't seem as though whatever happened on Wolf Mountain fits your premise the railroads helped establish the tourist industry in the Adirondacks. Hate to see you get sidetracked by an unsolvable riddle."

Blake stretched his back muscles. "I beg to differ. What happened on the mountain may have everything to do with Wordsworth's influence on railroad expansion."

Herb reset his reading glasses and resumed scanning the ledgers. "Don't follow."

"Transportation of people and goods proved to be very lucrative in the early development of the Adirondack wilderness. Like today, technological advancement brings criminal opportunity as well as mankind's betterment."

Herb bent his head to one side. "I'm aware of the evils the railroads afforded the devilish mind. Smuggling, as well as human trafficking, lined the pockets of railroad authorities willing to look the other way. Both illegal and immoral practices ran rampant."

Blake rubbed his eyes. He'd not slept well, and they had a long ride home. "I'm not accusing Wordsworth himself. Perhaps he had men of less noble character in his employ. His association with Reverend John Todd indicates Wordsworth was a godly man. Marci and I also researched the reverend's activities in northern New York."

"Ah, yes. I've heard of John Todd. Wasn't he the minister who offered a prayer at the joining of the two railroads, uniting east and west?"

"Yes."

Herb set down the ledgers. "Okay, you've got my curiosity up. How was he involved with Wordsworth?"

"He was friends with the older Wordsworth, the founder of the railroad. Todd was not only an abolitionist, he was also a leader in the temperance movement. The older Wordsworth was a devout Quaker, as was Felicity. If she became a disciple of John Todd, she would have a strong aversion to her husband's use of a good thing to promote a bad thing."

Herb closed the ledgers. "Wordsworth wouldn't have been the only corrupt tycoon in the late 19th century, who put his religion aside to honor his pocketbook. Maybe Felicity left him because he was a crook."

Didn't add up, nor did Herb's refusal to see any other opinion. "I don't think Wordsworth knowingly transported anything but wholesome commodities. Reverend Todd was a frequent visitor to the North Country and the Wordsworth estate. Young Wordsworth would have been brought up on his teachings. Personal journals of the older Wordsworth indicate he lived his faith."

"Bad apples can grow on good trees."

"Yes, and a bad tree can produce a few good apples." *And a bad apple can become a good apple. At least true for me, with God's help.* "However, most good apples come from good trees, and most good trees grow good apples."

"No argument there."

"Perhaps Wordsworth was duped."

"By whom?"

"Don't know until I do more research. Someone Wordsworth trusted, no doubt."

"Well, then, if you're determined to give the mountain a go, I'd like to climb with you." Herb rubbed his slightly bulged middle. "Could use the exercise."

"I appreciate the offer, but I'd hoped to convince Marci to join me."

Bianca, who'd stood next to Blake during his exchange with Herb, batted her lashes, her smile seductive, her intent clear. "Not tomorrow, though. Remember our golf date?"

Blake blushed. "Golf date. I wasn't aware we made a tee time?"

She leaned against him, her breath hot against his neck. "I did." Her lips rubbed his cheek just as her cell rang. "Oh, bother." She glanced at the caller ID, then raised her left brow. "It's Tad. Guess I'd better take this."

While Bianca stepped outside, Herb jabbed his elbow into Blake's side. "I envy you, Dr. Montgomery. Bianca's a very attractive young woman."

"Her attractiveness is undisputed, but something about her yells, 'Siren!'"

"Siren?"

"From Greek mythology."

"Afraid I'm at a loss, Blake."

"The Sirens, with their beautiful songs, lured sailors into cliffs and certain death. Jason and his Argonauts managed to escape the Sirens with Orpheus's divine music. I think I need an Orpheus to rescue me from Bianca."

Herb laughed. "I've known her a long time. She's harmless enough, I think."

"Perhaps, although I get the feeling she's hiding something. Sometimes I think I should get closer to find out just what. Then I think of the poor cat."

"The cat?"

"Curiosity killed him."

Herb's grin traveled the width of his face. "Ah, yes, and satisfaction brought him back. Don't worry, Professor. Bianca's meows aren't so treacherous."

"I'm through with the chase, Herb. I almost took Bianca up on her willingness, had an interesting evening planned last week. Thankfully, the best laid plans of mice and men aren't beyond God's intervention. Alfred called me with the news he'd been hospitalized before I crossed the line of no return. Not exactly a melody orchestrated by Orpheus. A successful pull-away, though."

"Alfred? Oh, yes. Your colleague. Sorry to hear he's been ill. How is he doing?"

"He hoped to be discharged by now. Every time the doctor comes in, he orders more tests."

"That's a shame. What's wrong? His ticker?"

"Initially, the doctor suspected heart trouble. Turns out, he has bleeding ulcers. Doc thinks he messed up his medications."

Herb pursed his lips. "You don't say."

"I'm going to see him tomorrow. Says he has important information he's learned on separate research regarding Forrest, the accountant."

Blake hitched a breath at Herb's fierce glance.

CHAPTER 23

Blake had offered to drive. Herb, however, succumbed to Bianca's insistence he take the wheel. When Blake opened the passenger door, she dragged him to the back and snuggled next to him. Couldn't argue. The Osprey was hers. He'd sighed in relief. They had opted not to spend the night in Long Lake, especially with Bianca along for the ride ... like placing a bottle in front of an alcoholic. Hopefully, they'd be back to Collins Bend sometime early morning. Perhaps he could climb Wolf Mountain tomorrow with Marci—if he could convince her to go with him.

He closed his eyes as he leaned back against the seat, the rhythm of the wheels against the pavement like a lullaby. The weight of something on his shoulder jarred him awake. Bianca had edged impossibly closer and rested her head against his chest, her soft purrs more of an annoyance than a prelude to seduction. Progress.

Herb put in a disc of classical music and nodded to its beat. He glanced into the rearview mirror. "Oh, good, you're awake."

"Where are we now?"

"Coming into Collins Bend in a few minutes."

"I must have dozed off for quite a while."

"A few hours."

"I should have helped with the driving so you could sleep."

"Didn't want to wake you." Herb's glance peered toward Bianca. "You two looked pretty cozy back there."

Blake pulled out his phone with his free arm to check the time. Already tomorrow. Long day and night but worth it. A low battery message glowed against his screen. Maybe enough to check his messages. Every time he'd tried, Bianca distracted him.

Before he could bring the list up, the screen went black. He should have charged his cell before he left the cabin.

As Herb parked behind Blake's truck, he lifted Bianca's head from his shoulder. "Wake up, little Susie."

She shook her tresses, her eyes wide with curiosity. "How do you know my name?"

"Your name? Am I missing something?"

She sat up straight and blinked. "I meant my middle name ... Susan ... although my friends used to call me Sis."

Blake laughed. "I didn't know. I quoted a line from an old song by the Everly Brothers. Way before your time. Mine too."

She shook her head. "Pity you won't sing me any morning lilts. I assume you haven't changed your mind about golf tomorrow."

"Bianca, I'm flattered. You must know we are not a good match."

"Says you."

"And a Higher Voice."

"Getting religious on me?"

Did he dare share his faith? The more of her shallowness Blake uncovered, the more Bianca lost appeal. "Still lots of summer left. Maybe we can have a lunch sometime, in a very crowded restaurant, and I'll explain."

"I have no use for religion," she harrumphed, as she stuck her long legs out of the car.

Before Bianca touched the ground, Tad Manning emerged from behind Blake's cabin and ran toward them, as if he'd been in wait for an ambush. He wielded a bat and straddled between Blake's truck and the Osprey. The car shook from the force of Tad's blows to the hood. Then he posed as if ready to use someone's head as a baseball.

Bianca screamed as she jolted from the vehicle. "Trevor ... stop! My car!"

Tad threw the bat on the ground, grabbed Bianca, twisted her arm, and pushed her against the car. Blake rushed out—a knight to a damsel's distress—and attempted to pull Bianca free. Bianca struggled and accidentally kicked Blake in the groin. He fell to the ground as Bianca freed herself from Tad's grip, then body slammed him against the Osprey with a move worthy of a sensei.

Tad rose as quickly as he'd fallen, pushed Bianca to the ground, and pounded Blake's abdomen and face. "Stay away from her. You hear me? Or you're a dead man."

By now Herb had circled in front of the Osprey and pulled Tad off Blake, twisting the attacker's arm and yelling, "Calm down, boy. Get in the cabin! Now!"

Tad slunk off like a scolded puppy.

Herb helped Blake stand. "You okay?"

He stroked his chin, feeling nothing untoward except stubble. "Might have a few bruises soon, but the new beard growth should cover them up."

Bianca giggled. "Aren't you funny."

Blake glanced toward Bianca who now leaned against the car. She stroked his cheek. "Are you hurt?"

"I'm fine. Remind me to be sure you're on my side the next time I'm in a brawl."

She laughed. "Tad's a boxer. You're going to have one sore cheek tomorrow."

"Is he always this protective?"

"Afraid so. Thanks, Galahad. Sorry you were roughed up on my account."

Blake laughed.

"Guess I'd better go in and talk some sense into my brother. Another time, Professor?"

Sometimes silence is golden.

She winked. "I don't take no for an answer." She sauntered off, and Blake caught the rhythmic sway of her hips, like drumbeats to disaster.

Herb got into the Osprey and rolled down the window. "I'll drive this over to Bianca and Tad's cabin and go have a fatherly talk with those two. Sorry you had to witness their temperaments."

"There are jail cells for men like Tad."

Herb laughed. "I wouldn't worry about Bianca. She's a black belt—First Dan, the highest order there is."

"I see she's fast and furious."

"Still plan on climbing Wolf Mountain later today?"

"After I see Alfred."

He rolled the window back up and steered the car across the lawns to the next driveway. Blake watched as Herb got out of the car and disappeared into Bianca and Tad's cabin. Marci had been right ... something was definitely odd about Tad and Bianca's relationship. And Bianca had called him Trevor—the name Marci heard at the restaurant. Herb seemed closer to Tad and Bianca than merely a friend of their father.

Perhaps Marci had been right all along.

If Tad and Bianca had sinister motives, was Herb involved? Distrust erupted. Blake had confided far too much in the man, a relative stranger.

Blake approached his cabin. As he reached for his key, he noticed the door ajar, the lock jimmied open. He hated guns and refused to learn how to use one. At moments like this, however, he understood why some people wanted to carry protection. What if the intruder were still in there?

He slipped from the porch and picked up Tad's dropped baseball bat. After taking a couple of practice swings, he returned to the front entrance and put his ear to the door to listen. No noises. Likely whoever broke in was gone. He couldn't call anyone with a dead cell. He glanced toward Tad and Bianca's cabin. Should he bother them? Maybe he could use a boxer and a karate master.

Probably best to let Tad simmer. He might yank the baseball bat from Blake's hand and do him in. Better to manage this crisis on his own.

He eased the door open with his left hand, flicked on the living room switch, and took a step back in disbelief. Cushions were strewn from one end to the other, furniture upended, his golf bag ripped, and the contents dumped onto the floor. He went into the kitchen. Cupboards were nearly disassembled and emptied, the entire floor littered with broken glass and dinnerware.

He tightened his grip on the bat and looked behind any place someone might choose to hide. He went to the bathroom and listened. When assured the room was empty, he raised his weapon just in case and entered. The medicine cabinet door swung on its hinges, and the shower door was cracked. The vanity had been smashed; shattered glass littered the tiles.

Why would anyone want to break into his cabin? The room looked as if the thief searched in a tornadic frenzy. Other than his Callaway golf clubs, his computer, and smart television, he had little of value. He checked the bedroom. Drawers had been ripped from the dresser, the contents strewn about. Wood shards jutted from the walls where the intruder had smashed drawers. Why this senseless destruction?

Blake went to his closet. His fireproof box had been pried open and his documents shredded, the hundred dollars he'd kept for emergency cash … gone. Let the vandals have the money. Maybe they'd buy a steak dinner and choke to death. He stepped back into the living room, righted a chair, and sat. He should report this. Which law enforcement agency had jurisdiction?

He returned to the bedroom and rummaged through debris. When he found his charger, he hooked up his phone to an outlet. At least he still had electricity. He scrolled through his messages. Two from the hospital and an odd one from Alfred's son. Perhaps he wanted Blake's take on Alfred's condition. He counted three messages from Marci. Should he be flattered or worried?

After confirming Paul's call had been made at three in the afternoon, Blake opted to check Paul's message first. "This is Paul Donahue. Afraid I have bad news. My father passed away an hour ago."

Blake sat in disbelief as he listened to the rest of the message: "I had spoken to Dad's doctor just this morning, and he had expected to discharge my father. Needless to say, this is a shock. Wondered if you knew something I didn't. I've arranged for a private flight into Saranac Lake Airport. I'll be there tomorrow afternoon. I hope you can pick me up so we can talk."

Sobs broke free of Blake's wearied spirit. Concern over a ransacked cabin now paled in comparison to this loss. Alfred's death made no sense. He was supposed to come back to his cabin, not home to eternity. He had more books to write, more rounds of golf to play—and he owed Blake another story about his boyhood days in Dublin.

The horizon cracked with morning light. Blake had not stirred from his chair for hours. His phone vibrated and brought him back from despair to the present. He checked the caller ID. *Marci.*

"This is Blake."

"Thank goodness I finally got you. Are you okay?"

"No, Marci, I'm not. Alfred's dead, and I've been robbed."

He caught Marci's gasp of sympathy. "Anna and I will be right there."

Marci found Blake slumped in a side chair, the upholstery so severely slashed, the stuffing stuck to the ceiling. Blake's gaze remained fixed on the bare spot by his chair as he spoke to Anna. "I'm sorry about all this. I'll pay for the vandalism."

"You'll do no such thing. I have insurance." She punched a number into her cell. "I'm calling the police now. Anything missing?"

"Only the cash in my box. Probably some drug addict needed a quick fix."

Anna scanned the room. "Nothing quick about this job. At least the cabin is still standing. That's about all. Appears to me this was not a simple robbery or random vandalism. Somebody was looking for something. I suspect whoever did this took the money as a ruse."

Blake smiled. "You're probably right. My computer and television are still here. What else would they look for except cash? If they were after money or valuables, why did they leave my computer and television?"

Marci picked up the pieces of what was once an end table. "Blake, what about Abigail's diary?"

"I gave it to Francine last night."

A state patrol car and a crime scene van pulled into the driveway. As the troopers approached, Anna squinted to see if she would recognize either one. "If I'm not mistaken, that's Gary Brentwood and Brenda Caswell."

Blake offered a faint smile. "Anna, is there anyone you don't know?"

She laughed. "Probably not. You might remember Gary from Briarcliffe. He was in my class."

"No. I don't recall him."

"Not surprised. He was a criminal justice major."

Marci rose. "Hello, Gary. Been awhile since we talked. Blake, Trooper Brentwood was on duty the night Matt was killed. He was very kind. You can trust him."

Gary shook hands with Blake. "I know who you are, Dr. Montgomery. I was at the banquet last week. I enjoyed your speech. I left soon after, so I doubt any of you saw me."

Gary was invited? And not me? Then Marci recalled how wealthy and connected Gary's parents were.

Blake shrugged. "Thanks."

"Wait out here. We shouldn't be too long." Gary and Brenda canvassed the cabin. Brenda took pictures and dusted for prints. Marci, Anna, and Blake found the upturned lawn chairs and sat in the driveway, a weary trio.

Marci dared to take Blake's hand in hers. "I'm so sorry about all this ... and sorry about Alfred. I know you were very fond of him. Anything I can do?"

"No." He squeezed her hand. "You're here. That's enough."

"They'll catch whoever did this. Someone must have heard something."

"Alfred was in the hospital. And Bianca was with me and Herb?"

Marci shuddered.

Blake grinned, a slight parting of the lips. "It's not what you think. I didn't invite Bianca along. She's one determined gal."

"And you didn't give her any encouragement?"

"Not on purpose, Marci. Look, I don't know what she wants from me. After last night, I'm convinced, like you, she has some ulterior motive for her feigned interest in me."

"Maybe one of the other tenants heard something."

Anna shook her head. "I expected to do renovations this summer, so I only rented out to Professor Donahue, the Manning siblings, and you."

Blake rose and stretched. "If Tad heard anything, I doubt he'd cooperate."

Anna arched a brow. "Why not?"

"When we got back, Tad used Bianca's Osprey for batting practice. Bent up the hood a little. Then he accused me of taking advantage of her. Punched me in the face."

"So that's how you got those red marks? You'll have some nasty bruises in a few hours."

"I used to be a scrapper in my younger days. I was no match for Tad, but Bianca was. Herb said she's a martial arts specialist."

Gary and Brenda came out and joined them in the driveway. "We're done for now, Dr. Montgomery. We found your prints. Otherwise, the place is clean. Perp probably wore gloves. Has anyone else stayed at your cabin? We found a couple of long black hairs on the bed."

Blake's face reddened. "Trooper Brentwood, I assure you, there have been no female guests in this cabin."

"We've bagged the hair as evidence. Could belong to the perp."

"You think a woman did this?"

"I agree, the degree of damage indicates the perp had muscle power. Could be he had a female accomplice."

Blake smirked. "And you found nothing else?"

Gary nodded. "I'm sorry, Dr. Montgomery. I know this is troublesome for you."

As the troopers left, Anna took one more glance into the cabin. "Blake, you can't stay here. These lawn chairs are the only furniture still in one piece. The carpet's slashed, and the bed's nothing but shreds. I'll arrange for you to move into a different cabin by tomorrow. It'll take me a day to get it ready. This mess will take quite a bit longer."

"I'll manage."

Anna glanced toward Marci. "Can't Blake stay with you? He'll need a few hours of sleep before he picks up Professor Donahue's son."

Blake bent his head. "Not necessary."

Marci tossed Blake her house key. "Go ahead. You'll have the place to yourself. Anna and I are going out for breakfast."

Anna's face was a portrait of confusion. "We are?"

"Yes. Your choice ... food or sleep."

Anna smiled and glanced back toward Blake. "Food, I guess."

Blake headed toward his truck, then turned. "Marci, I hope you believe me. Before this break-in, no one's been in this cabin but me."

A day ago, Marci would have labeled Blake a liar, like every man she'd known. As he stood before her, beaten, an image of despair, she knew he told the truth. "Did you want me to go with you to the airport?"

"I was afraid to ask. Afraid you'd refuse. Yes, I want you with me."

"We can take my car."

"Probably a good idea. The truck doesn't ride three very comfortably."

Should she heap more anxiety on Blake and share what she and Anna had discovered about Herb as well as their suspicions about Tad and Bianca? Not yet. Blake should rest first before she burdened him with more mystery.

Blake met her glance. "I know that look, Marci. You're afraid to tell me something you think I should know. Is your house booby trapped or something?"

She smiled. "No. You're right, though. What I have to say can wait. I'm not sure you're mentally in a place—"

"Marci, if there's one thing I've learned in the last week, there is never an optimum time for bad news."

CHAPTER 24

Except for a couple of truckers sitting at the booth nearest the window, Alexis's Café was empty. Marci and Anna sat toward the back, as far from the truckers as possible. Marci gazed out the window for an Osprey with a bent hood. Thankfully, the street appeared deserted.

"Marci, you should be home. Blake isn't the only one who hasn't slept."

"I promised I'd go to the airport with him, but I wanted time for us to talk."

Anna rubbed her face. "Nothing to talk about, unless you know how to commit the perfect murder."

"Justifiable homicide if you ask me. Although, doing Herb in won't get us any closer to finding out what those three are up to, not to mention behavior unbecoming a Christian."

"Don't preach to me, big sister. You've only been a Christian one day. I've got a couple months on you."

Their mutual laughter dispelled the tension.

"God has much to teach me, Anna. I hope you'll help me learn. We can start with church Sunday. This time I promise not to faint."

The waiter brought their coffee, then took out a pad and pencil. "Ready to order?"

Marci smiled. "I'll have a cheese omelet."

"And I'll have French toast." Anna pointed to the sign over the lunch counter: *Have it Your Way.* "And be sure to sprinkle mine with lots of powdered sugar and a dash of cinnamon."

Marci shook her head at Anna's resilience. "Living dangerously?"

"Says the lady who ordered a cheese omelet."

"Dr. Solomon suggested I do one pleasurable thing a day. Yesterday I had a cinnamon bun. Today, it's a cheese omelet."

"Good advice. Life is too short to park in a rut."

Marci sipped her coffee. A month and a week had passed since her last hike up Wolf Mountain. First to confide in Anna, then decide how much to tell Blake, without adding her own concerns to his. She set her cup down and turned it in circles.

Anna glared. "Okay. Something's on your mind. Spill, woman."

"How much did you know about Matt's affair?"

"Really? That's what you want to talk about? Now? After two years?"

"No sarcasm, please. Answer my question."

"I heard rumors."

"What rumors?"

"That Matt had been cozy with Elena Lopez, the college girl who sang in Matt's gospel group."

Marci sighed. How could she have turned a blind eye with so much evidence right in front of her. "Matt had talked about her all the time, praised her voice. He asked if I thought he should coach her, help her toward a career."

"And you agreed?"

"All I wanted was for Matt to be out of the house as much as possible, so I didn't have to think about how unhappy we were together. What did I do—push him right into her arms? If you knew, why didn't you say something?"

"Mere suspicion. Nothing concrete. I didn't want to say anything unless I was absolutely certain, although I thought I might hire a private detective on your behalf. Then again, if you ask me, your marriage was already on the rocks. There was no need to shove it off the cliff. Either Matt would change his ways, or he'd leave you. Either way, you and Matt had to figure out your problems by yourselves."

"Well, we didn't. I buried my head in the sand."

As Anna met Marci's gaze, her eyes misted. "I never told you before. My first husband had numerous affairs. Husband two left me for a movie star. Husband three ... well, he thought he could hide another wife from me. And then there was Robert and his male lovers. With all of them, I knew instinctively. The more I denied the affairs, the easier to pretend everything was fine."

"We've both known betrayal."

"And not just by our husbands."

"When the police called about the accident and told me another woman had been in the car with Matt, I couldn't pretend any more. There was a name. A circumstance. You can't hide from things like that."

"Again. Why bring this up now?"

"Here's the thing."

"There's a thing?"

"Not a thing ... a child."

Anna arched her back. "Whoa! Elena and Matt had a child together? Are you serious? How did they manage to keep a kid a secret? This is a small town."

"Apparently not that small."

Anna blew a breath. "I suppose I can tell you what I knew then. Apparently, the rumored affair ended after a few months and then Elena took a job in Albany after she graduated. I heard she moved back to Collins Bend a few months before the accident. I knew her parents had adopted a child while she was gone, but I never put it all together. How did you find out the kid was Matt's?"

Here it goes. Marci told Anna how she'd climbed the mountain, spoken with a wandering toddler, and thought she'd hallucinated the whole conversation. She decided to tell Anna about the remains later. Right now, she focused on Mark. How she'd seen the child again in the village, talked with his grandmother, and discovered he was Elena and Matt's son.

"What are you going to do?"

"What do you mean what am I going to do?"

"You have that look, Marci. What are you thinking?"

"Elena's parents have done a fantastic job raising Mark. They don't have a lot of money, but Mark doesn't lack for anything. I asked Gabriella if I could see him from time to time."

Anna clicked a *tsk.* "Do you think you should? What does Dr. Solomon say?"

"This is my decision. Don't you see, Anna? God has given me a chance to make amends."

"For what?"

"If I had confronted Matt about the affair, he'd still be alive."

"You don't know for sure."

"From what Gabriella said, Matt broke off with Elena to salvage our marriage. When he discovered she was pregnant, he did everything he could to support Mark. After he was born, Matt visited the baby at the Lopez's house."

"Then what was Elena doing in the car with him the day of the accident?"

"Gabriella said he'd taken Elena to the store to buy a gift for Mark's birthday."

"I'm glad he ended the affair at least. Still, I have no patience for husbands who cheat. If a man's unhappy, let him get a divorce. Infidelity is not the solution for a sour marriage."

Marci clasped Anna's hand. "Don't you see? God forgave Matt. Now the Lord has helped me to forgive him too."

"A Christian only a day and already you have a larger capacity for love than I ever will. What are you going to do now? Why are you telling me all this?"

Before Marci could explain, Anna's phone blared, and heads turned. "Oops, forgot to mute it." She gazed at the number bold against the screen. "It's Herb." She rejected the call and powered down. "If he calls again, he can go right to voice mail."

"Are you going to call him back?"

"Maybe."

"What will you say?"

"Nothing."

No use warning Anna. A complete waste of breath, like trying to blow out a gag candle. A sister had to try. "Anna, please don't see him again. Things are getting way too scary. Tad's altercation with Blake, his cabin ransacked. Don't talk to Herb until we know how he's really connected to Tad and Bianca."

"And that's precisely what I plan to wrangle out of him."

"Be careful."

"I will. I'll only see him in a public place. I promise." She glanced at her watch. "Right now, you need to pick up Blake and head to the airport."

CHAPTER 25

Saranac Lake Airport held no resemblance to the bustling hubs Blake normally used. One airline and small engines only. Ludicrous how the same word could be applied to both the massive and the miniature. Whether large or small, any airport required stringent security procedures, yet the process was laughable when shrunk to a single room for both arrivals and departures. Deplaning passengers walked from the plane through a set of double doors into the main area. Visitors remained behind a rail but within easy view of all operations.

Blake's cell vibrated, and he checked the screen. "It's Paul."

Marci nodded.

"Hey, Paul, what's up?"

"Apparently, there's a storm approaching Saranac Lake. My flight will be delayed. It's a fast-moving system, so my pilot thinks the delay will be about half an hour."

"Chartered flights have their ups and downs, literally. We'll wait for you."

Blake's stomach rumbled. So much for arriving early. Weary, Blake struggled to keep his eyes open. He'd rested for a few hours at Marci's place, though he didn't sleep— thoughts ran a marathon through his mind. The best way he could honor Alfred was to keep moving forward. He'd get through the rest of today, sleep, and then tomorrow, he'd hike up Wolf Mountain ... with or without Marci.

Certainly not with Herb, not unless he found some explanation as to why he lied to Anna. Blake could agree with Marci ... Herb's behavior veered toward suspicious. As to whether he was Marci's mystery man in the blue tuxedo, the quirky fisherman she saw at the market and the library, and the fatherly figure she saw with Tad and Bianca at the restaurant, only God knew for sure.

Blake ended the call and glanced around the one-room airport. He spotted a small lunch counter. "I'm starved. Let's grab something to eat while we wait for Paul.

Marci smiled, her eyes like lampposts lighting the black spot in his heart. "I'm full, but coffee sounds good. It's a beautiful day ... a balmy eighty degrees with a gentle breeze. The fresh air might do you good. We can order and take our food outside."

"I like the way you think, lady."

Blake paid for the order and found a bench outside the airport. Marci was right, the fresh air revitalized him. Why not live in these mountains permanently? He could ski in the winter and golf in the summer. So far, with the exception of Herb, Tad, and Bianca, who were relative strangers to Collins Bend, Blake found most of the town's residents to be very friendly.

Perhaps one of the area's community colleges had an opening for a history professor. He could always tutor or substitute until something turned up, even write books like Alfred had done. He'd taught enough years to secure his retirement. Why not try something different?

Blake gulped the rest of his coffee and discarded the trash. He helped Marci up, and they clasped hands. "Let's walk a bit." Her nearness comforted him in ways he hadn't thought possible. Ironic how he'd hoped to be the source of Marci's conversion—instead, a mop-headed preschooler cracked her spiritual resistance. Within his egotistical mission, he thought himself her solution. Yet she proved to be the very tower of strength he needed at this vulnerable time.

"I've been thinking quite a bit on how Herb managed to fool Anna. Not an easy feat. Though she might play the dumb blonde, in truth, she has a keen instinct about people."

Marci smiled. "Even as a kid. Anna's had some hard knocks in life, but she can take care of herself. Whatever Herb's agenda, he must have known Anna would eventually discover his ruse."

"Maybe he has a backup plan. He apparently is a master of disguises. Fooled me too."

"So, you believe me? What I saw at the restaurant?"

He kissed Marci's hand. "I believe you saw something strange. Who or what, I'm not certain. Forgive me for doubting you. The whole scene still sounds improbable."

Marci took a deep breath before she continued. "See, that's part of the reason I kept you at arms' length ... until yesterday. I was afraid I might be losing my mind. The things I saw made no sense to me, either."

"What's the other part?"

"I was drowning in my anger."

"About how I treated you? Marci, I explained why I was an idiot. Can't you forgive me?"

"I want to. I have in my head, at least. My heart will follow in time."

"What are you trying to say?"

"With Dr. Solomon's help and God's intervention, I've come to realize why I've been so angry. Things happened to me long before I met you. My pain started when my father abandoned us. Anger was the first knot in a chain of relationship issues, kind of like a tangled fishing line. Only time and patience will unravel the mess. At least now I'm hopeful."

"Somehow, we'll figure us out—where we go from here." He pushed her hair back from her face. "I believe if Matt had lived and with God's help, you'd have eventually forgiven him and made your marriage work."

"I'd like to think myself that noble. The truth is, I'll never know for sure. I'm grateful I finally know the truth. I have begun the process by accepting the Lord's forgiveness. I do wish I hadn't taken so long to do so. Before I can forgive Matt, I must forgive myself. A far more difficult endeavor. Yesterday, I made a *breakthrough*—as the shrinks say."

He stroked her cheek. "Lots of people have trouble with forgiving themselves, even after accepting God's plan for their salvation. Fresh starts can take time. Forgiving yourself takes a little longer than the instantaneous cleansing God gives us the moment we accept him. But I don't understand what you have to forgive yourself for. You were the victim."

She gave him a playful shove. "Not so fast, Professor. I might have been a young college student, but I was hardly innocent. I knew what we were doing. Perhaps a part of me was relieved when the romance ended. But that's not what I have to forgive myself for."

"Then what?"

Marci glanced skyward. A Cessna approached the runway. "Probably Paul's plane. We should go inside."

"We've got time before they deplane. Tell me, Marci."

"It's something no woman wants to tell a man, especially one she loves."

He pulled her into him, and they kissed. "I love you too." He reflected on their relationship. Revived affection?

No, not a resuscitation of old desires—rather, a freshness as if they'd fallen in love for the first time. "I have no right to judge you. Nor will I promise to understand. Of this much you can be sure—nothing you say will make me love you less."

She slipped from his hold and turned away. "Until the affair, Matt had been a good husband, kind and considerate. Most women were envious of the attention he lavished on me. Although I was incredibly fond of him, I never loved him, not as he deserved to be loved."

He lifted her chin. "You and Matt weren't the first couple who held a marriage together out of friendship."

Her eyes misted. "At first, we *were* happy with our fantasy world until reality clamored and woke us up." She hesitated, searched his eyes, her gaze pleaded for understanding. "I left our marriage bed."

Matt had sought comfort with another woman because of Marci's rejection. Something Blake understood—if not for God's intervention, he'd have fallen into Bianca's arms over Marci's refusal to give him a chance.

Marci stared, as if waiting for Blake to respond. What could he say? Excuse Matt's affair as Marci tried to do? Understanding and condoning were not two sides of the same coin. No wonder Marci struggled.

"Marci, if you want me to, I'll go with you the next time you see Dr. Solomon. I want to help you. Dr. Solomon may be able to give me advice too. Though I may not have been the cause, our breakup certainly is part of the puzzle."

She nudged his side. "Don't think more of yourself than you should. You are not the cause for my unhappiness. Looking for blame is wasted energy. Chances are, if we'd stayed together without God in our lives, our marriage might have failed too."

"How can you be so certain."

"Because things happened to Anna and me, causing me to distrust men from an early age. Our disappointment and Matt's affair added to an already warped perception of how the world worked. I became a prisoner of resentment."

"I think I know what you mean. I'd sooner forget my childhood too."

"We both had too much baggage to make us work as a couple. My mother had multiple partners. One of them thought my sister and I were worthy of his attention. Anna lured him to protect me."

Those few words explained so much. Her willingness to share such deep pain with absolute honesty deepened his love for her.

Marci pointed toward the airport. "They're probably deplaning by now. We really must go in."

Blake agreed. When they returned to the airport lobby, a youngish man walked toward the gate, his steps heavy. No need for an introduction, though Blake had never met any of Alfred's children. This man's features were a testament to his heritage.

Blake embraced Paul as a brother—united in grief and purpose.

"Paul, this is Marci. She attended Briarcliffe and knew your father."

Paul nodded in acknowledgement. "Glad to meet you, Marci. Thank you ... both of you ... for coming."

"I am so sorry about your father. He was a good man."

"My father thought highly of you too, Blake."

"He was more than a mentor. He was a dear friend. How can I help?"

Paul took out a piece of paper from his suitcoat pocket. "Can you give me a ride to the State Police Headquarters in Ray Brook? Here's the address."

A very odd request. Marci nodded. "Yes, I know how

to get there."

"I received a call from"—he glanced at the paper again—"a Trooper Brentwood."

"Yes, we know him."

"He asked me to come to the station as soon as I landed to talk to someone from"—he glanced a third time at the note—"from the BCI. Whoever they are."

Marci offered an explanation. "The BCI is New York's State Police Bureau of Criminal Investigation. Of course, we'll take you there."

"Trooper Brentwood thinks my father may been murdered."

CHAPTER 26

Blake excused himself to go to the restroom where he splashed water on his face. Thirty-six hours with no sleep had dulled his brain, and another long evening stretched in front of him. Paul's shocking news still burned Blake's heart. *Alfred, murdered? Why? Who would want a harmless, Irish storyteller dead?*

Blake met up with Paul and Marci in the airport lobby. What could he say to comfort Paul, a stranger, when Blake had no words to soothe his own ache? Alfred would have counseled his mentee to extend the hand of brotherhood in the face of personal loss.

They walked to the car in silence. Paul climbed into the back and placed his computer bag and pilot case on the seat next to him. Blake sat up front with Marci.

No one spoke for the ten-mile ride to Ray Brook. Blake gazed at the multi-story brick building. When they entered, Trooper Brentwood, accompanied by a stocky man in a gray suit and striped tie, greeted them. "This is Investigator Rabinowitz of the BCI."

Rabinowitz wasted no time in getting down to business. "Mr. Donahue, follow me." Paul and the investigator disappeared down a long hallway.

Brentwood motioned toward a large coffee station. "Help yourself and have a seat here in the lobby. When he's through speaking with Mr. Donahue, Investigator Rabinowitz would like to talk with you, Dr. Montgomery."

Not a request ... a command.

"Sure." What else could he say?

Blake opted out on the coffee. He sat and tapped his foot to stay awake while Marci, sitting next to him, literally twiddled her thumbs. "I assume you've never been here before?"

"No."

"I've been in police stations as a kid. Can't say things are much different than I remember. Cold place. I do like Trooper Brentwood, though. He seems conscientious. I'm sure he and Investigator Rabinowitz will get down to the bottom of whatever's going on."

Marci scowled. "Blake, you're babbling. Relax. We'll know soon enough."

Blake leaned his head against the wall and closed his eyes.

Marci jabbed him in the abdomen. "Wake up! Paul's coming back."

"Did I doze off?"

She glanced at the clock. "For about twenty minutes. I'm glad. You needed a respite."

Paul returned and sat on the other side of Blake. His red face indicated only one thing—the interview with Rabinowitz promised to be intense.

Brentwood knocked against a window, then slid a file through a slit to a clerk behind the glass partition. "Dr. Montgomery, would you come with me, please."

Blake followed Brentwood through the same bowels of law enforcement business that swallowed Paul earlier. The trooper opened a door into what must be an interrogation room. Plain white walls were set off by a large mirror. A long table sat in the middle of the room, a chair on either side.

Brentwood motioned toward the chair across from the door. "Have a seat. Investigator Rabinowitz will be here shortly." He left Blake alone, the hard click of the door echoing memories of boyhood confinement. His throat closed.

Calm down, Blake. It's only an interview.

Why did the police need to talk to him about Alfred? All would be revealed soon enough. Blake sucked in three deep breaths and drummed his fingers against the table for what seemed an eternity, his thoughts volleying like a ping-pong ball. Since he first drove into Collins Bend, one crazy event after another stretched this insane week into exhausting exasperation, his only joy, a reunion with Marci. He wished she were with him now to hold his hand—her renewed love a gift he didn't deserve.

The door opened. Blake glanced at his watch. Only ten minutes, yet those minutes seemed more like hours. Rabinowitz entered, his face taut with seriousness. By his tufts of gray hair and a slight droop around his lips, Blake guessed the man to be in his mid-fifties. Good. An experienced law enforcement officer would have a better chance of finding justice for Alfred. Blake shivered from the chill of an unstated accusation written on Rabinowitz's blank expression.

Blake moistened his dry lips. "I'll ask right out. Am I a suspect?"

Still standing, Investigator Rabinowitz smiled, cracking his stoicism to reveal a row of yellow teeth, probably the result of a decades-old smoking habit. "Not really, Dr. Montgomery. Let's just say you're a person of interest."

"What's going on? What happened to Alfred?"

"Where do you work ... how long have you been in Collins Bend ... what is the nature of your research?"

Investigator Rabinowitz began his interrogation with simple questions. Not once did he meet his target eye to eye. He cut off Blake's responses as if Rabinowitz already knew the answers. If so, why ask? Then Rabinowitz turned, sat in a chair across from Blake, and leaned in. "Were you aware of Professor Donahue's heart condition?"

"No. He never mentioned he had a problem. The man seemed healthy to me."

"You say he was like a father to you, but you weren't aware of his arrhythmia?"

"I told you, already. No, I didn't know he had anything wrong with him." Blake's cheeks heated as his heart raced and stomach acid swirled.

Investigator Rabinowitz flung a file into the middle of the table. "Professor Donahue was admitted to the hospital with suspicion of cardiac complications. He must have told you why he was in the hospital."

"Alfred told me the doctor suspected he might have had a mild heart attack. Alfred believed his trouble was nothing more than severe indigestion. As I've already told you, I wasn't aware of any cardiac problems before he went into the hospital. Alfred always downplayed his symptoms whenever he was sick, which wasn't very often."

"That's what his son said."

Blake leaned back. His saliva thickened. "Alfred mentioned his doctor thought he might have mixed up his meds. He laughed it off. So did I. Alfred is ... was ... far from senile. I brought his meds to the hospital at his request."

"We've confirmed much of your story with the nurse." Rabinowitz leaned in, his tone suddenly sounding friendly. "Here's the thing, Blake. Professor Donahue went into cardiac arrest before his meds were tested. Since his death appeared to be from natural causes, his physician released the body to the funeral home and subsequently to the crematorium per the family's request. We weren't able to do an autopsy."

"What are you implying?"

Rabinowitz opened the file and pointed to a photograph of two prescription bottles. "When the nurse packaged Professor Donahue's belongings, she noticed an odd residue inside these bottles. She brought them to Dr. Phillips's attention. He then sent the medication to the hospital lab for analysis."

Rabinowitz closed the file and leaned back. "The residue tested positive for arsenic. Naturally, the hospital contacted us. We did a subsequent search and found hair follicles on the professor's comb. They also tested positive for arsenic which means the professor was poisoned. For most people, the amount would not have been lethal. Given his age and preexisting condition, he ingested just enough to cause heart failure. For now, we're treating his death as a homicide."

"Could this have been due to a pharmacy error?"

"We're investigating all possibilities, including negligence. The fact still remains—you were the only known associate with access to his cabin. Your prints are not only on the bottles, but on the bathroom medicine chest as well as the kitchen counter and cupboards."

"I wasn't sure where he kept his medicine."

"You were the last person to handle the professor's medication before you brought them into the hospital. This makes you a person of interest."

"That's insane. I told you, Alfred was like a father to me—"

"And yet you claim you didn't know he had a heart condition?"

"And does your father tell you everything?"

Rabinowitz smiled. "No. I know you're still in a flux over the incident in your cabin. Trooper Brentwood tells me prints came up negative except for yours. Did you stage the break in?"

Blake swallowed hard. He was a suspect. "Why would I vandalize my own place?"

"To make it appear as if you were a victim—to cover up your crime?"

In his mind, Blake slammed his fist against the table, restraint difficult to muster. "I committed no crime. Do I need a lawyer?"

"I don't know. Do you? While the case is being investigated, I'll have to insist you remain in Collins Bend. For the moment, you're free to go."

Marci worried for Blake's spirit. They'd spent hours at the police barracks, with little conversation between them. The police gave Paul Donahue a ride to his hotel and allowed Blake and Marci to leave. He seemed so upset, she insisted on driving.

She pulled into her driveway and glanced at Blake, his near zombie posture worrisome. How long could someone go without sleep before collapsing? "Anna thinks your new digs should be ready by evening. You can rest while I fix a supper of some kind. I think I have a ham slice I can broil. I can nuke a couple of potatoes and open up a can of corn."

"Sounds good."

He clasped her hand as they walked toward the door. Marci stopped. Either she'd forgotten to close the door or someone had been here while she was gone. "Blake, the door's ajar."

He examined the splintered jamb, then pulled her behind him while he whispered, "Looks as if someone pried it open."

"You think someone might still be in there?"

"Possibly."

"Shouldn't we call the police?"

"Let me go in first. Wait here."

"No. I'm going in with you. If we need a weapon, Matt's golf clubs are in the entryway closet."

Blake pulled her back outside and went in ahead of her. "Call the police from out here."

Trembling, she fumbled in her purse, pulled out her phone, and punched in 911. She should have called the barracks directly and spoken with Trooper Brentwood instead of a nameless person on the other end. "I think my house has been broken into."

Marci gave the dispatcher the pertinent information. "Help is on the way, Mrs. Henderson. Don't go inside until the police arrive."

Too late. Even if warned, Blake would play the knight. Wielding a nine iron, he'd already vanished into the living room out of her field of vision.

She crept inside and grabbed a driver, then headed in Blake's direction. A scuffle, a grunt, a thud, like someone falling, and then retreating footsteps. She rushed into the living room. Blake pulled himself up from a prone position, his forehead bloodied.

"Blake, are you okay?"

He laughed. "Aren't you a menacing picture! Love to see what you could do with that club on the course. Bet you've got a heck of a swing."

"Not a time for jokes. Blake, you're bleeding!"

"Relax, I'm okay. Just a little cut. Someone pushed me from behind, and I fell against the table. I'll live. The perp probably left by way of the kitchen door."

Marci turned on the overhead light. The cushions were scattered, but nothing else looked amiss. "The police will be here any minute. Let me look at your wound."

He turned away. "I only need ice. Have some?"

Marci led the way into the kitchen and flicked on the light. "What in heaven's name happened here?" Drawers had been flung open and contents strewn on the floor. She grabbed an ice bag from the freezer and handed it to Blake.

"This can't be a coincidence, Marci."

"I agree."

"Anything missing?"

"I can't tell for sure, but I don't think so. I keep my emergency cash in a locked safe. Looks as if the robber started here, then went into the living room. Apparently, he didn't get far before we arrived."

Sirens wailed. "We better get back outside."

Marci nodded.

"I'm sure whoever comes will try to blame me. They already have me tagged as a vandal and a murderer. At least this time I have an alibi. I've been with you all day."

Sad, she'd have to burst his relief. "Not all day, Blake. I left you here alone while Anna and I had lunch. I picked you up here but didn't go into the house. Remember?"

"Oh, brother. Maybe this time, they'll lock me up. If they do, at least maybe I'll finally get some sleep."

"No one believes you had anything to do with all this, Blake. The police are simply being thorough."

Blake took her hands in his. "As long as you believe I'm innocent. You do believe me, don't you?"

Did she? Time changes people. Yet, commitment required faith beyond the circumstantial. "Yes, I believe you."

Blake shuffled his feet, anything to keep his eyes open while Trooper Brentwood completed his report.

"And you were the last one in the house, Dr. Montgomery?"

There it was—the sting of hinted accusation. "I know how this looks."

"We're through processing the place. There are several sets of prints. Matt Henderson of course is deceased. Anna Vincent, Mrs. Henderson's, and yours."

"Of course, my prints are here. Marci let me stay until the new cabin is ready, which I expect will be soon. And we've shared donuts and coffee in her kitchen. Are we nearly done?"

Keep your cool, Blake. Not wise to get snippy with a trooper, even a former Briarcliffe student. Sometimes thoroughness bordered on the inane.

His cell rang and he checked the number. "This is Miss Vincent. Perhaps my cabin's ready."

Trooper Brentwood nodded. "Go ahead and answer your call."

"Anna?"

"Blake, what's going on? Someone told me there're police cars at Marci's house. I called her. She said she's outside waiting for the troopers to finish their investigation. Someone broke into the house."

No way Blake would tell Anna the police thought him guilty. "Is the cabin ready?"

"You can come by for the key tonight."

"Marci shouldn't be alone in case whoever broke in comes back. Can she stay with you?"

"Of course, if she'll agree. You know how stubborn she can be."

Trooper Brentwood handed Blake a business card.

"Seems like I'm getting a collection."

Brentwood remained deadpan. Did troopers have no sense of humor? "We're done for now. Mrs. Henderson said nothing of value was taken. And there was very little vandalism. You say someone pushed you?"

"That's right."

"Take off your sport coat. Assuming your story checks out, we might find fingerprints or trace DNA on the coat."

"Assuming my story checks out? I told you the truth. Why wouldn't my story check out?"

"Anything's possible, Dr. Montgomery ... and you were alone in this house for two hours."

"What motive could I possibly have?"

"Throw us off track? Scare Mrs. Henderson into staying with you? Who knows?"

"You can't really think I had anything to do with any of this stuff?"

"Merely following the evidence, Dr. Montgomery. Be sure you do not leave Collins Bend."

Did they have the right to stop him if he wanted to leave? He hadn't been charged with anything. Forget retiring here. Time to contact the legal profs at Briarcliffe, clear his name, and shake the dust of Collin's Bend off his feet. He could finish his research from the comfort of his office computer chair. He'd had enough Adirondack adventure to last a lifetime.

CHAPTER 27

Blake dumped the last of his coffee into the sink. He wished Marci had agreed to stay with him, but at least she'd gone to Anna's.

He scanned his new cabin, glad his clothes, computer, and golf clubs had survived the vandalism. His sleep had been fitful, yet he did feel somewhat rested. Hopefully, he would manage to remain alert during church and Alfred's memorial service that followed. It was going to be hard to say goodbye.

At the advice of his legal counsel, he would stay in Collins Bend, cooperate with the investigation, and be patient. He was innocent until proven guilty. Eventually, the truth would be known—or would Alfred's unsolved murder be another footnote in Collins Bend history, another puzzle for locals to add their spin of suspicion?

Please, God, bring justice for Alfred.

Blake shook his head. Was his prayer only a selfish wish to clear his name?

He picked up his keys and drove to Anna's.

Anna seemed far too cheerful given the solemnity of the day. Her perkiness suited her, but Blake's taste in women veered toward demure and insightful. "Is Marci ready?"

"Almost. I thought I should drive myself, rather than go with you and Marci. I have plans afterward, and you'll need to take Paul to the airport."

"We should take Marci's car, then."

When Marci walked into the living room, Blake could barely breathe at the sight of her. Wearing a fitted purple dress, she was more beautiful than ever. Her glance spoke of love, different from their youth, yet far more precious. All the complications of the last week were worth this moment, to know, from this time forward, they would be together.

"You look very nice, Marci." His meager words muted what was in his heart, his true thoughts—how much he'd like to revisit the ecstasy they once knew at the cabin on Sorrel Pond. Or perhaps, at the appropriate time, the experience would be even more memorable. "Ready?"

"Yes. I wish I could say I looked forward to today."

"We're together. I'm glad you're with me."

Blake scanned the church, surprised at the full occupancy for someone who was only a part-time resident. The service had been arranged quickly since Paul would take Alfred's urn with him. Or was the turnout for Will Forrester, slated to give the main eulogy? Blake had no intention of voting for the man. No doubt the senatorial hopeful would optimize this tragedy to further his candidacy. Why Alfred supported a blowhard politician like Forrester escaped reason. At least he had the decency to honor a man who had worked so hard on his behalf.

The pastor of the historic church had abbreviated the morning service to allow preparation for the memorial service. He greeted Dean Foster and the delegation from Briarcliffe and introduced Paul to his father's colleagues.

Paul had asked Blake to give a brief statement. How could he sum up a lasting friendship in a few sentences? Hard enough to face this memorial service without the onus of suspicion hanging over him.

The pastor introduced Blake, and he took the lectern. He spoke of how Alfred had been his mentor. He'd been a friend who challenged Blake to be more than an educator, to live a life worthy of admiration. "Sadly, some life lessons are hard to learn. I stand here today a changed man because of Alfred Donahue, a man who taught me there is hope after failure."

Blake squinted toward the back of the church. He couldn't be certain from where he stood, but he thought he saw Tad and Bianca in the shadows behind the last pew. Other than a brief encounter at the alumni dinner, they had no association with Alfred. Then again, this was true of many sitting in the pews who attended to hear the celebrity rather than honor the deceased.

Will Forrester politely told of Alfred's faithful service. Otherwise, most of his comments, though cleverly disguised in rhetoric, sounded more like a campaign speech than a eulogy. Following his remarks, the service closed with the congregation singing Alfred's favorite hymn, "Amazing Grace."

Paul had invited Blake and Marci to join him in the processional and to take part in the reception line at the back of the church. Blake looked once more for Tad and Bianca, but they were nowhere to be found.

When the guests had departed and all protocols exhausted, Blake sighed in relief. "Long day, Paul. Yours will be longer yet, I understand."

"I received a call from my pilot. My flight will leave earlier than anticipated."

"Where to from here?"

"Ireland. Dad wanted his ashes buried in the family crypt in Dublin. Interesting. The land my father fled as a fugitive now honors him as a native son. I suppose fame often opens the door to forgiveness in ways obscurity cannot."

Blake smiled. "Something Alfred would say."

"I can't thank you enough for your help. Hard to believe this service was arranged on such short notice."

Blake squeezed Marci's hand. "Much of the credit goes to this beautiful woman."

Paul's eyes misted. "My parents were married for fifty years before Mother went to Glory. Not a day went by but what my father praised God for sending him a mate who stood by him through the good and the bad of life. You two have something special, I can tell. Blake, don't let this woman out of your life."

Blake kissed Marci on the cheek. "I don't intend to.

As the trio headed toward the airport, the whirlwind of the past few days blew through Marci's thoughts like a blizzard. As Blake parked, her cell rang. "Great Is Thy Faithfulness" replaced the solemn *Beethoven's Fifth* she'd had for the past few years. The hymn had been Matt's favorite. He closed every concert with his specialized rendition. Each time her phone chimed, she felt Matt's forgiveness, a permission to abandon her guilt, to find a new purpose and mission.

She checked the screen and met Blake's gaze. "This is Anna. You men go on ahead. I'll meet you inside."

Anna's voice sounded hesitant. "Marci, where are you now?"

"We're at the airport. The Briarcliffe delegation is serving as an honor guard while Paul and Blake lead the way into the airport. As soon as Paul's charter plane takes off, we'll probably grab a lunch in the village. Do you want to join us?"

"Maybe. Herb's with me. We just pulled into the parking lot. I'll see you inside." She giggled, a nervous laugh, then she disconnected.

CHAPTER 28

Marci surveyed the airport where they'd first met Paul Donahue. Once the urn was loaded into the cargo hold, Paul returned and shook hands with Blake. "I'm still in shock. I expected to visit my father next week and play golf with him, not escort his ashes for burial in a foreign land."

The honor guard waited to break rank until Paul's plane taxied and readied for takeoff.

Marci veered her glance through the double-glass doors. With a clear view past the baggage claim area and into the lobby, she caught a glimpse of the man Anna called Herb, the man Marci was certain wore a blue tuxedo at the alumni banquet, the man she would testify in a court of law she'd seen at the restaurant, and who had answered to the name of Tommy. He waved to Blake as if completely innocent.

Marci approached and gave Anna a hug. "I'm glad you're here."

An actress deep into character, Anna motioned toward the restroom. "Marci, come with me. You know I hate to go into these places by myself."

Should she leave Blake alone with the man who called himself Herb? Perhaps Blake would avoid confrontation, at least until she and Anna returned.

Marci checked the stalls. "We're alone. Now tell me what you found out so far."

Anna opened a stall door and sat. "I haven't told him I know he isn't who he says he is. God help me, Marci, I still want to believe there's a reasonable explanation for his charade. Whatever his motive, I really think he likes me."

"Of course, he likes you. After all, you own half of Collins Bend."

Anna's eyes filled with tears. "That was mean, Marci."

"You're a beautiful woman, Anna. You could have any eligible man you want. Don't fall for a con man's flattery."

"You're right. But why do I get the feeling I'm not the target of his con?"

"Isn't the nature of a con to be so thorough the victim doesn't know they're being conned?"

"And you still think there's a connection with everything else that has gone on?"

"Yes, Anna, I do."

She stood and slammed the stall door shut. "Forgive me, big sister, but you could be wrong. What should we do now? We don't have anything to go to the police with. And they're all hot to think your boyfriend's a murderer."

"We'll have to confront Herb."

"You're right. I knew we would. That's why I brought him here. I couldn't face him on my own. But I still refuse to believe his motives are malignant."

"I saw what I saw, Anna."

"When do you talk with Dr. Solomon again?"

"Next week."

"Maybe I should go with you?"

"Maybe one of these times. I'll ask Dr. Solomon."

Anna's face shriveled with impatience.

"Let me guess—you already called him and invited yourself to my sessions?"

Anna nodded. "Only because I love you, big sister."

"Or because you want to find out for yourself if I'm delusional or not?" Ire bubbled like lava.

"What do we really know other than he used a fake name to get close to me? Are you positive he's the man you saw in those other places?"

"Yes. I never met Herb before, so why would I imagine his twin in so many different places and with so many different disguises?"

Anna huffed. "There has to be a logical explanation."

"Okay ... give me one."

"Maybe he couldn't find a tuxedo other than the crazy blue one. Maybe he came to the banquet to ask me for a date. And maybe he likes to fish, and you only thought he had white hair. And maybe the three people in the restaurant only looked like Herb, Tad, and Bianca."

"Anna, you're grasping. You have to face the truth. Herb is a con man. Let's get this out in the open, once and for all."

Marci followed Anna from the restroom where they rejoined the men. "What did you guys talk about while we powdered our noses?"

Blake pointed to the television. "The golf tournament. What else?"

Herb nodded. "My money's on Bryson DeChambeau. He's had a good year."

People sitting in the bar area whooped as DeChambeau made a birdie.

Herb poked Blake in the arm. "What did I tell you?"

Marci nudged Blake.

Anna took Herb's hand. "Herb, we need to talk."

"Here?" Herb asked.

Anna scowled. "Or would you prefer the police station?"

Herb let go of Anna's hand and glared at Blake. "What's this about?"

This time Marci answered. "I'm about to prove my sanity."

The girls could have found a better spot to talk than this deserted section in the parking lot. There was nothing to lean on, and they stood under direct sunlight. Blake removed his suit coat, his throat parched, his shirt wet with sweat. Still, he couldn't be as uncomfortable as this man, whom they now knew as Tommy Osterman.

Marci and Anna harpooned questions as skillfully as any prosecutor. Outgunned, Tommy squirmed like a squirrel surrounded by cats. A comical scene if not for the fact Alfred had been murdered. Blake's instinct told him Tommy knew much more than he was willing to share.

"Anna, please believe me. I never meant to hurt you or anyone. In fact, you are the most delightful woman I've ever known. If things were different—oh, how I wish they were—I think I'd end up asking you to marry me."

Anna crossed her arms and scowled. "Fat chance of that now, you ... you ... there are no words worse than scumbag."

"Marci, you're not crazy. I was, indeed, the man in the blue tuxedo at the banquet. And, yes, the fisherman you saw at Bert's Tackle and again in the library."

"What about the restaurant? Did you follow us to Cold Creek?"

Tommy's head drooped. "Yes."

"And were Tad and Bianca with you?"

"Yes."

"Why?"

"It's complicated."

Blake swung his suitcoat over his shoulders. "Marci, I've heard enough. I think it's time we called the police."

Tommy sneered. "On what charge?"

"Stalking and impersonation for starters. How about breaking and entering and murder?"

"I didn't break in anywhere, and I certainly did not cause Professor Donahue's death."

"Then who did?"

"I don't know. You have to believe me." Tommy glared at Blake. "Anna says the police think you did."

"I'm innocent."

"Easy enough to say." Tommy paused.

Marci snarled. "You're changing the subject. You were following us. Why?"

"I'm sorry. I was ordered to."

"Whose orders?"

"I can't say."

Blake pushed Tommy against a parked black sedan. "Tad might beat me in a fight, Tommy, but you don't stand a chance. Out with it. Whose orders?"

"Go ahead and call the police. I think I'm safer with them."

Blake punched in Investigator Rabinowitz's number. "There's someone here you need to talk to."

CHAPTER 29

Blake put on his jacket and accepted the keys from Marci. "We're no closer to figuring this thing out than we were twenty minutes ago."

"At least we know I'm not delusional."

Anna's gaze remained fixed on the retreating patrol car with Tommy handcuffed and riding in the back. "Blake, what do you think will happen to him?"

"I hope they lock him up for a very long time."

She turned to Marci. "Do you think he meant what he said? Do you think he liked me? Loved me, even?"

"Doesn't matter. You deserve better. And you'll find better."

What man wouldn't say whatever he thought a woman wanted to hear to get out of trouble? Yet, from Blake's point of view, Tommy had been sincere when he wished he and Anna had met under different circumstances. Like the poem by Whittier—*What might have been* ... truly, the saddest words of tongue or pen. No matter whose biography, none would be void of regret.

"I'd like to know how Tad and Bianca figure into this. Are they under Tommy's nebulous orders, too?" Marci asked.

"He never told us their real names. I can only assume they, too, are not who they say they are."

"Did you have a chance to ask Dean Foster if he knew Verne Manning's children?"

Blake nodded. "I did. He said Verne had a son and daughter with those names, but he'd never met them."

Marci gave Anna a sisterly hug. "Will you be okay to drive?"

Anna straightened. She wore resiliency with as much class as she wore her Lord & Taylor wardrobe. "I've faced worse disappointments. I'll be fine. I do think I will go home and sink into a hot tub and wash off the memory of Herb Waycross."

The three walked to Anna's car. She drove off, tires squealing, and made a sharp left turn onto the main road. Marci fixed her gaze on Anna's hasty departure.

"What's the matter?" Blake asked.

"Her house is in the opposite direction. Wherever she's headed, it's not home."

Marci turned to face Blake. "Anna lied. Do you think she went to the police barracks?"

"It's a good bet."

"Should we go after her?"

"Absolutely not. She's a grown woman. I vote we get something to eat. We'll know soon enough what she's up to. If she wanted us along, she would have said so."

"You're probably right. I worry about her. The job of an older sister."

"You worry about Anna as much as she worries about you. However ..."

"However, what?" She shifted her weight and teased him with a smile.

"There's something else on your mind right now besides Anna. Something you don't want to tell me. Going after her would give you the perfect excuse to hide what you're afraid to say."

"Are you a mind reader?"

"Sometimes. Like now."

So much of what she'd seen had been proven to be real, not hallucinations or misinterpreted stimuli as Dr. Solomon had suggested. Truth brought more questions than if she'd been delusional. The events on Wolf Mountain had been explained, if not completely understood, except the scattered remains. Animal or human? Or perhaps they didn't fit into all this at all, merely oddly shaped stones reflected in the setting sun. What if they were as real as Mark? Shouldn't she tell someone?

"I told you how I saw Mark when I climbed Wolf Mountain last month."

"Yes."

"I didn't tell you the whole story."

"Then tell me now."

"When I realized Mark had not been a hallucination, I dared to believe everything else I saw was real. However, there's one strange thing I'm still unsure of."

Blake put his arm around her waist and steered her toward the car. "I'm listening."

Though she could not meet his inquisitive stare, she explained how the fright of a disappearing preschooler caused her to lose her balance and how she tumbled down a slope, nearly falling off the ledge into the crags below. She held nothing back, including the inexplicable debris resembling human bones. "I was afraid to tell anyone because I thought I was crazy."

"They might have been animal bones or ..." He hesitated as if searching for some other explanation. "Fossils. You did say the sun was setting. The glare could have affected your vision."

"I thought the same thing at the time. There was something shiny with the remains, like a piece of jewelry. I know I should have said something sooner."

"Marci, we need to make sure what's there before you report it."

A reasonable suggestion.

Blake glanced at his watch. "It's only two o'clock."

"You think we should go up there now? By the time we change, get gear together, and grab something to eat, it'll be late afternoon. We won't get back before sunset."

"We'll have enough light at the top. We should be able to make most of the descent before darkness. I'll bring flashlights, just in case."

Blake's cell rang. "It's the museum. I should take this."

Blake hit accept and slid in as Marci got into the passenger side. "Blake Montgomery," he answered, his tone needlessly official. If the caller was Francine, she'd not be put off by formality. He scowled, then offered, "I see. Thanks for letting us know."

Us?

"That was Francine. The museum was broken into last night, and Abigail's diary has been stolen. The police have already been notified. She thought perhaps we should be told as well."

CHAPTER 30

Marci paced the house while she waited for Blake to return. She'd dropped him off at his cabin to change and to pick up his truck while she scrounged for hiking gear, including ropes.

Marci had climbed Wolf Mountain a hundred times since she came to Collins Bend. Most of the trails were hiker friendly. However, if they were to descend the slope where she nearly met her end, ropes would be safer.

Nearly an hour had passed. Even the fastest climbers needed to plan on two hours to reach the summit. With or without a flashlight, the trails could be treacherous at dusk, let alone nightfall.

She put sandwiches, water, and snacks in a backpack, knowing to climb on an empty stomach was not wise. She checked the window every two minutes. With each pull on the curtain, she rehearsed a speech to convince Blake to wait until the morning. Why rush?

Blake's knock hinted at his grim determination. No amount of begging would change his mind. If she didn't go, he'd try to find the remains himself. He'd be safer with her as his guide than trying to find the spot by himself.

She opened the door and flung her backpack over her shoulder. "I'm not sure this is wise."

"We'll be fine."

"Then let's go before it gets any later."

When Blake eased onto the road, the white Osprey, parked near the end of the block, pulled out behind them. From her view in the mirror, the hood appeared dented. "Do you see the car behind us, the white Osprey? Is the hood dented?"

Blake glanced into the mirror. "Too far back to be sure."

"Didn't you say Tad hit Bianca's car with a baseball bat?"

"Gave it a good whack, yeah."

"Pretty sure she's following us."

Blake glanced into the mirror once again. "We can't be sure. There are a lot of cars with dented hoods. Lots of deer in these woods. If she is following us, so what? Let her follow us. I'm not interested in Bianca, or whatever her real name is—Susie or Sis."

Marci gasped. "Susan? I think I know where I've seen her before. You said she's a really good golfer?"

"Amazingly good."

"When Matt and I first moved to Collins Bend, the pro at the golf club had a daughter, a phenom. She was well on her way to national championships when her parents were arrested for embezzling from the Country Club. She went into a foster care home, started using drugs, and eventually was placed in a youthful offender program in Albany. Far as I know, she never returned to Collins Bend. I wonder if this is the same Susan."

"Possible, I suppose. Though, why pretend to be someone else unless she's involved with whatever scheme Tommy's trying to pull."

"If Bianca and Tad are fake names, do you suppose they aren't brother and sister either?"

"Pretty good bet. Tad did get beyond jealous. More than a brother might."

"Do you think they could be behind Alfred's murder?"

"Anything's possible. One mystery at a time. Let's figure out what you saw on Wolf Mountain. The rest will unravel as we go along. When we get back, we'll give Rabinowitz a call and tell him what we suspect about the so-called Manning siblings."

Blake turned his radio to Christian music. Only a week ago, she'd have tried to tune the words out. Now, they comforted her.

"You're deep in thought? Care to share?"

She gazed out the window. "Matt tried so hard to convince me to be a Christian. I let him down in so many ways."

"Who's to say? Perhaps you and Matt were part of God's plan all along. We weren't Christians when we dated. Your appreciation for the human side of history touched me, made me a better person. After we broke up, I felt lost without your moral compass. Perhaps our legacies of regret ultimately led us to faith."

Blake pulled into the museum parking lot. "We're here." They both looked up as the white Osprey pulled next to them. Bianca brazenly waved, then sped off toward the main road.

Blake glanced at Marci. "I suppose I should feel flattered by Bianca's obsession, but I don't. I know her interest in me is hardly romantic. I'm not irresistible."

"Go ahead. Flatter yourself. You are irresistible ... to me, at least. Back then and even now."

Blake swept Marci into a kiss.

She gently pushed him away. "Not the time. Let's move."

He threw the ropes over his shoulder, then stuck two flashlights into Marci's backpack. They climbed in silence, reserving their breath for the tasking ascent. They clipped as fast as their lungs could handle, hoping they'd reach the apex before dusk and Marci's find was not too far down. Still, they'd likely run out of natural light on the downward trip.

A small crowd milled near the mansion. "Guess this is a popular place. I'm surprised to see anyone still up here this late in the afternoon."

Marci removed the backpack from her shoulders. "Might as well eat our lunch while we wait for the area to clear."

"I'd rather no one see us tramp through an area clearly marked as treacherous. Might raise suspicion."

They sat on the bench and devoured everything Marci had packed ... breakfast but a distant memory. Soon, the group disappeared down the longer trail to the road. Finally alone, Blake scoped the mountainside near the ruins. "Now where did you take your slide?"

A uniformed man came from behind the mansion cinders, waved, then disappeared into the woods. Blake whispered to Marci. "Did you know rangers came up here?"

"People are supposed to sign in at the trail bottom and sign back out. Not everyone does, so rangers will make a precautionary check at the end of the day to make certain everyone's left the apex. There's a short trail behind the mansion leading to the ranger station, about a quarter mile. Only the locals know it's there."

Blake snickered with the small comfort. If Marci and Blake plummeted to their deaths, the ranger would know where to look for them. Blake scanned the view. "You're right. Not much ground before the drop off and a very long way down, indeed. I see three large boulders creating a faux barrier. Is that where you saw ... well ... whatever it was you saw?"

Marci nodded.

He played with a nearby cement post jutting from the ruins. "Looks secure enough." He fastened the ropes, then tugged to make certain the pole would hold. "I'll head down first. Then you follow."

"No, Blake. I know where the remains are. You follow me."

She eased down, hesitant, but assured of her footing. Blake followed.

When they reached the boulders, Marci pointed to an area five feet west, under the dilapidated balcony. "There."

They inched over. Blake took out his phone. Only one bar. He tried to call Anna but couldn't connect. He snapped pictures. "Might not be able to call out, but at least we have proof."

A shiny object, surrounded by what looked like human bones, glistened in the fading sunlight. Marci gasped as she clutched the matching necklace Mrs. Tierney had given her, the one Felicity had bequeathed to her servant. "Do you know what this means?"

Blake photographed the necklace and slipped it into his pocket. "Yeah. We may have found Felicity's grave. My hunch is she was murdered and tossed over the balcony. The killer probably thought her body had gone into the ravine below." He looked toward the sky; the sun was sinking rapidly. "We better get topside now."

Blake's line suddenly slackened. He shuddered as the once tethered end slithered to his feet. He bent to pick up the rope, lost his balance, and slid toward the drop off. Fortunately, he managed to grab hold of a bush, preventing his fall to certain death. Marci eased her way to him, and together they pulled to the top.

They unhitched Marci's rope just as Tad stepped out from behind the ruins. He wielded a Glock and tilted it sideways, leaving no doubt as to his intent. "Fancy meeting you here, Dr. Montgomery."

CHAPTER 31

Blake held his hands up. "Put the gun away. I'm sure we can work out our differences. I'm not in love with your sister."

Tad's eyes darted first to Marci, then to Blake, a wildness visible even in the diminishing twilight.

"Do what you want to me, but let Marci go."

"Sorry you got mixed up in all this, Mrs. Henderson. You're a nice lady. Crazy ... but nice."

Blake inched forward. "Tad, be reasonable. We've done nothing to you."

"Oh, but you have, Dr. Montgomery. I told you to stay away from Sis. You didn't listen. Now you'll pay."

A ranger came from behind the mansion, glanced their direction, and moved slowly behind them.

Best to keep Tad talking.

"Okay, maybe we flirted a little, but Susan isn't interested in me. Besides, I'm in love with Marci. Put the gun down before you do something you'll regret."

"Too late for that, Dr. Montgomery. Thanks to your meddling, I'm facing a bunch of felonies. Breaking and entering, not to mention murder."

"You killed Alfred?"

"Didn't want to. I liked the man. He told great stories."

Anger rose and caution fled. Blake lunged just as the ranger swung a two-by-four, knocking Tad to the ground.

The ranger retrieved the gun and helped Blake tie Tad's hands behind his back.

Blake blew a sigh of relief. "Thanks. Glad you happened by. Now the question is, how do we get him down?"

The ranger shook his head and took out a high-powered flashlight. Using a shoulder com, he called for a helicopter.

"After I saw you two idiots near the drop, I noticed this kook with a gun, I figured he couldn't be up to any good. Rather than confront him, I followed. I'm glad I did. I'll ride along in the helicopter if you don't mind. Pretty boring day today until now." He poked Tad in the arm. "Guess you weren't thinking this through, buddy. Didn't you know this historical landmark is guarded?"

Marci flipped open another magazine. If only she could lean back and snooze like Blake did. They had been in the lobby for two hours, waiting for their turn to be interrogated. Ranger Artie, as they now knew him, had been brought in, questioned for ten minutes, and left, offering a wink and a smile as he walked out of the barracks.

Investigator Rabinowitz finally came into the lobby, his face deadpan, no indication as to what would come next. Rabinowitz glanced toward Blake who rubbed his face to stay awake. "Long day, Dr. Montgomery?"

"Guess so."

"Almost over. I've reviewed your statements, and I'm satisfied you had nothing to do with any break in or Professor Donahue's death." He pointed a finger over his shoulder. "Our friend in there made a full confession."

"Then he *was* behind the vandalism and break-ins?"

"So he says."

"I get why he wanted to kill me. Jealousy makes people do unreasonable acts of violence. But what motive did he have for killing Alfred?"

"Everything will be explained in due time. First, there're two people who'd like to talk to you."

The door opened, and Trooper Brentwood entered along with Anna and Tommy.

Marci and Blake exchanged glances. Her eyes probably were as large and full of confusion as Blake's. "I don't understand. Anna, what's going on? Why are you with Tommy? I thought he'd been arrested."

Investigator Rabinowitz leaned against a counter. "Except for scaring Mrs. Henderson with his disguises and using a fake identity to woo Miss Vincent, our man here is not guilty of anything. The real culprits are Susan Brannigan and Trevor Winston, aka the Manning siblings. Trevor is on ice, but I'm afraid Susan has left the county. We have a warrant for her arrest, and we've put out an order to be on the lookout for her."

Marci gulped as Investigator Rabinowitz shook hands with Tommy. "Sorry for detaining you, Agent Hollingsworth." The investigator left the room, leaving Marci with a gazillion questions unanswered.

Anna leaned her head against Agent Hollingsworth's shoulder. "See, Marci, I knew this man really cared about me."

He showed his FBI badge. "Samuel Hollingsworth is my real name." He pointed toward a row of chairs. "Like Lucy, I know I've got a lot of explainin' to do."

Blake frowned as he glanced at his watch. "Sometime before morning would be good."

"The situation's very complicated."

Anna sat next to Marci. "True."

"Trevor and Susan work for Will Forrester. The FBI has suspected him of campaign fraud, and I've been working undercover as his assistant for about a year. A few months ago, because of his popularity in Collins Bend, Forrester enlisted Professor Donahue to head up his Adirondack campaign. Alfred didn't know I was undercover, nor had we ever met until I came to Collins Bend."

Blake chewed his lip. "Still doesn't explain why Alfred was killed."

Marci thumbed her necklace. "Or why the diary was stolen."

"I'm so sorry about Professor Donahue's death. If I'd had any idea his life was in danger, I'd have blown my cover and extricated him." Agent Hollingsworth turned toward Blake. "Forrester is a friend of Dean Foster and a large contributor to Briarcliffe. When Forrester learned of your sabbatical ambitions, he sent me, Trevor, and Susan to make sure you stayed away from researching the Wordsworth estate."

Blake shifted—his impatience evident. "Why?"

"Forrester is a descendent of William Forrest, Wordsworth's accountant. Apparently, William escaped to New York City, changed his name, and pledged to live a respectable life. The Forrester family name has been synonymous with philanthropy for generations. No one knew of William's crimes until a few years ago, when Senator Forrester decided to sell the New York City mansion. In the process of packing up the old library, the cleaning crew discovered a journal tucked behind an original edition of *Moby Dick*. The journal contained the accountant's full confession to the murder of Felicity Wordsworth, the arson, and human trafficking. He also confirmed Wordsworth had no knowledge of the cargo.

Why the accountant wrote the confession, we'll never know."

Marci's tears welled in sympathy for the much-maligned Felicity. At last, her innocence would be known. "Then those are her bones?"

"Forensics may or may not confirm the remains are Felicity. They'll perform DNA tests on the bones and the necklace and compare the results to her personal effects taken from the ruins."

Although she suspected, Marci asked anyway. "Did William say how Felicity died?"

"As a matter of fact, his journal was quite detailed. Felicity discovered William's activities and confronted him. When he pushed her, she hit her head on the fireplace mantel. He dumped her body over the balcony, believing no one would find her remains in the thick terrain below."

Blake inched to the edge of his seat. "Wow. So that's why Forrester sent a team here? Was he afraid I'd uncover the truth? Did Alfred discover something incriminating? Did Forrester order a hit on poor Alfred?"

Hollingsworth sighed. "While undercover, Forrester authorized me to use bribes or whatever was necessary to keep the events on Wolf Mountain a secret."

"Why go to such lengths? He didn't have anything to do with what happened to the Wordsworths."

"True. But the family's fortune was made through human trafficking and the sale of drugs. Forrester did not want this truth to leak."

"Are you saying he *did* order Alfred's murder?"

"Alfred wasn't killed to keep the nefarious Forrester name a secret."

Blake straightened. "Then why?"

"The day before his hospitalization, he'd discovered discrepancies in campaign funds."

"Discrepancies?"

"Odd transfers he couldn't account for. Forrester got wind of Alfred's snooping and told Trevor to make Alfred's snooping stop—permanently. Trevor gave up his boss in a plea deal."

Blake's eyes misted. "You didn't know about Alfred's discovery?"

"Not until Trevor's confession. I'm so sorry, Dr. Montgomery. If I could have prevented his death, I would have. He shouldn't have gone rogue detective and called the police at his first suspicion. We'd have protected him. Trevor is a crook, a liar, and a hothead—but I never pegged him capable of murder."

Anna pinched Agent Hollingsworth's arm. "Samuel, did you put my sister in harm's way to save your precious cover?"

He rubbed his arm. "No, I'd never knowingly put a civilian at risk."

Blake squeezed Marci's hand as he glanced toward the agent. "What will happen to Trevor and Susan?"

"Trevor will be charged with first degree murder. If he continues to cooperate, the DA will offer a reduced sentence. He'll still do serious time. Will Forrester is bigger game, and Trevor is the key to putting Forrester away. As for Susan, she'll probably be charged with aiding and abetting."

"At least Alfred will get justice." Blake said.

And so will Felicity.

EPILOGUE

Marci gazed one last time at the ruins. October winds had brought an early snow to Wolf Mountain, covering the estate in a thin, white blanket. Joy filled her as she viewed the new legend plaque near the ruins, words that spoke of Felicity's strength.

Hard to believe a year and a season had passed since she and Blake were married. How drastically life had changed for them both. They looked forward to a new chapter with Blake's position as History Department Chair at Adirondack Community College and her appointment at Saranac Lake High School.

Blake squeezed Marci's hand. "The newspaper said they'll put up a monument on Felicity's fresh gravesite, next to her husband."

"I'm glad she has a proper burial place and is not forsaken on a mountainside."

"This town owes you a huge favor, Marci. You believed in her innocence when no one else did. Thanks to you, history will be rectified, and Felicity's name will be synonymous with charity rather than scandal."

Marci turned to face the trail. "We should be going. Gabriella is bringing Mark over for the weekend."

"He's a great kid. I'm glad I can be part of his life."

"I didn't know you were so fond of kids."

"I've always liked kids. Why do you ask?"

"Do you like them well enough to give up your office?"

Blake's obvious confusion made her smile. In so many ways, he was like a child himself, yet he'd be a wonderful father. His eyes softened with insight. "Marci, are you—"

"Yes. I thought the chance for motherhood had passed me by. God knew differently, I suppose."

Blake laughed. "We're not quite as old as Abraham and Sarah. I'm not fifty yet, and you're still in your early forties. We've got a lot of good years to offer a baby. And yes, I'll gladly remodel my office into a nursery." He pulled her into a kiss.

Marci sat on the stone bench where she'd once fought for sanity and gazed back at the ruins, once a legacy of tragedy. With Felicity's innocence proven, she'd now be remembered for her generosity and as a lady of substance. Marci sighed with gratitude, rather than sorrow. Because of faith, her legacy of regret had been traded for hope.

THE END

ABOUT THE AUTHOR

The author has been fascinated with the beauty, history, and mysteries encompassed in the Adirondack region, the perfect backdrop for *Wolf Mountain Legacy*. Find out more about the author on her website, www.lindarondeau.com, and signup for her newsletter to stay informed. The author is available to speak to groups, in person or online.

Visit her on Facebook, Twitter, Instagram, MeWe, and Pinterest.

AUTHOR NOTES

The Adirondack Mountains are perhaps some of the most beautiful in the East Coast. Some have compared them, perhaps not in height but in majesty, to the Rockies. I love to set my stories in this historic and magical place. Perhaps why Theodore Roosevelt proclaimed the Adirondacks to be "Forever Wild."

The fictional town of Collins Bend was inspired by the real town of Saranac Lake, New York. If you want to take a breathtaking drive, traverse the highway between Saranac Lake and Lake Placid, the home of both the 1980 and 1932 Olympics. Visit the historic White Face Mountain, the inspiration behind Wolf Mountains tourist attraction.

The Adirondacks was known for summer homes and huge estates of the millionaires in late 1880s. There are still many opulent homes in the northern peaks and waterways of Northern New York. The late 1880s through the first few decades of the 1900s saw the rise of many hotels catering to the wealthy, the inspiration behind The LaGrande Hotel (fictional) but placed in the very real Lake Placid.

The railroad expansion brought trade and tourists to the North County as well as human trafficking of Native Americans into the sweatshops and brothels of New York City.

Reverend John Todd did indeed offer a prayer at the Golden Spike ceremony of the transcontinental railroad and was an active abolitionist, influential in the Underground Railroad through New York State.

Wordsworth is a fictional family name and any similarity to actual people or events is accidental.

EXCERPT FROM THE GHOSTS OF TRUMBALL MANSION

QUICK SYNOPSIS

A romance writer and her estranged publisher husband spend a summer together in her Connecticut estate. He sees ghosts. She believes his sightings are excuses to remain separated. As the couple move toward a possible reconciliation, even Sylvia begins to experience the fury of forces bent on keeping them apart.

(to be released by Elk Lake Fall of 2021)

PROLOGUE

FIFTEEN YEARS EARLIER

Sylvia Moore Fitzgibbons steadied herself against the balustrade surrounding the upstairs promenade. Henry stood at the door, much like Scarlet O'Hara's Rhett. In her mind, Sylvia could hear Scarlet say the words, "Oh, Rhett, whatever will I do without you?"

She expected the same final condemnation to pass from Henry's lips. "Frankly, my dear, I don't give a ..."

Sylvia screamed her petition. "Henry, don't go."

He paused—his gaze sorrowful as he opened the double-paneled door. "I'm sorry, Sylvia. I told you last night. I can't live here."

She pushed away from the rail, her knees wobbling, wanting the floor to swallow her whole. How could she live in a world where Henry no longer shared her bed? She summoned the author within. If she were to survive, Lana Longstreet must completely take over. "Then go."

He glanced toward the marble-floored ballroom. "I tried, Sylvia. For a brief while, I thought I might eventually learn to manage the commute." He pointed toward the infamous ballroom. "But whatever's in there is real. And it hates me."

Of all the excuses she'd ever written, Henry's fiction surpassed Lana's most creative pages. "Will I still see you Wednesday?"

"As agreed—a weekly business meeting at Chez Phillipe."

With that, Henry was gone, leaving Sylvia to mourn the life she'd lost. Only Lana could help her make a new one. What now? She surveyed the staircase and the portraits of the ancestors. Lana Longstreet would not let sentiment stand in the way of enjoying this mansion, a piece of New Haven history. She laughed at Henry's idiocy.

Sylvia surveyed the lower rooms, the lure to the old Trumball Mansion, now known as the Donner Estate. Every room, even the servants' quarters on the left wing beyond the ballroom remained as the edifice was when Trumball built the place. Of course, she'd modernize the kitchen for Rosalie. She couldn't expect her cook to manage with a wood stove.

Anger heated her cheeks as she surveyed the perfect symmetry and Georgian architecture. How could Henry have resisted the breathy charm filling each room, the engraved woodwork, and Plaster of Paris etched ceilings?

Last night's sharp criticism still stung. "Of all your impetuous designs, this is the craziest thing you have ever done," Henry had said. Lana Longstreet thought her decision to buy Trumball Mansion the smartest move she'd ever made.

She walked through the living room to the kitchen, then looked out the window at the rose gardens—the only feature Henry found alluring, though he couldn't name a single species. She'd laughed while Henry referenced each bed by its color and location rather than use their common name.

Apparently, not even the roses were enough to keep him here. He'd rejected her gift and threw their marriage to the wind in the process. He made his choice—now Lana Longstreet would make hers. The once bustling Trumball Mansion would live again through twenty-first century galas, and Lana Longstreet would emerge as New Haven's sauciest socialite.

A last tear trickled down Sylvia's chin. She pulled out a hankie from the sleeve of her knitted long-sleeved tee and wiped her eyes. No more regret, no more conniving. She'd salvage what she could from her broken marriage and find contentment within her alter ego's independence. Though Henry refused to call the mansion his home, he would not divorce her. Lana Longstreet's books were the cornerstone of Fitzgibbons & Associate Publishing, and Sylvia had controlling interest. If love didn't motivate Henry's faithfulness, the fear of poverty would. And, they would have Wednesdays at Chez Phillipe's. A little perfume, sultry helplessness, and Henry would take her to his bedroom, a small part of him better than none at all.

She gazed at the beveled archways gracing the entrance to both the ballroom and sitting room. She'd fashion a life for herself and the children here. Let Henry keep his predictable Manhattan existence. Lana Longstreet's genius needed surroundings that juiced the creative spirit, one that would be richly fed in this historic home.

She scanned the open ballroom—the cornerstone of Trumball's influence on a nation in the making—the place where Henry claimed ghosts danced.

Ridiculous.

She joined thirteen-year-old Julie in the ballroom. Her daughter and son were perhaps Sylvia's greater claim to fame than all of Lana Longstreet's books, and mothering the only arena in which Lana was not permitted.

A residual pungency coated Sylvia's throat. "Let's get out of here. Smells like rotten eggs. Tomorrow, I'll hire a cleaning service to purge these odors."

Julie stood with cocked head, her gaze fixed on the angel-engraved marble fireplace. "They're gone, Mother. They jumped back into the walls when Daddy left."

OTHER BOOKS BY
LINDA WOOD RONDEAU

A Christmas Prayer
Fiddlers Fling
Hosea's Heart
It Really IS a Wonderful Life
Miracle on Maple Street
I Prayed for Patience: God Gave Me Children
Second Helpings
Snow on Bald Mountain
The Fifteenth Article
Who Put the Vinegar in the Salt